ORPHAN TRAIN TO
CATTLE BARON

T0244152

JACK SLATER

ORPHAN TRAIN TO CATTLE BARON

JOHNNY GUNN

THORNDIKE PRESS
A part of Gale, a Cengage Company

Copyright © 2017 by Johnny Gunn.
Thorndike Press, a part of Gale, a Cengage Company.

ALL RIGHTS RESERVED
Thorndike Press® Large Print Softcover Western.
The text of this Large Print edition is unabridged.
Other aspects of the book may vary from the original edition.
Set in 16 pt. Plantin.

LIBRARY OF CONGRESS CIP DATA ON FILE.
CATALOGUING IN PUBLICATION FOR THIS BOOK
IS AVAILABLE FROM THE LIBRARY OF CONGRESS.

ISBN-13: 978-1-4205-1723-1 (softcover alk. paper)

Published in 2024 by arrangement with Wolfpack Publishing LLC.

Printed in the USA
1 2 3 4 5   28 27 26 25 24

ORPHAN TRAIN TO CATTLE BARON

1

Wind was howling through the streets of Brooklyn, blowing leaves, horse crap, dirt, and filth into the blistering cold late afternoon. One of the boys said it felt like it would rain at any given minute, and Jack knew that he would face another miserable night huddled in some alley, just waiting to freeze to death. He was hungry, cold, and about to get wet, and had no answers to any of the above questions. All he knew was, he was alone, and he had never been alone before.

It was frightening on the one hand, exhilarating on another, but it was the fear that was at the forefront most of the time. And the big question, why? Where was his mama, why wasn't Pa here? He whimpered "Why?" when he wakened, when he slipped into sleep, throughout the day.

He had stumbled into these other three boys, all orphans or runaways, just like him, hoping that maybe they had some food or blankets or a place to get warm. It wasn't to be, not that night anyway. No one cared, he thought, as he shook from the cold, got shoved to the cobbled street by one of the other boys, fought off another boy from trying to take his ragged coat.

He was cried-out, he had no Mommy, no Pa, and didn't know why. They just left him in that ditch half filled with putrid water, left him to wander the streets of a city he didn't know anything about. The worst part, he was only ten-years-old.

The streets of New York, in October 1872, were home to hundreds, possibly thousands of homeless children, roaming, stealing, and dying. Some blamed the recent war, some the economy, some just didn't care. Jack Slater was ten years old and in one instant went from being a loving son to being a cold, frightened orphan when a carriage carrying his mother and father overturned into a ditch on a rain slickened road.

Mr. and Mrs. Reginald Slater were pronounced dead when their bodies were brought out from under the carriage after being underwater for several hours. No one was aware that Jack lay, unconscious, in the deep grass mere yards from the wreck. He awoke to find himself alone, cold, and wet.

For him, it was just the beginning of a long nightmare of trouble.

Slater was large for his age and strong. He worked right alongside his father on their farm. He had dark wavy hair that fell across a broad face that shown with large brown eyes. Jack's wide mouth was more often curved in a smile than not, and he had a strong jaw line. Until that terrible wreck, Jack Slater had never missed a meal, had never known fear, had never found himself totally alone and helpless.

"You boys, there," the big policeman yelled. "Stop now."

"Copper," one of the boys yelled, and the four started running, but Jack tripped on some garbage in the alley and went face first onto the hard paving stones. He tried to struggle when the policeman grabbed him, but of course, that was a losing proposition.

"Now, now, laddy-buck, let's not have any of that," the copper said, holding Jack by his coat collar. "Calm down, now boy. What's your name?"

"Jack," he said through blubbering tears, still jerking to get free of the big man.

"Well now, Jack, I'm sure there's more to your name than that. You and me are gonna take a little walk, boy, down to the Children's Aid Society, and we can do that nice, or we can be dumb and rough. Which way do you want it, boy?" he snarled, shaking the little boy like a terrier would a rat.

"Well?" the policeman growled. "Nice?" and he shook the boy hard, "or rough?" and he gave the kid a hard swat across his head, knocking his cap about ten feet down the alley.

Jack's head throbbed from the hit and he blubbered, "Nice, sir, please. I didn't do nothin'."

"That's better, boy. Come along now," and for the first time in several minutes Jack could feel his feet touching the ground. "You hungry, boy?"

"Yes, sir," jack whispered. "And cold."

"They'll feed you and keep you warm at the aid place. How old are you?"

"I'm ten," Jack said.

"You're a big boy for bein' just ten. Me own John is almost twelve and you're about his size. Well, now, here we are, the Children's Aid Society. In you go, now," the officer said, escorting Jack through the large double doors into a broad and open main reception room of the society.

"Got another one fer ya, Maybelle. Says he's ten and 'is name be Jack. Says he's hungry and cold. Ain't they all?" He stood

Jack in front of a large counter behind which was a young woman, pretty in a plain sort of way, seated so she was about eye level with Jack. She had large brown eyes, dark hair that was wound into a bun, and simple drop pearl earrings.

"Hello, Jack," she said, giving him a warm smile. "Thank you, officer Hank, you've done a fine thing bringing this boy here and off the street." Jack felt the big paw of the cop slowly let go of his coat, and saw him turn and walk out the door.

He wanted to run, but it was warm in this building and the lady had a nice smile. Was this a jail where lost boys were kept? Would they feed him? He had only eaten a few scraps in the last two or three days and the copper said they had food here. "Have a seat, Jack," Maybelle said. "Do you know where you are?"

"The big policeman said something about a society. I don't know what that means. Am I going to jail? The policeman said it's warm and I would be fed. I'm hungry."

"I bet you are, Jack," she laughed and said he was definitely not going to jail. She stood up and walked around the counter and took Jack by the hand. "Let's go see if we can find something to take care of that little eating problem and I'll tell you all about where you are and what we'll be doing." They walked, hand in hand, down a wide corridor and into a room filled with long tables and benches.

At the far end of the long room was a serving counter stretched out far enough to hold great tubs that would be filled with food at mealtime. Behind that was a kitchen and Jack could see several people, including some children, working there.

"Well, Maybelle, who have we got here," a large woman in a bright yellow and orange apron said, her hair up in a net, and a smile with crinkly eyes beaming at Jack.

"Jack is going to be with us for a time, Beatrice, and he says he's a bit hungry. Think you might find a nice sandwich and cup of milk for the boy while I start his paperwork?"

"I'll bring it to the table meself, Maybelle," Beatrice said, reaching down and giving Jack's cheek a little pinch. "You certainly have some color in those cheeks, sonny," she said, waltzing back into the kitchen. For the first time in many long days there was a smile working across the boy's grubby face.

"Let's see what we can find out about you, Jack," Maybelle said, walking the boy over to one of the long tables. "You sit there, and I'll sit across from you." She pulled a notebook from her skirt pocket, a pencil from her blouse pocket, and sat down. "This won't take long."

Beatrice was there in an instant with a large roast beef sandwich and a cup of warm milk. "This will make you feel better," she said, that wonderful smile filling her face.

"Thank you, Ma'am," Jack whispered, looking at a platter with more food on it than he had eaten in a week. It had been more than a month since he lost his parents, he told Maybelle, and he didn't know where they went or why they threw him into the grass along that road. He hadn't slept in a bed, had a bath, or eaten a fair meal in all that time.

"Eat that nice and slow, Jack," Beatrice said. "Don't wolf it or you'll make yourself sick."

"What do we know about this new boy?" Rudolph Morrison asked as Maybelle brought the paperwork to his office. "Will he be able to join the next train?" Morrison was close to fifty, overweight, and rarely smiled. He had no outside activities that anyone knew about, spent twelve hours a day in his office. Morrison had never married and considered each one of these lost children his, and his passion was finding them a home.

Morrison was meticulous in his affairs, personal and business, did not approve of anything less than perfection from those who worked for the Children's Aid Society. "Those families in the west are expecting a full train," the gentleman said, looking over Slater's paperwork.

"I just got the boy, Mr. Morrison. My first interview with him is scheduled for this evening. I'll give you a full report following my meeting with hm. He isn't one of the typical street boys, he's had some schooling, I believe, seems very frightened, and was famished." Maybelle was one of the long-time employees of the society and enjoyed helping the street urchins get some kind of life for themselves.

The street people were ugly and mean, often so hungry they gave no thought to killing for a crust of moldy bread. The children found themselves fighting full-grown adults just to survive, and the only safety net was the Children's Aid Society.

The society found that getting homes for these children, some orphaned by disasters and accidents, some simply flung onto the streets for economic reasons, and some runaways, were very difficult to place with eastern families. City families simply didn't need several children as farm families did. Extra children were often a burden rather than a help.

The street children were generally non-educated, tough and feisty, and independent. They arrived in rags, filthy dirty, and often suffering from open sores or some disease or other. The number of street urchin deaths was high, even higher during the winter months.

On the other hand, families in the west, at the edges of civilization were desperate for help on their farms and ranches, and welcomed youngsters to their families. To run a farm in the 1870s took many people and many animals, and being able to take in children to help was a Godsend. The society had placed thousands of children with families in Kansas, Nebraska, Minnesota, the Dakotas, and other farming areas, some right on the far edge of the frontier. Trainloads of children, thousands of orphaned children, were sent west yearly.

The War Between the States was over, and the Indian problems in the plains seemed to be coming to an end. Railroads were moving west, people were moving west, cities and towns were springing up, and the young plains farming families needed help. There was a dearth of men looking for work, people were not available to work on the farms, and the farm families didn't have money to pay for hired help, anyway. The Children's Aid Society seemed to have the answer in thousands of children who suffered on the cold streets without hope of finding families.

The Children's Aid Society was started by Charles Loring Brace, with help from the business community and others, in the 1850s, and was a thriving enterprise when young Jack Slater was dropped off by that friendly copper. The farming communities were more than willing to take these children, but the kids sometimes weren't necessarily that enthusiastic about the program.

The children were adopted into the families, were required to be given an education, and when they reached the age of sixteen, were to be given a wage. Some of the children were thrilled with the possible adventure involved, others sulked that they were simply not wanted and had been thrown out by society. There were a few that rebelled and were recalcitrant in every way.

Maybelle had seen them all over the years, and felt that Jack Slater was not the typical New York City street urchin. Maybelle wanted to bring Jack home with her, but knew she felt that way almost every time a youngster was brought in to the home. She was not married despite being rather attractive and well educated.

It was her choice, she often told friends. "Most of the men I've discovered are beasts at best, and I'd rather not share myself with one. I have my small farm, my fruit trees, and my horses, and on nasty days and cold nights, I have my books. I would not care to replace any of them with a man."

Despite all of that, Maybelle wanted a family. Working so close with so many children that wanted a family as much as she did, brought a constant ache to her heart. "The only way I can have a child is to have a man, and that just isn't fair."

2

"So, Jack, now that your tummy's full, let's have a talk, eh? I'm going to ask you a few questions that you should be able to answer and then we'll talk about what your future might hold in store. Make yourself comfortable, and we'll start."

Maybelle's little office was off the main reception area, with a large hardwood desk that she sat behind and two chairs on the other side. There was one window that looked out onto a playground behind the main building. The floors were polished to a mirror finish, and the walls, above the wainscoting were intricately patterned wood panels. At one time the building had been an elegant home.

Jack walked to the window and watched children playing with balls, rolling hoops across the open area, laughing, jumping, having fun. It had been a long time, he thought, since he ran for fun, since he laughed, even. Maybelle stood next to him, put her hand on his shoulder, and with a smile, asked him to take a seat.

She asked him to say his name and age again, then asked the first of the important questions. "Why were you alone and running loose on the streets, Jack? Where are your parents?"

"I don't know where Mommy and Pa are," he said, tears beginning to well. "We were in the buggy coming into town, and that's the last thing I remember until I woke up with a very sore head in the grass at the bottom of a ditch."

"You haven't seen your parents since that time?" she asked, getting a tearful nod back from the large boy. "Do you remember what day that was?"

"It was the second weekend in October, because Pa wanted to spend some of the corn money to buy material for Mommy to sew on. We were going to have dinner at a hotel and spend the night. Where did they go?" he bawled. "Why did they leave me in the ditch like that?" He couldn't stifle the tears, and his body was wracked with spasms of grief. Maybelle knew she couldn't, but she wanted to gather the boy up and just squeeze him for hours.

"We'll see if we can find that out, Jack,"

she said, doing her best to hold her own tears in check. "I want you to sit quiet now for a couple of minutes," Maybelle said, picking up the sheet of paper she had been writing on and walked out the door. Tears were coursing down her cheeks as she headed toward the superintendent's office.

"I fear a tragedy, Mr. Morrison," she said, handing him the paper. Mr. and Mrs. Slater may have suffered an accident that left Jack by the side of the road."

"I'll send Mr. Whipple to find out immediately, Maybelle. Thank you, and see what else you can find out about the boy. He seems very bright."

"Bright indeed," she said, "and very mannerly. He's had a good family life up to this point, sir."

She walked back into the office and found Jack reading from a volume of essays that Maybelle kept in her office. "That's rather advanced for a boy of ten, Jack. You like to read, eh?"

"Oh, yes," he said, closing the book and handing it back to her. "My Pa has this book and we read it together sometimes. Pa says reading philosophy expands the mind."

"Yes it does," she noted. "Were you going to school regularly, that is, before this accident?"

"Yes, and I work in the field with Pa, too. We have wheat and corn, and raise hogs and sheep, too," he said, his eyes bright with remembrance. "Pa says I'm a good worker. I can run the team with all the equipment except the thresher. Pa says that's too dangerous for a boy to run."

"Your Pa must be a good man," Maybelle said. "Do you have any other family members close by, Jack? Do your grandparents live close, or aunts and uncles?"

"Ma and Pa came to America two years before I was born, and no one else came with them. I don't have any relatives that I know of. If there are, they're somewhere in England, I guess. Will you be able to find my parents? I'm really scared."

"I know you are, Jack, and I want you to know we are working on it. Right now, let's get you a good hot bath, some fresh clothes, and find a comfy bed for you to sleep in. We have dormitories upstairs, you know where the dining hall is, and after you get all cleaned up, I'll have one of the other boys give you a tour of our little home here."

Whipple was a slight man, aged and bent, mostly bald but with a flowing white beard that he kept immaculately brushed and trimmed. He had a long and sad face on his best day, his eyes almost sagging in their gloom, and a sharp beak-like nose that was often quite red. He was slow and angular as he walked the streets of the city, but was even more sad looking as he entered Morrison's office.

"I'm afraid there is no good news today, sir," he said, offering a large manila envelope to the headmaster. "The Slater couple were killed in a buggy accident several weeks ago. Those that found the tragedy apparently missed the boy, unconscious in the weeds."

"Oh, dear," Morrison said, reading through the packet that Whipple brought back. "Maybelle was right, this Jack Slater isn't your typical street urchin. He will be a perfect candidate for placement on a farm on the frontier. Thank you, Whipple. Would you find Maybelle and ask her to come see me right away?"

"Well now, young Master Slater, don't you look fine," Maybelle said when Jack came back downstairs after his bath and getting dressed in almost new clothes. "Clean trousers and bright new shirt, your hair combed and clean, you're a find looking lad, indeed," she said. "Please take a seat, Jack,

I'm afraid I have some very bad news for you."

Jack sat dazed for less than a minute after receiving the news of his parent's death, and then the tears started with mournful sobs, the large boy's body wracked with the horror of knowing he would never see his Mommy or Pa again. Jack's father had instilled a sense of independence in the boy and it slowly filtered through the terror of his mind to the surface.

In less than half an hour Jack had slowed then stopped the sobs and tears, and Maybelle could almost see a transition take place. He squared his shoulders, sat very erect and looked deep into her eyes. "What do I do now, Miss Maybelle?" he said, very softly, not childlike. She saw a determination in his face, knew that whatever happened, he would be responsible, he would make the decisions. "How will I live?" he asked, but not pitifully.

"The laws concerning this type of situation are not very helpful, I'm afraid," Maybelle said. "Being under age you cannot own the old farm, and it will be sold. That money will be held in an account for you, and will be yours when you reach eighteen. All the paperwork will be made available to you at the time."

She settled back in her chair looking at the boy, smiling. "We have a program for children that find themselves in your position," she said. "Let me tell you something about what the next several years of your life might be like."

Maybelle spent the next hour explaining the concept of the Orphan Trains and relocation to a farming or ranching family somewhere on the frontier. Maybelle had never been east of the Hudson River, The Slater farm was on Long Island, so the concept of the great plains was difficult for her to describe and even more difficult for Jack to understand.

"Pa says I'm a very good worker on our farm, I love animals," he whispered. "Do you think this would be the best thing I could do?" He already missed his pony, knew he'd never see his mother or father, and wanted to cry some more. Maybelle realized she may be talking to a young man whose mind is far older than his body.

Would this be the thing I could do? he asked, and I would expect that question from someone much more mature that Jack. She was enjoying this conversation very much. He sat very still and Maybelle had enough sense to just let him think it out, not talk or question.

"I was afraid every minute I lived on the streets, and I loved every minute I lived on our farm. I'm big and strong, Miss Maybelle, but I'm a little afraid."

"I bet you are, Jack. We have a train leaving in two days and there is room for you on that train, and a family at the end of the journey just waiting to meet you. You don't have to make your decision right now. Sleep on it, eat well, and let me know tomorrow."

"I want to go. I really do because I don't like the city at all. I don't have my books and I guess I can't take my pony," he said.

"I will get you some books, Jack, but no, you can't take your pony. You're a wonderful boy, Jack, wonderful," Maybelle said. "Some family way out there on the frontier is going to be very happy having you join their family. We'll spend tomorrow getting you some books, plenty of fresh clean clothing, and make you ready for your long journey to a new life."

3

"Mornin' Pete," storekeeper Lucius Walters called out from behind a stack of feedbags. "Looks like fall has left and old man winter has come. River's running mighty high right now. How's your place lookin'?"

"Wet and muddy like ever thing else 'round here. Fool question to ask," Peter Jablonski snarled in answer. "Need seed, Walters. Come in yet?" Jablonski began and ended each day angry, had few friends, and never a wife. He wasn't yet forty but often acted as an old and tired man. On the other hand, those that knew him said that once riled he would start a fight on a whim.

The Jablonski place was about five miles south of Fargo, Dakota Territory, on the Red River. He raised corn and wheat, some market vegetables, and hogs. It was a fight every year to find people to work the fields until he discovered what had been advertised in Kansas as an orphan train. Jablonski had taken in three children in the past three years, a nine-year-old girl named Mims, a twelve-year-old boy he called Skeeter, and another boy named Jason, a ten-year-old.

The mean hearted man fulfilled the contract with the Children's Aid Society, but didn't go one half a step further. He said they wore clean clothes, said they were well fed, and said they attended what schooling was available. The one thing missing from the picture was kindness and the love of a family. The concept of an adopted child being shown family love wasn't in the scene.

There were questions right from the beginning about a single man adopting children, but Jablonski made promises, signed affidavits, and was accepted. No one ever felt it necessary to do an on-the-scene inspection since there had been no complaints filed or even suggested.

Many of the farmers and ranchers in the area had taken in children to raise and treated them as part of the family as it should have been, but Jablonski felt that he was simply feeding and clothing field workers that he didn't have to pay as well. The children should have carried his last name but he refused them that honor. Mims was rescued by the Society when she was an infant and doesn't actually have a last name that she knows of.

"Next shipment due in sometime next week Pete. That is if we don't flood out with all this warm weather. Johanson's place is underwater right now, and that's a pretty heavy snow pack that's building up out there."

"Yeah," is all Jablonski said. "Here, fill this order and put it in my wagon. I'll be in the Barrel House. Don't short me, Lucius," he hissed, slipping out the door and across the muddy street to the Barrel House Saloon for a morning bracer.

"I've never shorted anyone in my life," Lucius called out, "and you know it. Miserable old fool." Pete Jablonski was well out of hearing by then but Walters didn't care. "If you threw that man a party he'd complain about something." The commentary continued as he filled the Jablonski order and had his one employee take it out to the wagon.

The morning bracer came in multiples and Jablonski was seen to weave just a bit as he made his way back to the wagon and the short trip to the farm. "Get your butt out here Skeeter and get this wagon unloaded. Where's Mims?"

The children were aware that when Pete

went to town he would come home in his cups, as they called it, and that often led to them being verbally, never physically, abused in some way. As Mims was heard to say often, "Walk on eggs, boys."

"She's in the kitchen, Pete, fixin' lunch." Jablonski would not allow the children to call him pa or papa or anything resembling a family association. "Jason got hurt feedin' the hogs and she's been tendin' him too."

"Darn fool boy can't do anything right. Might just send him back where he came from," he muttered walking up the steps to the back porch of the large old farmhouse. "Mims, where are you?"

"I'm right here, Pete," she said. "I'm just puttin' some stuff on Jason's leg. He cut it on that fence that needs fixin'. Dinner is almost ready, if you're hungry. We'll eat and get back to our chores."

Pete walked over and looked at a gash on Jason's leg, just below the knee, but didn't say anything. "Better fix that fence after eatin' something," he said and walked down the hallway toward his bedroom. "I'll be out to check on you later."

Mims was just ten but had the airs of a grown woman at times. She was small for her age, very thin, with deep golden hair that streamed out behind her when she ran full tilt across the yard, her blue eyes danced with joy most of the time, and she was always there to help the boys when Pete was on the prowl.

"He said he would fix that fence, Mims, and I thought he did."

"I know, Jason, let it go. After dinner, you and Jason fix the fence, and then we'll work on those drainage ditches. It's really wet out there. We need some snow to freeze all this water up," she said. "And then Pete will blame us for that, too," making Jason laugh a little through the pain in his leg.

Mims picked up the newspaper that Pete left on the kitchen table and saw an advertisement that Pete apparently had circled in pencil. "Look at this, Jason. There's another Orphan Train coming in a couple of weeks. I bet Pete is going to try to adopt another boy or girl."

"If he does, I hope it's somebody I like," Jason said. "Skeeter scares me and I don't like him."

Jason was small for his ten years, a little frail, susceptible to any germ that passed through the territory, and vowed that he would never spend another day on a farm if he could get away from this one.

Skeeter on the other hand was large for his twelve years, tended to be a bit of a bully, pushing Jason around often. He did not push Mims, nor did he attempt to bully her because the only time he did try, he got a bloody lip and black eye for the effort. Nobody, including Pete most of the time, pushed Mims around.

"It would be nice to have a sister," Mims said, putting the newspaper back on the table. She went back to the stove to stir a large pot filled with great chunks of pork swimming in a sea of beans. "Gonna be a good dinner, pretty quick," she said, shooing Jason out of the kitchen.

4

"I've never been this close to a train before," Jack said, walking down the passenger boarding platform. "It's really big." Maybelle and Rudolph Morrison had twelve children in tow along with luggage and all the necessary paperwork that went along with the children, in hand.

Jack's face was lit up like a gas lamp on Broadway as he all but danced down the wooden platform. He stayed awake the whole night thinking about his journey to the great unknown of the frontier. He thought about the long train ride, about the possibility of hostile Indians, about having a new family. "I'm not afraid," he told himself several times during the night.

His thoughts strayed from this great-unknown back to the known and the loss of his family and everything he had ever known. His time was spent in looking forward to his new life and then remembering his past life. He was alternating from crying over this horrible loss to great joy in anticipation of a new life. There was that constant thought of being alone.

I'm with all these people here at the Society, but really, I'm alone, and it's just not fair. He smacked his pillow a good solid blow, and let his mind continue putting him to sleep amid thoughts of a frontier farm with horses, maybe Indians, and most importantly, a family.

The twelve children getting ready to board the train ranged in age from Claudine's eight-years to Charles's twelve, and were evenly split between boys and girls. Maybelle called the children's attention and said, "Charles, I want you and Jack to do what you can to see to it that the younger children are taken care of. Remember the rules, do what the train conductor tells you to do, and enjoy this wonderful train ride to a whole new life."

They were hustled aboard by the train people and assigned to their staterooms. Jack had tears in his eyes saying goodbye to Maybelle, and she almost held hers back, finally letting the cascade flow, hugging the big boy goodbye. "You be a good boy, Jack. I want you to write me often, and remember that we will be holding your money from your farm's sale."

"I will, Maybelle. Thank you for being a friend." She felt as if she were saying goodbye to an adult, and gave Jack a kiss on the top of his head. *If I ever get married, this is the son I want,* she thought, smiling through her tears. She and Morrison hurried off the train and stood on the platform waving to the children as the train huffed its way out of New York City, toward the great plains in the far west.

There were twelve little faces plastered on half a dozen windows, smiling and laughing for the most part, waving goodbye back. There were two children assigned to each of the staterooms, and Jack would be rooming with Charles. The two got to putting their stuff away, hanging the clothing, and getting to know each other, but jumping to the windows at every opportunity.

"You ever been on a train?" Jack asked, opening one of his suitcases on his bunk.

"Ain't never even seen one before today," Charles said. "Just look how fast we're going," he said, wide-eyed, pointing out the window. The buildings and open lots of the city were flashing past as the train began picking up speed. "We're going faster than my old mule could run," he said.

"You had a mule? I had a pony that I rode

all the time. I don't think he could run this fast, either." The two boys stood by the window for a few more minutes before getting back to work on their belongings.

There was a gentle knock on the door and a small black man stuck his head in. "Is one of you boys named Charles?" he asked, holding his porter's cap in his hand. "I'm Ephraim, the porter for this carriage."

"Hello. I'm Charles," the boy said.

"I'm Jack," Jack piped up with a big smile.

"We'll be together for several days now, boys, so let's talk for a few minutes about what this trip is gonna be." He wasn't much taller than Charles, had just a fringe of snow-white hair surrounding a shiny bald head. His smile was wide and friendly, but Jack noticed that his hands were gnarled and one was twisted painfully as well. Ephraim put his porter's hat back on and took a seat on Jack's bunk, indicating the boys should sit across from him.

"Here's our schedule for meal times, and it's important that you children all come to the dining car as a group. We won't allow for any loud talking or yelling, and certainly no roughhousing. This is a long trip you're starting, so let's make it just as pleasant and enjoyable as possible."

He was firm in his delivery but Jack could

see warmth in his eyes and the way he smiled. Ephraim handed Charles the schedules and asked that he make sure each child got one. "I know you'll have lots of questions, and I'll be close to try to answer them if I can." Ephraim stood up, nodded to the boys, and slipped out of the stateroom.

Charles left two schedules in the room and followed the porter out the door to give the rest out. Jack sat on the end of his bunk, and peered out the window at the passing scene, which slowly changed from big city to small farms to open wild-land.

They were no longer in New York, already in an environment that Jack understood. There were farms, large ones and small, and he had pictures in his mind of the one he would never see again. As he watched, he saw wild rivers, magnificent forests, large open pastures filled with animals, and even more open land.

After getting his things put away Jack decided to take a walk through the train cars, so he would know where things were. He had a curious mind, wanted to know how something worked, why it worked that way, and just what might be around the corner or on the other side of the fence. Being on a railroad train was more than a dream come true for him. He located the restrooms first and then started for the dining car. As he moved through the new Pullman coach where the children were housed, he bumped into Claudine.

"Hello," he said. "Isn't this wonderful? Have you seen the restrooms? I've never imagined anything like a railroad train before."

"Hi, Jack," she said, lowering her eyes a bit, almost overwhelmed by his enthusiasm. "I'm kinda scared. Aren't you?"

"No, not me. What an adventure we're on. We're going almost clear across the country, clear to the wild frontier." His smile covered his entire face, his arms were swinging, and his eyes were as bright as brown eyes can get. He was excited, his face glowing in anticipation of the unknown, almost dancing in his pleasure. "I'm going to try to find the car where we'll eat. Do you want to come with me?"

"Is it okay to do that? Do we need permission?"

"Of course it's okay," he said. Claudine was just shy of her ninth birthday and Jack was well into his tenth year, but towered over the girl. Working on the farm right alongside his father had given him a set of muscles few ten-year-old boys had, and he had a sense of adventure and natural leadership locked into his genes as well.

"We're going to be on this train for a week or more, so we better know our way around. Don't be afraid, come on, let's go explore."

She hesitated for just a few seconds and finally got a cute little smile on her freckled face and said, "Okay, but don't run off and leave me." She put her little hand out, almost tentatively, and Jack took it up, and the two walked down the aisle toward the back of the coach. Ephraim noticed them and gave a little nod of his bald head, smiling and chuckling lightly.

"Do you know who your new family is going to be?" Claudine asked as they came to the door that opened onto the next car. "I'm going to be with the Fuller family in Minnesota."

"Maybelle said that I'm going to Fargo, in Dakota Territory, but I won't know the name of the family until I get there. We're going to change trains in Chicago." They moved between the two cars, with Jack holding tight to Claudine's hand. She had a death grip on his, her eyes wide in fright. The noise of the train was ferocious, and the blast of cold air was trying to push her around.

Jack held her tight but didn't seem to

notice her fright. "I looked at some maps that Maybelle had in her office. It's a long way from New York," he said. "Fargo is close to the Minnesota border, and we'll be on the Northern Pacific Railroad when we get there."

"You're really smart, Jack. Thank you for being my friend," she said as they moved into the next coach. Her fingers were getting numb from gripping Jack's hand so hard.

Jack's smile said everything because he discovered at that point that he couldn't talk. They stood just inside the next coach, and he felt warm and very happy. He hadn't had much contact with girls, there were a couple at the school he attended but they stayed by themselves and talked about dresses and dolls and other things that boys didn't. He looked into bright green eyes and noticed freckles and blond hair that hung in curls, with a sensational smile aimed right at him.

In such a short space of time, Jack Slater had changed dramatically. He was a big strong farm boy when that carriage ran off the road and overturned and he became a dirty, hungry, street urchin. From the moment the copper caught him up and brought him to the Children's Aid Society, he had grown to be a man, albeit a very young one.

"I know you're scared, Claudine, but I won't hurt you and I won't let anyone else hurt you." His shoulders, wide and strong, were set and he started off down the long aisle way.

Claudine was looking into big brown eyes on a face that was mostly a mile-wide smile. She decided that she was a very lucky and very happy little girl. "I'm not very much afraid now, Jack," she said. "We won't get to play outside or anything on this trip. What will you be doing?"

"Maybelle gave me a nice box of books, so I plan to read a lot. My Pa and I used to read a lot to each other. Do you like to read?"

"I haven't had much time to read. We kids didn't go to school much. Is it hard to read big books?"

"No, it's really fun," Jack said. "I like the kind where people do all kinds of things. One that Maybelle gave me is about some men that are chasing whales and another is about men and women moving to the Ohio Valley a long time ago.

"Maybe I could help you learn to read good," he smiled to her as they walked down the coach aisle toward the next car. "Did you have a big family?"

Claudine's eyes misted up as she told him about her brother and two sisters, and how everybody was killed in a horrible fire. Jack slipped his arm around her shoulder and held her for a minute. "You'll be okay when you meet your new family," he said, continuing their trek toward the dining car.

"Where have you been, Jack? I was starting to get a little worried," Charles said as the big boy entered their room.

"Me and Claudine went to the find the dining car, and the porter there let us sit at one of the tables. He brought us some iced lemon-aid. I've never had anything like that, ever. It's really good. And, we had some cookies, too."

"I don't think we're supposed to do that. Did you get in trouble? Maybelle said we aren't supposed to get in trouble, you know."

"We didn't do anything wrong. You can't get in trouble just seeing what was on the train. You'll like the dining car. The waiter guy wouldn't let us go to the next car, though. I guess it's just for grown-ups. We could see some men in there smoking cigars.

"Have you ever smoked a cigar? It looks like fun. Those guys sat at tables, some had

41

newspapers, some were playing cards, and they blew all that smoke into the air. I'll be glad when I'm grown up."

He sat down on his bunk staring out the window as the train raced toward the great unknown. He was just as enthusiastic watching the country flash past as he was leading Claudine down the coaches. "You don't seem very happy, Charles. Do you know where you're going, who your new family will be?"

"Somewhere in Kansas is all I know," he said. "I didn't want to go but Mr. Morrison said I had to."

"Why don't you want to go? Don't you want a new family?"

"Don't you understand, Jack? They're sending us where the wild Indians live. They eat children. Aren't you scared?" Charles had never been outside his little neighborhood in New York until this day, had run with a gang of little street thieves until brought to the Society by a copper.

"Indians don't eat children," Jack said, almost laughing. "Where did you hear that? The Indian wars are almost over, don't you know that?"

"No, that's what I heard, and I don't want to go there." Jack watched Charles hold back tears of serious fright. "I'm going to go find Thomas," he said, slipping out of the cubbyhole of a stateroom. Just the opposite of Charles, Jack was hoping that there would be wild Indians where he was going, wanted to be a part of the open frontier of the far west, wanted all the excitement of this new life to flow through him.

Jack looked through his stuff until he came up with a notebook that Maybelle gave him, and a pencil. He wrote at the top of the first page, 'My Journey to the Great Plains, By Jack Slater.'

A couple of hours later, Ephraim knocked and said, "Supper will be served in half an hour." He said that twice at each door of the childrens' coach. Jack looked over the several pages of fine penmanship, and tucked the notebook and pencil back into a drawer.

"Better get washed up. I could smell some good food when me and Claudine were in the dining car," he muttered, taking just another minute to watch the great wilderness pass by his window.

5

Some of the children had learned good manners and proper behavior from their parents and relatives, while others had never heard nor contemplated the concept. Their first encounter with table manners had come at the insistence of Beatrice in the dining hall at the Society. Maybelle had suggested that Charles should see to it that the children behaved themselves, but it was Jack Slater who became their leader.

The porters and dining car waiters had a section set aside for the group and Jack helped the porters get the children settled in. "Just like back at Beatrice's tables, let's not forget our manners," Jack said after getting everyone settled. "Claudine, maybe you can help Sherryll with her knives and forks, just like you did at the Society."

The children bowed their heads and said a quick prayer as the food was distributed. The waiters were kindly to the children, reminded them that the dishes were hot, and got chair boosters for a couple of the smallest children.

"I don't like this stuff," Terrence said, pushing the plate away. "I'm not gonna eat it."

"Don't be rude, Terrence," Jack said. "If you don't like something, you don't have to eat it, but you must eat something. Just like Beatrice always said, eat a little bit of what you don't like, and eat everything else on your plate." The kids laughed because Jack sounded just like Beatrice, and he even stood tall and folded his arms across his front just like she did.

One or two little squabbles happened but Jack got things settled quickly and the children were overjoyed when the waiters came out with chocolate cake for dessert. Even picky little Terrence cleaned up his plate as fast as the others.

Jack helped herd everyone back to their coach and settled in next to the window to watch the first day settle into dusk. Farmland stretched out, mile after mile as the train plowed through the early evening mists. He fought as hard as he could but couldn't hold back the tears seeing so many farms, so many fields neatly plowed and harvested, so many lights shining through farmhouse windows.

Thoughts of Mama and Pa flooded through his mind, while thoughts of what was going to be coming his way fought to be understood as well. The worst part of evenings like this was not having Pa to read with, not having anyone to talk with or read with. It was difficult for a ten-year-old to understand that he was alone in the world, yet on a railroad train full of people.

I'm not like all these other kids, he thought, seeing a grand sunset way out west. *They are all city kids, scared of things that are different. Some of these kids are not going to like living on a farm,* he chuckled, thinking of cleaning hog pens and horse stalls, and getting their little hands dirty.

Charles was with one of his friends in another stateroom, Claudine was with her friends, and Jack Slater was alone. He watched the slowly darkening landscape until it was dark and then slipped out of the room to find someone to talk to. He hadn't been at the Society long enough to make any friends, and it seemed to him that many of the boys and girls he met weren't able to talk about things like planting fields of wheat and corn, harvesting those same fields, didn't understand the pleasure of riding his pony or driving a team of horses through the fields.

They were city kids for the most part and Jack was a farm boy from the first day. He could talk to Maybelle about the farm and life there, but not to Charles or Claudine, or Terrence. *"I'll be glad when we get to Dakota Territory,"* he said to himself. *"I'll be living on a farm right on the edge of the frontier."* He knew that in just a few years he would have enough money because of the sale of the old farm that he could buy a farm of his own.

Ten years old and he was already plotting out his life and fighting off the horrible things that had changed it so dramatically. The first person he saw when he stepped into the aisle way was old Ephraim, sitting on a bench near the back door of the coach. "Hi," he said, walking right up to old porter.

"Hi, yourself," Ephraim said back, smiling at the boy. "Can I help you with something, boy?"

"You ever been on a farm?" Jack asked, sitting down on the little porter's bench.

"Oh, yes sir, I have been on a farm. Do you know where the Cumberland country is? My Pappy and Mammy and us'ns were slaves on a big farm in the Cumberland before the War Between the States."

"What happened to them?" Jack asked.

47

"My Mommy and Pa had a farm before they got killed in a buggy accident. I'm going to join a family on a farm in Dakota Territory."

"My folks died during the war. I'm so sorry to hear about your folks. What kind of farm did they have?"

The conversation between the old former slave and the bright young boy went on for more than an hour, as they traded stories about driving teams through aromatic black soil so rich you didn't dare drop a seed, about fighting bitter cold winters getting water to the stock, and about bountiful supper tables groaning from the weight of fresh food.

"Oh, Master Jack Slater, I could spend hours talking with you about our lives. Let's do this each evening of our trip, okay with you boy?"

"Thank you, sir, I would like that very much."

"Good, and now, young man, I think it may be a little past your bedtime. Get yourself tucked in and have a good night's sleep. You'll see some beautiful country tomorrow as we fly through Pennsylvania and into the great Ohio Valley."

As the days slid from one to the next, Jack

found himself more and more taking care of the other children. Charles simply wasn't up to it. With no outlet for pent up energy, some of the children found themselves getting into difficulties with each other, with Ephraim, with some of the waiters and porters in the dining car, and with Jack.

One boy in particular, Richard, ten-years-old, and a bully by nature tended to push the little children around, always had to be first in line, and challenged Ephraim's authority. Richard shoved Claudine aside one morning as they walked toward the dining car, and she fell to the carpeted floor, skinning a knee.

Jack helped her to her feet and told Richard to apologize to the girl. "She got in my way. I ain't got nothin' to apologize for," he snarled back at Jack. "You don't like it? Too bad for you," and he turned to walk away.

Jack reached out and grabbed Richard by the shoulder, spinning him around. "I said, apologize to Claudine. You were rude, Richard, and you know Beatrice would not allow you to get away with being a bully."

"Beatrice ain't here and you ain't my boss. Let go a me," and he tried to jerk away from Jack's strong grip. "Let go."

"Not 'till you apologize," Jack said. Richard tried to slug Jack and Jack ducked the swing and wrestled Richard to the floor, pinning him down. "Apologize and never, ever try to hit me again."

Richard was beat, and as so many bullies in the past, when confronted by someone that can't be bullied, gave up in shame. He mumbled an apology and Jack let him up. Richard went on to the dining car, his head bent down, and tears flowing across his face.

After breakfast, Jack found Ephraim and told him about the incident. "Everybody's upset because there's no playing time. There's no running, no jumping, no way to play anywhere."

"I see this all the time, Mister Slater," Ephraim said as the train plowed its way toward Chicago. "These boys and girls have all the energy in the world right now. They could not be more rested, they've been fed the finest food, and just like all the young ones in the world, they want to run and jump and howl with joy." The old man chuckled as he pretended to howl, to Jack's delight.

"I know I want to," Jack laughed, howling right back at the porter. "So, what do we do about this?"

"I think I may have an idea," Ephraim said. "Let's you and me go talk to the conductor."

A most serious pair of gentlemen walked up the aisle toward the dining car where Ephraim expected to find the conductor. The train's engineer may operate that great engine but it is the conductor who is the big boss on a railroad train. The two found Mr. Orion Bounty seated at a table, a sheaf of paperwork spread out in front of him.

"Mr. Bounty, sir, have you had the pleasure of meeting Mr. Jack Slater?"

"No, Mr. Clairidge, I don't believe I have," Bounty said, putting his pen in the inkwell and looking right in Jack's bright brown eyes. "How do you do, Mr. Slater? Is there something I can do for you?"

"My pleasure, sir," Jack said, offering his large strong hand. "Ephraim thinks he may have an answer to giving the orphan train children a chance to burn off some excess energy."

"He does, does he? It has been a problem since the beginning of this program. Well, Ephraim, what is your idea?"

Bounty was a sprightly fellow, probably near forty or so, with a full head of dark red hair that hung in waves to just above his shoulders. He wore a massive moustache that made him look like a walrus, Jack thought, and thick bushy eyebrows that danced about as he talked. He sat back in his chair and pulled a beautiful watch from his vest pocket. "Let's hear it, Ephraim."

"Well, sir," Ephraim began, "these children are so full of energy and have no place to burn it off, and it's just about at this point in our trips that they tend to get quite rowdy, to put it bluntly. We have one of our longer coaling and watering stops coming up, and quite often many passengers take that opportunity to detrain and walk about some.

"I believe it might be a good spot to let the children off the train for half an hour during the coaling, and let them romp about some. I believe that with some help from Jack, here, that we could then put a dozen very tired young people back on the train and they would be fine for the rest of the trip into Chicago."

Bounty sat quietly for a couple of minutes, looking at Jack, then at Ephraim, and finally, a little cough to start things off, gave his full approval. "Splendid," he said. "Now, Mr. Clairidge, Mr. Slater, you will now organize what needs to be done, and I would like a full report on how this turns out. It may come pass that all the orphan trains in the future will have one stop designated as an exercise stop for the children." He smiled to the two and turned back to his paperwork.

52

"Thank you," Jack said and he and Ephraim made their way back to their coach. "This is a really good idea, Ephraim. You've been thinking about this for a long time, haven't you."

"I just needed someone like you to come along and give me a chance to say something. Most of the kids that make these trips are city kids and they don't know why they're being rowdy, why they're getting in trouble. It took a good old farm boy to push me into doing something." They laughed and shook hands before entering the coach.

"Come, young Jack Slater, let me show you something," Ephraim said, walking toward a closet at the far end of the coach. "I've been putting together some of the things that would be needed for such as this."

Jack found half a dozen balls of varying sizes, some hoops for rolling, some ropes for jumping, and other items that use up lots of energy. "I hope you children wear these out," Ephraim chuckled, giving Jack and nice pat on the shoulders.

6

Before he led the children to the dining car that evening, Jack called a meeting to outline Ephraim's plan. "We've been cooped up in this train for several days," he said, getting grumbles back from everyone. "Tomorrow morning the train will be making another long stop to take on coal and water, and Ephraim has set it up so we can get off the train for half an hour and play."

There were whoops and laughter from all the kids and Jack let them show their excitement for a couple of minutes before he continued. "Let's remember now, when we're at supper tonight and breakfast tomorrow morning, that we're ladies and gentlemen, and then we can run and jump and yell all we want when they let us off the train tomorrow."

Supper was a happy event, almost everyone behaved, and the talk was about being able to run tomorrow. Jack sat in front of his window and watched night fall across the open land. They would be in Chicago in just a couple more days and he would be put on another train for the trip to Fargo.

What would his new family be like, he kept wondering? What if they didn't like him, or what if he didn't like them? Charles kept talking about wild Indians but Jack was more anxious about his new family than wild Indians. Jack was not aware of problems in the Black Hills, had no knowledge of the anger building between those moving into the vast plains, and the natives who had called those plains home for several thousand years.

Those in the east had unreasonable expectations of the army being able to pacify the warrior nations and make the frontier a safe place to live. Seldom was anything said to the children about what they might encounter in their new lives. Jack went to sleep with dreams of seeing great fields of wheat and corn dancing in a summer's breeze, and Charles had nightmares about wild Indians eating children.

Twelve very fidgety kids managed to get through their breakfast. In anticipation of getting outside and romping around for half an hour. Ephraim and another porter helped get the kids off the train when it finally stopped for coal and water, and Jack and Ephraim brought all the balls and hoops and ropes out. Terrence didn't want to play, he said, but as soon as someone threw him a ball, he laughed and threw it back.

Jack challenged anyone and everyone to race him and it surprised him when Richard almost beat him. "You're really fast, Richard. Let's race again," Jack laughed, and the two took off, raising a storm of dust around a corral near the water tower.

Claudine told Jack later that day that Richard was fast like that because he was always running away from the coppers.

The first play stop for orphan trains was a huge success, Ephraim said in his report to Conductor Bounty.

The train moved slowly through endless stockyards filled with cattle, then through grimy industrial neighborhoods before pulling into an incredibly busy train station in Chicago. "This is where we part company, Jack," Ephraim said. "You and several of the children will now board a Northern Pacific train for your trip to the Dakota Territory. Many of the children will be heading southwest toward the Kansas areas.

"You have a good life, young sir," he said, holding back tears. Ephraim Clairidge had come to love this sparky boy who was more adult sometimes than many the old man had to work with. He handed Jack an envelope, "I want you to wait until this evening, when you're sitting in front of the train window before you open this. I hope we meet again sometime."

Jack threw his arms around the frail little porter, sobbing. He tried to control his tears but couldn't, and just hung on tight. Ephraim let his dam burst as well, and the two rocked back and forth, bawling their farewell. "I'll always love you, Ephraim," Jack swallowed as he finally let the man go.

"Yes, Mr. Slater, I too, will always love you." He helped Jack and a couple of the other children load their luggage and boxes of personal goods onto a cart to be transferred to the Northern Pacific line. Jack followed that cart to the rails holding his next train and boarded, giving all the paperwork for the children to the coach porter.

"It looks like it's you, me, Richard, and Terrence for this part of the trip," Jack said to Claudine as they scurried down the aisle to their cabins. "Want to take a walk around this new train after we get settled?"

Claudine found herself looking down at the ragged carpet of the coach as she mumbled her yes to Jack. There was a definite smile on her face, and his lit up as well. "Come on, Terrence, let's you and me get settled in," Jack said, nudging the boy down the walkway. "Richard, it looks like you'll have a room all to yourself.

"Just another few days now and we'll have new homes and new families. Where are you going, Terrence?"

"I don't know," he said, putting his little suitcase on a bunk. "It's in the papers you gave the porter. I guess he'll tell me when we get there."

"Didn't somebody at the Society tell you where you were going?" Jack was a little confused about this since almost all the other kids had talked, sometimes at great lengths about where they were going.

"I think Beatrice said something, but I don't remember. It doesn't matter, 'cuz they won't like me anyway. Nobody likes me," he said, his body quivering as the tears began to flow. "I don't like trains."

"I'll talk to the porter and find out where you're going and we can talk about that later, okay?"

"I guess, but they still won't like me," Terrence said, fighting to get his suitcase opened. Jack reached across and opened it for him, and continued working to get his stuff put away. He held the envelope that

Ephraim had given him, wanted to open it right then, but remembered the old man said to do it tonight while sitting in front of the window.

Jack glanced out the window when he felt the coach jerk and begin to move. He caught a glimpse of his old black friend ushering Charles and the other children onto their new railroad coach. "I'll miss you, old man," he murmured, waving a little, even though he knew Ephraim couldn't se him.

There was a tap on the door and a rather rotund gentleman stuck his head in the cramped room. "Are you Jack?" he asked. "My name is Chuck Foster, the coach porter."

"Hello Chuck. Yes, I'm Jack and this is Terrence. Claudine has the room next to ours, and Charles is next to her. I guess it's just the four of us, now."

"I have all your paperwork put together. You'll eat together at the same table, and after your long journey from New York, I guess you know all the rules and stuff. Have a good trip," he said and started to back out of the stateroom.

"One thing," Jack said before he could get out. "This is Terrence, and he doesn't know where he's going or who is supposed to be picking him up. Can you help him, Chuck?"

"I think I can," Chuck smiled. "Come on with me Terrence, and we'll take a look at some of the papers and get you all set up for your new family."

Chuck and Terrence slipped out and Jack found himself sitting in front of the coach window, watching Chicago go by, faster and faster. *It was so flat coming across the last couple of days, and even right now, I can't see a hill anywhere. We had hills near our farm, with big trees and creeks and ponds. I wonder what Fargo is like? Maybe Chuck knows,* he thought, letting the clickety-clack of the rails almost put him to sleep.

It was another tap at the door that brought him back to reality and he opened it to find Claudine standing with a big smile. He put the envelope on his bunk, slipped into the aisle way, took her hand, and headed for the dining car. "I hope they have some cookies or ice cream," she said, with a little giggle. It was more than an hour before they got back to their rooms.

"That was fun, Jack," she said. "How long is this trip?"

"We have to go through Minnesota, and you'll get off in two days, I think, then another couple of days before I get off in Fargo. I don't know where Terrence is supposed to get off, and neither does he," he said, still wondering why the boy doesn't know or not seem to even care.

"Terrence didn't want to come at all," Claudine said. "At the society, all he did was sit in his room all day. He wouldn't come and play or anything. He didn't even want to play the other day, remember? You had to almost push him off the train."

"I think he's just scared," Jack said. "He's very young, and so small, and I think he's just scared. I hope he gets a nice family."

Chuck tapped on the door to announce that supper would be served in half an hour, and Jack hurried to wash up and put on a clean shirt. "Supper time, Terrence. Better wash your face."

"I don't want any," the little boy said, sitting on his bunk.

"You have to eat, Terry. You know what Beatrice said." He looked at the boy, sitting so forlorn, ready to burst into tears at any moment. "What did Chuck tell you?"

"I'm supposed to get off at some place called Twin Falls, no, that's not right. Twin something, anyway I can't remember. It doesn't matter 'cuz they won't like me anyway."

"Come on, Terry, wash your face and let's

go eat. You can tell us about it during dinner. The dining car porter told us we're getting chocolate cake for dessert. I could eat a whole cake," he said, his face lit up like a lantern in the dark.

It took a little more coaxing, but he finally got Terrence moving, found Claudine waiting for them in the hallway, and headed for supper. *I guess Richard went on ahead, without us,* he thought, wondering why Richard was so thoughtless.

They could see lightning flashing in the distance as they ate their dinner, and with every crash of thunder, Terrence jumped up. Jack had a hard time calming the boy down. Richard teased him, almost to the point of having the boy crying.

"Stop being a jerk, Richard," Jack exploded at one point. "You're rude, you're a bully, and you better stop being stupid. Terry is a little kid who's afraid of lightning. You ever been afraid of anything?" he sneered. Jack chuckled then, and said, "Yeah, you have. You're afraid of me, Richard. Do you want me to make fun of you like you make fun of Terry?"

Richard got up from the table without asking to be excused and went back to his room without dessert. Jack held back a smile as best he could, got a big smile from Claudine, and went back to talking about lightning.

"Thunder and lightning can't hurt us in the train, Terry," he said, over and over. After cake and ice cream, the three children made it back to their rooms as the train moved right into the center of a massive early winter storm. Jack sat by the window after getting Terrence ready for bed and half-way calmed down, and watched snow fly through the air, saw great flashes of lightning, and felt the coach tremble with some of the claps of thunder.

He pulled the envelope from Ephraim out of his notebook and slowly opened it. There was a two-page letter inside, written in a beautiful hand. "I wish I could write like that," he murmured. "Mama always said I needed to practice my penmanship more."

In Ephraim's letter, the old man outlined his life, first growing up as a slave on a farm in Virginia, and then being freed and moving north after the terrible war, and going to school for the first time, as a grown man.

The old man wrote about learning to read and write, and then about getting the job on the railroad. He said, "Meeting you brought many memories back, some not very good, others extraordinary. You too have had a hard time and there are big changes in your life coming up. You're a very smart boy, big and strong, and you are on your way to a long life. I want it to be a good life for you, and you might find that you will have to work hard to make it so.

"Don't give up, Jack. Don't let problems force you to do the wrong thing or make the wrong decision. You're a big, brave, and wonderful boy, and strong enough in your mind to make a good life for yourself. I just wish I had gotten married and had a son, a son like you. I love you, boy," and he signed it Ephraim (Pappy) Clairidge.

Jack sat very still in front of that window, tears rolling down his broad face, watching the huge storm and thinking of Ephraim. "Pappy he called himself. If I ever see that man again, that's what I'll call him, too."

7

One thing that could be said for Pete Jablonski, he never hit any of his children, never spanked one, never cuffed one, and yet, was abusive in many other ways toward them. Extra work was one form of control, withholding food was the worst abuse, and from the time Skeeter, the first of the orphans arrived, there was never any love shown toward the children.

The first major winter storm blasted through the Dakota Territory, shutting down all but the basic work on the Jablonski farm. Feed and water the animals, keep the drainage ditches clear and flowing, keep a full load of firewood for the kitchen and living quarters, and keep the pathways as open as possible. These jobs were done by the children, without question.

"I walked by the barn," Jablonski said after everyone was seated for supper, "and the ice had not been broken in the cow's trough.

Wasn't that your responsibility, Jason?"

Jason, ten-years-old but the size of an eight-year-old, knew what was coming and started crying immediately. "Well?" Pete Jablonski said in a very loud voice. "Speak up, Jason. Wasn't that your job?"

"Yes, sir," Jason blubbered through his tears, shaking all over.

"Mims, take his plate away." She got up from the table, hating to have to do this to her littlest brother. "Now, Jason, you sit there and watch the rest of us have a fine supper of roast pork with corn and potatoes. And," he said, almost proudly, "when we're through, we're going to enjoy an apple pie that Mims spent the afternoon baking for us.

"You'll be going to bed hungry, Jason, because you failed to do your job. Because you failed to do your job, the cow didn't get any water today. Now you'll know how the cow felt about that."

Nothing more was said at the supper table that night. Not one word was spoken. Mims and Skeeter were forced to eat everything on their plates, were forced to have apple pie for dessert, and Jason was forced to sit and watch. No one in New York, at the Children's Aid Society knew how Jablonski treated his orphans.

"Why didn't you say something to Skeeter or me about not breaking the ice," Mims asked Jason after supper. He was helping her do the dishes while Skeeter was feeding the hogs.

"I tried to break the ice with the ax but I couldn't," Jason was still bawling like a two-year-old. The boy was frail in build, unable to do most of the chores that Mims and Skeeter handled with ease, and suffered the fire of Pete Jablonski's anger regularly.

"But you didn't say anything," Mims said, frustrated at the boy. "You know Skeeter and I will help anytime. It's stupid not to ask for help, and Pete will go out of his way to catch you not doing your chores."

"I don't want to be here," Jason blubbered.

"Well," she said, "we don't have much choice in that matter do we." She wasn't quite four feet tall, stood in her apron, her fists knotted up and on her hips, shaking her head in anger and frustration at the boy. "Grow up," she said, jerking the apron off and heading for the barn to help Skeeter with evening chores.

Jablonski was a terror around the farm during the long storm and after three days he finally announced why. "I'll be going into town tomorrow and won't be back for two days. Skeeter, you see to it that all the chores are done, all the animals are taken care of, and Jason, you better shape up."

"Why are you going to be in town for two days, Pete?" Mims asked.

"I'll be picking up another boy for the family," is all he said, walking out to inspect the barn and hog pens.

"I knew he was trying to get another kid," Mims said, "but I was really hoping for a girl. Sometimes working with you two I feel more like a boy than I do a girl." She was as strong and worked as hard as Skeeter even though she was two years younger, and couldn't remember the last time she wore a dress. All three of the kids wore twill pants and heavy wool shirts along with leather boots most of the time.

"I hope he's big and strong, not like Jason," Skeeter said, bringing a gusher of tears to Jason's face.

"Don't be cruel, Skeeter. Jason can't help it if he just isn't really big and strong. You were here first, Skeeter. Was Pete always mean like he is now?"

"I was nine when I got here, three years ago, and he's always been just like he is now. I sure wish we had a pa and ma. Those kids at Reverend Thomas's farm have a real family and we have Pete. As soon as I'm sixteen I'm leaving here."

"Where would you go?" Jason asked. "Wouldn't you be scared? Who would feed you?"

"I wouldn't be scared," Skeeter said, "and I'd go anywhere I wanted. I'd go into the mountains and eat deer and stuff, that's what I'd do," he said, and headed out the door to work on his chores. Until Skeeter arrived at the Jablonski farm he had never spent a minute outside New York City, and since he arrived in Dakota Territory has been off the farm less than ten times.

"I'm going to go to work in one of the stores in town when I get old enough to leave this farm," Mims said. "You better head out to the barn if you want supper tonight, Jason," she said, putting on a heavy winter coat and leaving the warm kitchen.

"I'm going to think about you every day, Jack," Claudine said while Jack was helping her get all her bags and boxes off the train. "I hope we get to see each other again, some day."

"Me too, Claudine," Jack said watching her give him a big smile. He liked her freckles and the way she wrinkled her nose sometimes. "I don't know the name of whoever I'm supposed to live with, but I have the name and address of your new family, so I'll write to you, if it's okay."

"I'd like that Jack. I'm not very good at reading and writing, but I'll write to you, too."

The train gave a couple of blasts on the steam whistle and Jack jumped back onto the coach, waving goodbye to Claudine until the porter finally forced him to get all the way into the coach so he could shut the door. "She sure is a pretty little girl, isn't she?" he said, nudging Jack in the ribs.

"I like her a lot," he said. "How long now until we reach Fargo?"

"Probably two days, son, if we stay on schedule. That storm slowed things down a little, but we've been making good time today. You're the last of the children on this run. Is there anything I can get you before I get back to my business?"

"No, sir. I'm going to go to my room and read for a while. Sure glad we got Richard off this train but I'm going to miss Claudine."

"That Richard was a pisser, wasn't he? I'll knock when it's supper time," the porter said, leaving Jack to head to his station at the other end of the coach. Jack slipped into his stateroom, now all alone in the world, once again.

He sat by the window and watched Minnesota fly past, forests full of big trees, not a mountain or hill in sight, but it seemed like every mile or so the train would be going across a bridge over rushing streams and rivers. There were large farms, now coated in their winter white, that he could imagine filled with fields of wheat and barley and corn.

I wonder what my new family is going to be like. Will I have brothers and sisters? I'll always have my Pa and Mama, but what will my new pa be like? He tried to match what he was seeing out the coach window to what he would find in Fargo and that didn't work. Finally, he got his notebook out and read what he had been writing for the last several days on this trip of a lifetime.

He re-read the letter from Ephraim again and once more, holding back tears of love, and laid his head down on the pillow and slept soundly until the tap on the door announced supper time. He found that he would be sitting with a man and his wife and small son and liked that idea.

I guess I'll never get that out of my mind, his thoughts rumbled through his head as he made his way to the dining car. *I'm alone, and I'm surrounded by people. Do other people have these thoughts? Until that terrible day when I lost Mama and Pa, I was never alone.*

"How do you do," Jack said, scooting into his chair. "I'm Jack Slater, soon to be of Fargo, Dakota Territory."

"I'm pleased you're joining us, Mr. Slater. I'm, Thomas Kennedy, my wife Mary, and our son Joshua, who's almost three. We're going to be homesteading in the Wyoming Territory. It's high up in the Rocky Mountains and we'll be raising sheep and cattle."

"We had sheep and hogs on our farm in New York," Jack said, "but I don't know what kind of farm my new family will have. We raised wheat and corn, too, and I've sure seen a lot of wheat and corn on this trip."

Kennedy laughed at that, agreeing with him. "Yes, Jack, I don't think I've ever seen as much wheat and corn as we've seen. So, what I understand about your situation is that you lost your family and are being relocated to another family in the territories? Is that right?"

"That's being awfully blunt, Thomas," his wife said. "It must have been terrible to lose your family."

"Yes, it was," Jack said, fighting the desire to let a gusher flow. "All I know is that there is a family waiting for me on a farm in

Fargo. I really miss my Pa and Mama and our farm, but I'm also excited about what I'm moving to."

"Well, you're a big boy, Jack, and I'm sure this new family will come to love you just as your parents did. I'd love to have a big strong boy like you to help us get our ranch started in Wyoming. Joshua will be big and strong like you in just a few years. How old are you, twelve?"

"No, sir, I'm ten," Jack said.

"Oh, my, then you are big and strong," Thomas Kennedy said, giving the boy a full look.

Small talk filled the table, supper was good, dessert was chocolate cake again, and Jack found himself alone once more, watching the Minnesota sky turn to full dark. He could see clouds building on the western horizon as the train continued westward.

Jablonski drove the team to the livery stables across the street from the Fargo Hotel and grabbed his carpetbag from the back. "I'll be here for a couple of days, Mr. Forrest, so take good care of these boys. If you need me, I'll be at the hotel."

You'll be at the bar, you mean, Forrest thought, nodding to Jablonski. "Old man Walters said the next train is supposed to have seed for this next spring. Thought you might want to know." Jablonski just grunted something back and trudged across the street to the hotel and took a room.

He emptied the carpetbag and put his things away. *They said I would be getting another boy, and I sure hope he's a big one. I should never have accepted Jason and now I can't give him back. Even a girl would be better than that little pip. I need a drink.* Pete Jablonski went back out on the streets of Fargo and turned immediately to the open doors of the Barrel House Saloon and Parlor.

"Hello, Pete," Lucius Walters said when Jablonski came through the doors. "Got seed coming in on the next train."

"Yeah, I heard." He motioned to the bartender for a drink, pulled a cigar from a box on the bar and lit it. "Hope it's better seed than last year. Rotted in the ground, it did," he snarled.

"Nobody else complained," Walters snapped back. "Probably planted too deep."

"Bah," Jablonski said, and walked away from the bar, toward tables near the front window. *Planted too deep. Bah. What would a storekeeper know about planting corn, anyway?* He watched as a couple of men from the kitchen brought out the free lunch food and set it up near the long bar. *I'll have a roast beef sandwich then I've got to get to the bank and get those papers signed.*

On the way to the bank he ran into Reverend Thomas and his wife. "Hello, Thomas," Jablonski said, nodding and tipping his hat to Mrs. Thomas as well. "Walters just told me that a seed shipment would be on the next train in from the east."

"Train will arrive tomorrow. That's why we're here. That seed last year was about the best that we've had for several years. My corn crop was far superior to the year before.

"What do you know about flax, Jablonski? I've been told there's a fair market for it in the east."

"Don't know about flax, Thomas. I'll stick with corn and wheat, and my hogs. There's a good market. Hogs. Sent hundreds of them into Wyoming Territory and down into Colorado country last year. Good market for hogs.

"Well, I don't want to be late at the bank. Nice to see you, Thomas, Missus. Good day." He walked down the long boardwalk toward the bank muttering about corn, planting too deep, and flax, whatever that was. Ray Bennett, Fargo National Bank was waiting for him.

Bennett had been acting as an agent for the Children's Aid Society for many years, helping to find homes for the children among the farmers and ranchers in Dakota Territory. He had placed all three of Jablonski's children, along with many other families.

Bennett was more than large. He stood near the six foot mark, and carried more weight than a man should. "Good morning Pete," he said. Looks like you're about to have another member of the Jablonski family. I have the paperwork right here. Sit down, please."

Jablonski and Bennett were among the very first to settle in the area, even before Centralia, now Fargo, became a community. "You know, Pete, it's only been a couple of years since we re-named this old town in favor of Mr. Fargo when he helped bring that railroad here. Everyone can move their crops and we get the finest ware from the east.

"Fargo isn't on the far edge of the frontier anymore, Pete." Bennett had a grand smile on his face, almost beaming in his thoughts of prosperity. "That railroad will soon stretch all the way to the Pacific coast to our west, and with connections, it goes all the way to the Atlantic Ocean.

"Well, you know all about that, but it's true, we're a part of the history of this territory now. And, you're a family man with a fine farm, and you should be a leader. I worry, Pete, that you have limited vision when it comes to the future. Your new son will be here tomorrow."

"Hello Ray," Jablonski said. "I hope he's a big strong boy, this time. That frail little Jason boy is a waste. I should never have accepted him."

"The idea, Pete, is to provide a loving home for orphan children, not to simply get free farm hands. Maybe I should take a closer look at your qualifications. You know, we stretched the rules a bit allowing you, a single man, to adopt these children."

"I know the rules and I know the program, Ray," Pete said, showing his anger. Then he realized what might happen and put a small smile on and said, "I'm just frustrated with the boy. Skeeter and Mims are doing fine, and there's no need to change what we have." He tried hard to give Bennett a smile, and coughed gently to help it along some.

"Very well, then. Here's the paperwork on Jack Slater," and he handed a sheaf of papers across the desk. "He's ten-years-old, large for his age, they say, and was raised on a farm that grew corn, wheat, and raised hogs and sheep, so he should fit right in."

"That's very good, Ray, very good, indeed. Right now, Skeeter and Mims are having to do all the work with almost no help from Jason, so this Jack boy should work out very good."

"All right," Bennett said. "Here are the forms that need to be signed," and he handed a couple of sheets of paper across to Jablonski, "and here are the adoption papers naming you Jack Slater's new parent, changing his name to Jack Jablonski." Bennett sat back in his massive leather chair and lit a cigar, blowing a cloud of blue smoke toward the ceiling.

"According to what I've been told, Pete, this will be your last adoption. They have put a limit of four for you. Maybe it's because of you not being married, I don't know, but this will be the last." He sat back in his leather chair and took a long look at his old friend.

"By the way, I talked with Reverend Thomas yesterday and he's going to be pulling some of his wheat acreage and planting flax this next spring. Have you given that any thought? There's a pretty good market for flax from Chicago east is what I'm hearing."

"Don't know nothing about flax. I'll stick

with wheat and corn, thank you. My big market is hogs and I'm sure going to increase that product. You know how much I shipped last year. There's your good market, Ray. Hogs."

"Your hogs will always find a good market, Pete, I know that, but with linen becoming so popular and so many uses for linseed oil, I would give just a thought to finding out more about flax."

Pete gathered up all his paperwork, shook hands with the banker, and walked back to the hotel. *I wonder what the flax thing is all about,* he thought, putting the papers on the table in his room. *I think I need to talk to someone about it. Thomas is pretty smart and so is Bennett. Do you eat the stuff, or what?*

8

"Well, young Mr. Slater, this will be our last meal together," Thomas Kennedy said as he and Mary with their son Joshua joined Jack in the dining car. "You must be very excited about what will be happening the rest of today."

Jack had a bowl of oatmeal sitting in front of him along with a sweet roll and a glass of milk. "I'm very excited," he said, his big brown eyes dancing in the early morning light. "I'll meet my new parents in just a couple of hours, and maybe find out that I'll have brothers and sisters." His stomach had been churning all night, was still active this morning, thinking about what he would find when the train stopped in Fargo, Dakota Territory.

He managed to finish his breakfast, made light conversation with the Kennedy family, and made his way back to his coach. He spent half an hour putting his belongings into the suitcases and carpetbags, made sure his face and hands were well washed and his unruly hair half way under control, when he felt the train begin to slow down. As it slowed down, the butterflies in his stomach got even more active.

Fargo, he discovered wasn't very big, just a dusty farming community on the outskirts of civilization, although this morning, he found out immediately, it was mud, not dust, in the streets from the storm that had passed through. He said goodbye to the porter and stepped onto a bare wood platform, watching several men begin to unload merchandise from two rail cars.

The train was a mix of passenger cars and box cars, and Jack was amazed at just how much merchandise could be hauled in one of those cars. Great bags of seed were brought out, large packing crates filled with who-knows-what were wheeled onto the platform and moved into waiting freight wagons. Jack was amazed and stood almost with his mouth open, watching.

There didn't seem to be anyone inside the little station and there certainly wasn't anyone on the platform, other than those unloading. The fright of finding himself alone once again settled like a heavy weight on his heart. As he looked quickly in every direction, hoping to find someone looking for him, the fright almost became panic.

Something's wrong, kept cropping up in his mind, and it was almost a full minute of fear before he spotted a man in a wagon, at the far end of the platform waving his arms and motioning for him to hurry up. Jack had a suitcase and carpetbag full of his clothing and personal belongings, and a large box or crate filled with books and other personal things.

He dragged the suitcase and bag several feet, then went back and pushed the crate up and beyond the bags, then went back for them. The man in the wagon hollered at him to hurry up, never stepping down from the wagon to help. One of the men unloading a boxcar stepped over to help Jack.

"Here, son, let me help you with that. Got yourself quite a load here."

"Thank you, sir, and yes I do." The man picked up the crate and grabbed the suitcase while Jack manhandled the carpetbag up to the wagon.

"Sure glad you were able to help this boy, Pete. You really are a mean-hearted old man. This your new farm hand, I mean, son?"

"Get in the wagon, boy," Pete Jablonski snarled, "and mind your own business, Walters. Just throw that junk in the back and get in the wagon," he said again, taking up the reins.

Walters and Jack got the three pieces in the back of the wagon and Jack climbed in and started to move to the seat next to Pete. "Just stay back there, boy. We're late now," he said, twitching the horses with a buggy whip into a trot out of town. Jack sat down in the back of the wagon wondering what kind of a man this was.

Is this my new Pa? What am I getting into? This isn't what Maybelle told me I would be coming to. It was just five miles, less than an hour back to the Jablonski farm and Jack watched mile after mile of corn and wheat fields, nestled in their winter's best, that is cold mud and frozen fronds. *Looks like good farming country. Maybe this man is just one of the farm hands and not my new Pa. I hope so,* he thought, seeing a large two-story house with a big barn and other outbuildings come into view.

Jablonski never slowed the horses down from their trot after leaving Fargo and didn't put them into a walk until he turned in at the lane leading to the house. Skeeter and Mims came running out to meet the wagon as soon as it turned into the lane. Jason slipped out of the barn just as the wagon pulled to a stop.

Jack stood up and lifted the suitcase over the side, then the carpetbag, but wasn't able to lift the crate over. Skeeter jumped into the wagon and helped him get it over the side where it crashed into the mud next to the suitcase. Mims stood watching with Jason standing next to her.

"He's just as big as Skeeter," Jason said, watching the two big boys begin to move all the stuff inside the house. "I thought he was supposed to be your age, Mims," he said.

"Mims, get these horses and wagon taken care of," Pete snarled, stepping off the wagon. "Give 'em some hay and a good brushing. Skeeter, get this stuff put away and then take the boy on a tour of the farm. Make sure he knows where everything is and what the rules are.

"Jason, get those stalls cleaned and all the animals watered. We've missed two good days of work now, and that's not good. Move it, Jason," he threatened, and walked into the house, not attempting to help Jack and Skeeter with Jack's belongings.

"Is that your Pa?" Jack asked. "I mean, is he going to be my new Pa?" Jack could feel the rebellion begin, and the worry. It had been in the back of his mind from the moment he stepped on the train back in New

York. *What if I don't like my new family? What if they don't like me?* He tried to talk to Charles about these fears but Charles was too fearful of the Indians to worry about whether his new family would like him.

"He's not a very nice man," Jack said, watching Pete Jablonski walk into the house. "Is he mean to you?"

"No, sometimes he isn't very nice. We aren't allowed to call him Pa or Papa. We have to call him Pete. What's your name? My name's Skeeter."

"Skeeter? That's a funny name. I'm Jack Slater." The two big boys managed to get Jack's stuff upstairs and into a large room. There were four beds separated from each other by curtains of wool blankets hung from twine.

"This is your bed, here," Skeeter said, moving a blanket aside. "Put your stuff at the end of the bed and under the bed." Skeeter put the carpetbag on the bed, pushing the crate toward the end.

Jack stood very still for a minute, taking the scene in. There was a curtain on one side of the bed that wrapped around the head of the bed. At the foot of the bed was a space of a couple of feet and the wall, and on the other side of the bed a space of maybe four feet and another curtain.

There was no dresser, no table, no chair, and no lamp. "When you get settled, come down to the kitchen and I'll tell you all about Pete Jablonski and our chores and rules," Skeeter said, stepping out of the little cubicle, letting the blanket fall back. "Better put some work clothes on," he said skipping down the stairs.

Jack sat on the edge of the bed, could feel the tears as they rolled across his cheeks, and tried with all his might to not cry. *This isn't right,* kept ringing through his mind. *Skeeter is afraid of Pete, and I'm not going to let him make me afraid. I'm big and I'm strong, and I'm not afraid.* He was afraid, he knew it, felt it, that's why he was crying, but he told himself three more times that he wasn't afraid.

Jack wiped the tears away with a hefty swipe of the back of his hand and sorted his clothing, changed quickly, and headed down to the kitchen, where he could hear the other children.

Skeeter introduced Jack to Mims and Jason, the two in the kitchen waiting to meet their new brother. The four kids walked out of the kitchen and over toward the barn. "Pete'll probably have you working with the hogs, Jack, but you'll also have to chop wood every day, chop the ice from the water troughs, and clean the barn stalls. We have to work hard during the winter to keep the ditches from clogging up with ice.

"When we sit down for our meals, there's no talking unless you are spoken to first. You must eat everything you're served, and if you have done something wrong during the day, your punishment is to sit at the table with no food and watch everyone else eat theirs."

"We all take turns cleaning the house, doing the laundry, and cooking," Mims said. "It's very hard."

Jack felt afraid at first, and then got angry instead. He looked at Mims and saw a very strong girl, a set to her mouth that intrigued him, not soft and with a pretty smile like Claudine's, more determined and with a touch of anger, more like Beatrice's back at the Society. He knew that Skeeter would never stand up for himself, could see that the boy was afraid of Pete, but was sure that Mims was the leader of the children.

Jack saw to it that Mims gave him the rest of his tour of the farm and the two spent the rest of the day together. The equipment was in fair shape, but much of the working harness needed repair or at least upkeep, the rolling stock was not taken good care of, and the general condition of the corn and wheat bins was poor.

"Who is supposed to maintain the harness? It hasn't been oiled or cleaned since the harvest," he said, holding a collar and hames. "These need to be cleaned and taken care of before spring work."

"You know a lot about farms, don't you," Mims said.

"Me and Pa worked a farm like this one. You haven't said what it is that Pete does around the farm. Pa was always right there doing everything."

"Pete tells us what to do," she said with a sly grin. "He's the boss and we're the farm workers. That's how he explains it. You need to be careful, Jack. If you try to tell him what needs to be done he'll get really angry. He don't like to be told things. He'll tell you that he's the boss and he says what's to be done.

"He'll punish you by taking your food away."

"He'll only do that once," Jack said quietly. They walked toward the hog pens, Jack's favorite animals, except for horses. "We had hogs and sheep on our farm," he said. "I really like working with them. Cept'in for the big old boars. They can be mighty mean."

Mims walked like she owned the world,

squared up shoulders, arms swinging with authority, and her head erect, her eyes taking in the whole farm. "I brought some good books with me that they gave me at the Society. I didn't see any lamps in our bedroom area. Where do you read?"

"I don't even know how to read, Jack," she said. "Ain't nobody ever taught me how. We don't have any books, besides, at the end of the day, after supper, all I want to do is go to bed."

"Don't you go to school? Maybelle said we would be going to school."

"Ain't never been to no school. Pete wouldn't let us go even if there was one. I guess there might be one in Fargo, maybe."

Jack pitched in with Skeeter and Mims for the rest of the day, helped Jason break the ice in the water troughs and was told by Skeeter that they weren't supposed to help Jason. "He's just a little kid," Jack said. "It's hard for me to break that ice, that's why he needs help." Mims gave him a nod and a smile when he helped Jason.

"Just don't let Pete find out," is all that Skeeter said.

The four children heard the supper bell being rung by Pete and headed out of the barn toward the big house. "I could eat a horse," Jack laughed as they trotted up the porch. "Haven't eaten since breakfast on the train. I guess I must have missed dinner with you guys."

"We had just finished when you and Pete arrived," Mims said. "I wish you'd said something, I could have fixed you something. I put a big shoulder of pork in a Dutch oven and it's been cooking all day, so you'll eat hog tonight, not horse," she laughed, giving him a poke in the ribs.

9

Jack was more than a little nervous as he washed his hands and face before settling in at the large table in the center of the kitchen. Pete Jablonski was already seated at one end of the table and Mims had hold of a big heavy cast iron Dutch oven ready to move to the table.

"Here, let me help you with that," Jack said, taking a step toward the stove. "Looks pretty heavy, Mims."

"Sit down, Jack. That's her job," Pete said.

Jack stopped, gave a questioning look at Mims, and stepped toward the kitchen table. "I just thought she might need a little help," he said, and pulled his chair out to sit. Skeeter and Jason were already seated. Skeeter had a little grin on his face, which seemed odd to Jack, while Jason was cringing just a little bit, as if expecting to be reprimanded.

Mims hefted the pot onto the table and

pulled the lid off. The pork shoulder was falling off the bone, with roasted potatoes, carrots, and onions mixed in the natural juices. "That really smells good, Mims," Jack said as she settled in next to him.

"We don't talk at the table, Jack, unless we're spoken to first by me. I'll let this slip tonight, but don't ever speak again unless spoken to." Jack was startled by the anger in Pete's voice and the idea of not talking at the supper table was just the opposite of how he had been raised. Again, he caught just a hint of a smile from Skeeter.

He could picture his Mama and Pa full of happiness at supper, talking about the day's activities, asking him questions about his day, planning the future, talking about the past, and here was Pete telling him that there would be no talk during supper. He wanted to say something, almost did, and Mims must have seen it coming because she gave him just the slightest nudge.

"I read the stuff the Society sent, Jack, and see that you have some experience living on a farm. It says you can drive a team pulling a plow or cultivators. Is that so?"

"Yes, sir," Jack said. "Pa taught me how to plow for both corn and wheat, and how to take care of the animals and equipment, like harness. I also helped with the harvest."

"I don't want you talkin' about your pa. He ain't here no more, so don't mention him again. Says here that you also raised hogs on that farm." Jack nodded yes, anger flushing his face at what Pete said about his Pa. Pete either didn't notice or didn't care, and continued. "I have a large shipment of hogs that I send out twice a year, mostly west into Wyoming and southwest into the Colorado country, so you better know your stuff."

Supper was short and silent, and Jack had hundreds of ugly thoughts raging through his head as he ate. He had just as many questions, and wanted to tell Mims how good her roast pork was. He was about to ladle out another helping of vegetables when Pete stopped him.

"Just what do you think you're doing, Jack?"

"I wanted some more vegetables," he said, looking at Pete, then Mims, and back to Pete, the ladle still in his hand, and big questions written across his face.

"We don't just take seconds," Pete said, "without permission."

Jack answered without thinking first. "How could I ask for permission if I'm not supposed to talk?" he said, getting a little giggle from Jason, which brought a huge storm from Pete.

"Alright, that's enough. This supper is over. All of you, leave the table now. Mims, take care of the food, Skeeter, go to your room. Jack, Jason, there will be no breakfast for either of you in the morning. Don't you ever talk back to me like that again, or you'll wish you had never met me. Go to your rooms now, both of you," he stormed.

You're right, Pete, I wish I had never met you, Jack thought climbing the stairs to his little blanket walled 'room'. Even when Mims finished her work and came up to the room, there was no talk among the kids. Jack started to say something and Mims shushed him immediately.

His mind was a fury of action, as he remembered Pete telling Skeeter to make sure that Jack understood all the rules of living there. *He didn't tell me anything. That's what that grin was all about. He walked me right into getting in trouble. You are now on my list buddy, and you might be older but I'm just as big.* He recognized that he had a friend in Mims, and then thoughts of his Pa and Momma crept in, and he wanted to cry. *You won't ever make me cry, Pete, never,* he thought.

After just a few minutes he laid his head on the pillow and could hear Jason crying himself to sleep, and heard Pete tromp up the stairs and go into his large bedroom, muttering to himself.

Jack's last thoughts before drifting off to sleep had to do with how he was going to survive over the next few years. He was well aware that he wouldn't come into his own money until he was eighteen, but also knew that when he was sixteen that he was supposed to get paid for working on the farm. He made a vow that by the time he was sixteen he would be ready to walk off this farm, go as far away from Pete Jablonski as he could get.

Over the next several weeks Jack learned as much as he could about the farm, about Pete's ugly temper and his lack of farming knowledge. He wanted to send a letter to Maybelle at the Society in New York, but wasn't sure how to go about that. Mims said that Jack wouldn't allow that. She told him that the only way he could do it would be to ride with him to Fargo to help bring in supplies, and when Pete went to the saloon, to sneak a letter to the post office.

After missing a couple of meals because of his quick mouth, as he put it, Jack started putting together a stash of food that could be hidden and wouldn't rot or go bad right away. Mims discovered what he had been doing after a terrible time at supper one night.

"I've had just about enough from you, Jack," Pete said as everyone sat down for supper. "This is my farm and it's going to be run my way. I heard what you said to Lucius Walters when we were in the store today. How dare you question my way of doing things around here.

"Mims, take Jack's plate away. You will not get supper tonight. You just sit there and watch us enjoy our supper. Do it now, Mims," he snarled at the frightened girl. Jack sat straight in his chair and spent the next half hour glaring at Pete, never took his eyes off the man, and only blinked when he had to.

He was fast approaching his eleventh birthday, and felt like he was never going to make it to sixteen. He did everything he could to help little Jason, but all that did was get him in more trouble, and it seemed that a lot of the trouble that came his way come by way of Skeeter. Skeeter was fast to tell Pete that Jack helped Jason, that Jack helped Mims, that Jack didn't like the way Pete treated the livestock and the kids. *I'm going to have to start paying more attention to what I say and do around that little brat,* he snickered to himself after missing another meal.

Late that night Mims heard Jack get up and get dressed. She did the same and silently followed him downstairs and out to the barn. He slipped a few pieces of harness aside and pulled a box out, opened it, and was munching on some biscuits and jam when she startled him.

"One smart boy, you are, Jack," she said, a smile spread across her face. "Do not let Skeeter know about this, or Jason either. Skeeter would tell on you right away, and Jason would too, but accidentally."

"I know," Jack smiled, offering Mims a biscuit. "He's a real tattle-tale. He's going to get it someday, though, and I'm going to give it to him."

They laughed at that, and as their eyes met, a pact was written, sworn to, and sealed on the spot. The two sat in the straw eating biscuits and jam for some time that night, talking about what a miserable life they had, and making plans on how to get Skeeter, and how to get out of there.

"When I'm sixteen, I'm leaving," Jack said. "I'm not going to stay until I'm eighteen. I'm already as big as Skeeter, and my Pa was really big, so I know I'm going to grow a lot bigger and be a lot stronger."

"Where would you go?" Mims asked. The two sat with their backs to the barn wall, their legs stretched out in front of them. "I know I've thought about running away, but I don't know where I'd go."

"People in New York always talked about California and Texas, about gold, and about cowboys. I'd go south to Texas, just as fast as I could get there. Heck, Mims, I could get jobs on farms, stay for awhile, then move more south until I would be in Texas."

"You're not afraid of anything, are you?" she asked, her eyes bright, and her freckles dancing with her smile. "I'd be really scared."

They spent well over another hour in the barn talking about what each of them wanted, with Jack wanting to be as far away from Pete as he could get, and working on a farm or ranch in Texas.

"When I'm eighteen, I have some money coming. When my Pa and Momma were killed in that buggy wreck, the farm had to be sold and the money is in a bank in New York, and will be mine. I think I'll buy a small farm in Texas."

"I like doing all the chores around here," Mims said, "but I don't think I want to live on a farm for the rest of my life. I've gone to Fargo a couple of times with Pete, and I want to live in a town."

10

As animosity between Pete and Jack brewed and steeped, Jack's personality brewed and steeped as well, he became quite a different boy from the one who stepped off that train. He loved the work on the farm, fought almost daily with Jablonski on how things should be done, found that Skeeter continued to be a troublemaker and bully, and loved Mims with all his heart.

She was a rascal at heart with a brilliant sense of humor that kept Jack on guard regularly. A splash from a pail of water, a foot stuck out from nowhere, or little kiss on his cheek or hug for no reason, then a giggle, dancing freckles, and Jack would find his heart racing.

It was Jablonski's mis-use of his equipment and intolerant attitude toward the children that bothered Jack the most. Pete tormented little Jason, allowed Skeeter to bully the boy, and forced Mims to do more work than either Skeeter or Jason. Skeeter constantly worked to get Jack in trouble, telling outright lies, or in some cases, plotting to make Jack do something Pete would not like.

Jack was relentless in maintaining the farm equipment, and challenged Pete regularly on just how wagons, plows, threshers, and cultivators should be kept. Jack simply took it on himself to keep the harness leather in shape, and the wheels on all the equipment turned on well greased axels.

By the time Jack was twelve he was bigger than Skeeter at fourteen, towered over little Jason, and was able to do a man's work every day of the week. During harvest, it was Jack that cut the most corn, reaped the most wheat, and stacked the most hay for the winter. Pete found that Jack was amazing with all the animals, in particular the horses used with various pieces of equipment.

Jack taught himself how to use the forge, how to do simple iron work with tongs and hammers. He fixed plows and cultivators, wagons and wheels, and found that he had a knack at leatherwork as well. Mending harness and fabricating leather harness and saddle pieces came to him almost as if he had been taught.

"Skeeter, I want you to work with Jack today fixing that wagon that's trying to fall apart. Do you have enough material to fix it, Jack?"

"Yup, but I'll have to fire up the forge to fix that double tree that broke. Need to get the iron on there good and hot or it won't stay long. Might have to fabricate some pieces as well. Sure would like to talk to Mr. Walters at the store about getting some iron. There's lots to be fixed around here and I don't have much scrap iron left."

"I'm going to town, so I'll ask about that, and I'll expect that wagon to be ready to haul corn when I get back," Pete said, putting a saddle on his horse. "Mims will be working with Jason. Don't take no breaks 'ceptin' for dinner," he said, as he rode toward Fargo.

I'll take a break when I need one you dirty pig, Jack said to himself, glaring at the man's back as he rode off. "Ought to just darn well take a break right now, Skeeter," he said, slipping into a heavy leather apron. "Darn right, let's take a break."

"If you do, I'll tell," Skeeter sneered. Jack reached out and grabbed him by his shirt-front, spun him around twice, and pushed him hard, sending him face first into the muck at the front of the barn. "You got a bad attitude, Skeeter. You threaten me again and I'll break your jaw. Go running to Pete about this, too, will you?" He kicked dirt in Skeeter's face and went to get his tools.

Jack was good with a drawknife. He sat down with a slab of oak, pulling that knife toward him over and over, turning the chunk of wood, and had a double tree ready for its iron pieces within a couple of hours. He had to keep on Skeeter to get the wheels off the wagon, one at a time and grease the axels. Jack walked over to the harness area and pulled his secret box out. He had a large biscuit and jam in his hand and offered one to Skeeter.

"You're not supposed to do that," Skeeter said. "I'm gonna tell Pete."

"You open your mouth to Pete and you'll be talking through bloody lips, Skeeter. It's because of you that Jason gets in so much trouble around here, doesn't get to eat like a boy should. You better stop being a bully to him and you better stop trying to get me in trouble all the time, too."

He took big bites of the biscuit and chewed long and slow, letting Skeeter know just how much he was missing. "I offered one, it's up to you to take it or not," Jack said, licking some jam off his upper lip.

"Mims sure makes good biscuits." By the time Jack had his third mouthful about chewed, Skeeter walked over and picked one up and slathered some jam on it. Jack smiled knowing the snitch couldn't say anything now without getting himself in trouble.

Mims had roast pork sandwiches and fresh apple pie for them at dinner, slipped an extra little piece of pie onto Jason's plate. "Shouldn't do that, Mims," Skeeter said. "Pete won't like that."

"Ain't no reason for Pete to know," she said back. "You tell on me and I might just have to mention that Jack's been teaching you to read. Just to make things a little nicer around here," she smiled. "Why don't you mind your own business."

Skeeter jumped up from the table and it looked like he was going to take a punch at Mims. He didn't get his second step and found himself flat on his back, his lower lip split and blood flowing. "Ever try to hit her again and I'll beat you half to death," Jack said, standing over the boy, his fists knotted, muscles tensed and ready to strike.

Jason started crying immediately and Mims was startled, then got just a hint of a smile, looking at Jack. She turned her head when he started to look at her, and got Jason quieted down, still smiling, her eyes as bright as the sun.

"You better watch yourself, Skeeter. Jack's a lot bigger than you are now. You might push me and Jason around, but you ain't gonna push Jack around." Mims heart was pounding with joy as she wiped the tears from Jason's face. *Just once I wish Jack'd look at me like I was a girl. I know he likes me, but I want him to like me like I'm a girl.* She found she was blushing and turned back to help Jason some more.

Skeeter ran out the door toward the barn and Jack stepped up close to Mims. "I won't let anyone hurt you, Mims, ever," he said, smiling down on her pretty face. "He'll tell Pete as soon as the old man get home, so I'll be in trouble again." His big brown eyes were looking deep into Mims' bright eyes, and he felt a twinge he'd never felt before. He reached up and gently rubbed her cheek, and just as quickly drew his hand back, as if getting an electric shock.

Mims stood stock-still, felt that same electric shock, and slowly closed her eyes, wishing for much more. It didn't happen, and she opened her eyes and found Jack still staring into hers.

"I bet he won't say anything, Jack. He's really scared of you, now. I'll make up a little basket for your hidey-hole, though, just in case," she said, giggling. She wanted to throw her arms around Jack, actually almost did, but he turned for the door before she could.

After dinner Jack fired up the forge and finished the iron pieces so they could be fitted to the double tree. "You work the bellows, Skeeter, keep that fire good and hot. I gotta get these pieces red hot, fit them onto the double tree, then get them cooled off so they're just as tight as all get out.

"Go ahead now, pump the bellows. Come on Skeeter, put your back into it." Skeeter had never been punched, more or less knocked on his butt, and was angry as all get-out at Jack, at himself, and at Mims for what she said, too.

"You had no cause to hit me, Jack. I'll get you," he said, pumping the bellows.

"You ever try to hit me you better be prepared to get hurt. And if you ever try to hit Mims again, I will hurt you bad." Jack had a four-pound hammer in his hand, and a set of tongs with some iron attached in his other hand, his legs spread slightly, and was glaring at the boy. "Just pump the bellows, Skeeter. I might only be twelve but I'm twice the man you are."

It was probably Jack's background that allowed him not to become a hurt and angry boy because of the way Jablonski treated the youngsters. Instead, Jack remembered the good times with his Momma and Pa, the good times on their farm. He remembered being taught table manners, how to act in public, and more important than anything else, to be responsible. He was taught to be respectful toward his elders, and that was probably his biggest problem with Pete. *I got no respect for that man, and the papers now say he's my pa. He ain't never gonna be my pa. My name will always be Jack Slater.*

At night, curled in his blankets he knew he was still alone. He was living in a family with four children and he was alone, wasn't able to relate to a life he didn't understand, wasn't able to share love and joy, and vowed that he would leave this farm the day he turned sixteen. "I signed those papers, so I have an obligation even if Pete won't live up to his."

Pete Jablonski would say and do things to Jack and the other kids that went against everything that Jack Slater believed in, and it got him in trouble. He just simply could not, would not, hold his tongue. He would have been a skinny little twerp like Jason because he missed so many meals. Mims laughed that Jack kept a two-week supply of food in the harness bin at all times.

Jack stood almost six feet tall when he turned fourteen, had broad strong shoulders, a deep chest, and almost no hips. His legs were like tree trunks, and his massive hands, with long strong fingers, could almost wrap around Mims' waist. One night after missing another supper, he crept out to the barn to find Mims waiting for him.

"I'm glad you're here, Mims. I talked with Mr. Walters last time I rode into town with Pete and he told me things that I didn't know. I have written several letters to Maybelle at the Society and never gotten one back from her. I figured she just decided that once I was gone, that was the end of it.

"Well, Mr. Walters, you know, he's the one that handles all the mail in and out of Fargo, well, he said that Pete never gave him any letters from me to mail."

"That's not right," Mims said, reaching out and taking Jack's hand. "Pete just threw your letters away? He's so mean," she almost whimpered. She was squeezing his hand, felt tremendous strength in his fingers, and wanted those strong arms wrapped around her.

"Well, I wrote another letter right there in the store and Mr. Walters promised it would be sent out on the next train. Walters said he would hold any letters that come for me and give them to me personally. When I hear back from Maybelle, I'm gonna start making plans to leave here. I'm not gonna wait until I'm sixteen."

"Oh, Jack, no, no," Mims cried. "If you leave, Pete will take it out on me, Skeeter will get just as mean as Pete. No, Jack, if you leave, take me with you." She flung herself on him, scattering biscuits all over both of them. "Don't leave me," she cried.

Jack had never had his arms around a girl before, and found it to be very pleasant, indeed. He held her tight, and she had her arms around his neck, almost squeezing his breathing off. He rubbed her back, felt her hot breath on his neck, pulled his head back a little bit, and they kissed, very gently for the first time. He let his hands roam up and down her back, pulling her to him as hard as he dared.

"We'll start making plans right away, Mims. I don't want to leave you, Mims, but I don't think I can take you with me." She tensed up when he said that, and held her even tighter. "It won't be easy, you must know that, but I'm big and strong. It is possible, I suppose," he continued, "I'm good on a farm, and you're excellent in a kitchen, so maybe we would be able to make it."

Mims stayed in the barn with Jack as long as she dared, talking about what she wanted in life. "You taught me to read, Jack, and because of that I know about things in this old world, and I want some of them," she teased. "We could leave now as far as I'm concerned."

11

"There you are, Jablonski, I've been hoping to run into you. We need to have a talk." The banker, Raymond Bennett stepped into Lu Walker's general store. "I have some correspondence from the Children's Aid Society that pertains to you. Come over to the office before you leave today."

"I'm in a hurry today, Bennett, but I'll stop by. Jack, get this wagon loaded as soon as Walker pulls the order." Jablonski handed Lucius Walker his order list and followed Bennett out the door. "Darn boy's a real pain, Bennett. Thinks he knows everything."

The two men walked across the muddy street and into Bennett's bank, scraping their boots on the wooden sidewalk. "I received a letter from Mr. Morrison at the Society that claims you haven't been following the directions that the Society demands." They walked into the office and Bennett indicated that Jablonski take a seat.

Bennett sat in his big leather chair and pulled a letter from the top drawer. "Here, I'll let you read it yourself." Jablonski took the letter, glanced at it and handed it back.

"I don't have time for this, Bennett. What's it all about?"

Bennett hid a slight grin as he realized that Pete Jablonski couldn't read. To cover, he reached for a cheroot and took his time lighting it. "What it's all about, Pete, is this. The Society has asked me to come to your farm and sit down with the children for an interview. It seems that you may have been mistreating the kids."

"Nonsense," Pete snarled. "I have rules they must follow and they are punished if they don't follow them. Nobody's been mistreated."

"It seems that you have not been providing them with schooling, which is part of the program, and that you force the children to do more work than they are able to do, and when they don't do their work, they are denied food.

"Is that true, that you deny the children food? That would certainly be mistreatment, Jablonski."

"There ain't no school out there, and how would they get their work done if they were in school, anyways. Jack's behind this, isn't he," he snarled, already planning to deny Jack his supper that night and maybe even breakfast the next morning. "Those kids eat plenty. Ain't nobody sick."

"I'll be at your farm tomorrow morning, Jablonski, and I'm bringing Reverend Thomas with me. I plan to spend most of the day with the children, so don't interfere. The Society wants answers and I plan to get those answers for them."

Pete jumped up from the chair and stormed out of the office, and straight to the Barrel House Saloon. "Jack's behind this, I know it, and I'll get that boy. I need to think, I need to punish him bad," he muttered all the way across the street and into the saloon.

"I got a letter for you Jack," Waters said when Jablonski and Bennett left the general store. "Came on the train yesterday. All the way from New York," he marveled handing an envelope to Jack. "Looks important. Mr. Bennett got one just like it."

"Thank you," Jack said, pulling his pocket-knife and slitting the letter open. He stepped out into the sunlight on the porch to read what Maybelle had to say.

My dear Jack, it was such a pleasure to get your letter, and I was saddened by what you had to say. I was afraid you had forgotten all about us here in dreary old New York City.

I found it hard to believe that Mr. Jablonski just threw your letters away, but since I never received any, I must, I guess. I gave your letter to Mr. Morrison and he was very upset by your comments about mistreatment. He is making a demand that our agent in Fargo, Mr. Bennett, investigate and talk with each of the children.

Do keep in touch, Dear Jack. I will always hold you in my heart.

Maybelle

Jack walked back into the general store, tears running down his face, and asked for some paper from Mr. Walters. He penned a quick note back to Maybelle and asked the storekeeper to send it off on the next train east. "Did Pete ever ask you about getting some iron? We almost don't have any scrap iron left out there and he's always demanding that I fix things that need iron."

"I told him how to order it but he said it was too expensive and he wouldn't pay that much. He must be a hard man to live with, Jack. As big as you are, I would think that you'd have moved out by now. You're a big smart boy, you should be able to find work on just about any farm or ranch here on the frontier."

"That just might happen, Mr. Walters. It just might. Looks like Pete's had his whiskey, so I better get ready to drive the team back to the ranch. Thanks again for taking care of my mail."

The ride back to the farm was filled with foul language and angry insults as Pete Jablonski railed the entire five miles. He was still howling mad when Jack pulled the team to a stop in front of the kitchen porch at the farmhouse. "Jack you get this stuff taken care of, Skeeter, get that barn cleaned out, Jason, clean up the hog wallows, and Mims, you make sure there is only food enough for me and three children, not four.

"Jack, you will not get supper tonight, nor will you get breakfast in the morning. Now, move it," and he stormed into the house. Mims' eyes were wide in fright and amazement, and Jack just gave her a little smile as he piled off the wagon.

"Not to worry, my little Mims," he said. "There just might be some changes around here." Skeeter and Jason couldn't believe what happened next. Jack walked right up to Mims, put his arms around her and lifted her into the air. She threw her arms around his neck, and he kissed her square on the lips.

"I do believe I love you, Mims girl," he laughed, leading the horses into the barn. "Let's get this wagon unloaded and all the stuff put away."

"He just said you weren't getting supper, Jack. Why are you so happy?" Mims was as confused as Skeeter and Jason.

"Gonna be some changes, I think. I got a letter from Maybelle, and the Society is complaining to Mr. Bennett at the bank about how Pete treats us. Mr. Bennett had some hard words with Pete, and he will be here in the morning to talk with us. Gonna be some changes, I think," he sang again, hefting a bag of grain that weighed more than Jason. "Jason, you mind your manners and get a good meal tonight, and Skeeter, if I hear that you tried to get Jason or Mims in trouble, I'll beat you black and blue." He was almost dancing as he put the sack of grain with others.

Mims had a generous pot of stew bubbling on the stove when Pete called everyone in for supper. As they sat, Jack said, "None for me tonight, Mims, thank you."

Pete almost came off the chair he was so angry at the boy, and screamed at him to sit down and not say another word. Jack sat down, folded his hands on his lap and

smiled at the furious man. The rest of suppertime was very quiet, and Mims let her
leg bump Jack's several times. Jack just sat
and smiled at Pete the whole time.

When the table had been cleared, Pete
spoke to the kids, more a growl than simple
talk. "Mr. Bennett, the Society agent, will
be here tomorrow and wants to talk to you
kids," he said, looking at Skeeter, but not
Jack, Jason, or Mims. "Jack told some lies
about me to the Society and Mr. Bennett
will ask you about them.

"Jack, you'll be fifteen next month. I want
you off this farm at that time. Between now
and then, you will sleep and eat in the barn.
Move your belongings out there now. You
are not welcome inside this house from the
time you have moved your stuff. Move it,
now," he howled.

Jack smiled, nudged Mims, and started
for the stairs. "Thank you, Pete. I appreci-
ate that." It took about half an hour for him
to get his bags and boxes moved to the barn
and he made a nice little nest in one of the
empty stalls. He spent the next hour or so
arranging his belongings, deciding what
would go with him when he left, and what
would be discarded.

He also knew he would take Mr. Bennett
aside tomorrow morning for a little private

117

chat. *I have quite a bit of money coming to me when I'm eighteen, and that's only three years from now. I wonder if Bennett would front me enough to get me out of here. I would need a horse and a pack mule, I have a bedroll but I would need some utensils, and I would need a rifle.*

He was about to lie down and sleep when Mims slipped into the stall. "Jack, I'm so scared. What are we gonna do? What's gonna happen tomorrow? What will Pete do to us?" She was bawling, and Jack took her into his arms, letting the two of them ease down into the straw. He held her close, kissing her deep, feeling her breath slow down, enjoying her arms wrapped tight around his neck.

"I'll talk with Mr. Bennett in the morning and probably be out of here in the next few days. I won't be able to take you with me, Mims, you know that, but I'll find us a place. I'll find a good farm or ranch, and I'll send for you. Will you wait for me? I do love you."

"I want to come with you, Jack. I can't stay here without you. Skeeter will be so nasty and mean, and I don't know what Pete will do. I wish you could take all of us away from here."

"I'm going to see to it that you and Jason

118

are well taken care of," Jack said, rubbing her back, holding her close, understanding that he was holding a well developed young woman and enjoying that very much. "Mr. Bennett will hear everything that Pete does, and I'm going to work hard to get him to find new homes for you and Jason. You'll be safe, I promise."

It seems like I have been taking care of people all my life, and after tomorrow I'm going to be alone, still, again. Is this what I can expect for the rest of my life? To help others, and still feel terribly alone? It wasn't very many fifteen year old boys living on the frontier in the mid 1870s who carried such a burden, and Jack's burden felt heavy.

Mims stayed with Jack through most of the rest of the night, cuddled in his strong arms, kissing him a thousand times, wanting to do more, frightened to even think about it. They slept wrapped up together, and Mims slipped away just before dawn, getting started in the kitchen before Pete awakened.

It was a grand confrontation later in the morning when Ray Bennett and Reverend Thomas arrived. Thomas brought his wife Helen along, and their big ranch dog had followed whether they wanted him to or not.

119

"I don't want no dogs on this farm," Pete said when they drove up to the kitchen porch.

"Well, just tell him to go home, then, Pete," Thomas said with a smile. Bennett chuckled helping Helen out of the buggy.

"Morning, Pete, got all those kids ready for us? How about some coffee to take the dust down some."

"Mims," Pete bellowed. "Put some coffee on and call Skeeter and Jason to come in."

"What about Jack?" she asked, knowing that would cause a conniption. "Isn't he supposed to be at this meeting, too?"

"He's not allowed in my house," Pete snarled. Reverend Thomas and his wife were startled. Thomas was about to say something but Bennett beat him to it.

"Well, he is today," Bennett bawled, his bushy eyebrows gathered in a frown. Then he smiled and said, "Call all the children in, Mims, if you please. Reverend, Helen, after you," he bowed slightly, ushering everyone into the large kitchen. Mims started to make the coffee and Helen Thomas took the pot, said she'd do it, and Mims headed for the barn to find the kids.

"Sit down, Pete," Bennett said. "This is pretty serious, and you will need to control that temper of yours. What did you mean that Jack wasn't allowed in the house? Where does he live? I've had my doubts about you and the children, but what Morrison wrote to me, I would not have believed." He sat down at the large kitchen table and pulled the envelope from his frock coat pocket.

"Morrison said that Jack complained about the children not having their own rooms, that meals were withheld for punishment of simple rule infractions, that there was no schooling, and that you had not allowed the children to send letters."

Helen Thomas spoke right up. "The children all sleep in the same room? My heavens, Skeeter is almost seventeen, and the other three are fifteen-years-old. Mims can't be sleeping in the same room with three teen-age boys. My heavens," she said again, as shocked as she had ever been.

"Pete," Bennett said, "this is very serious, and right now, Reverend Thomas is of the impression that I should remove the children from your care for their own good. I want to hear from them before I make that kind of decision, and I want to hear from you after they make their comments.

"I won't allow any theatrics, Pete. When the children are talking, I don't want any interruptions, and there will be no threats.

Is that understood?" Pete sat down hard, glared at Thomas, ignored Helen, and nodded to Bennett. "Good," the banker said as Mims led Skeeter, Jack, and Jason into the kitchen. The coffee was boiling and Helen poured cups for those that wanted some, and everyone sat around the table. Jack sat down next to Ray Bennett, directly across from Pete.

"I'll keep this as short as possible, but it is important to understand that some serious charges have been made that could alter everyone's lives," Bennett said, unfolding the letter from Morrison. "Mr. Morrison from the Society wrote to me after receiving a letter from Jack here, outlining several problems. First the issue of being denied food."

Jason started crying immediately and Mims moved to calm him down. "Sit down, Mims. Let the little baby cry," Pete snarled.

"Pete, what do you mean by that? That boy is frightened," Mrs. Thomas said, getting up from the table and moving to Jason's side. Mims paid no attention to Pete and was now on the other side of Jason.

"Jason isn't able to do many of the things that Pete demands of him," Jack said, "and when he can't, he is then denied supper, sometimes even breakfast the next morning. Jason, Mims, and I are the same age, Mr. Bennett, and as you can see, Jason is frail and not very strong. He has missed many meals in the few years I've been here."

Jack watched Pete close his fists repeatedly, glaring at the boy, flexing his muscles, wanting to reach out and punch Jack hard. Jack smiled at him and said, "Moving Mims and Jason out of here is the best idea I've heard in a long time. Skeeter's a tattle-tale and trouble maker and Pete can't hurt me. I'm not afraid of him."

Reverend Thomas and his wife said, almost together, that Jason would be going home with them when the meeting was over. "This boy needs nourishment and love," Helen Thomas said.

"Why aren't you small and frail, Jack?" Bennett asked. "I understand you were denied many meals as well."

Mims was chuckling when Jack told about his hidey-hole in the barn, and Pete almost blew a gasket. It took Bennett a few minutes to get order restored at the table. "Mims and I did what we could to get extra food for Jason, but he is so afraid of Pete that he was even afraid to eat it when we did," Jack said.

The little meeting at the kitchen table went on for another two hours, and it was

Pete who finally broke it up. "You've all had your fun, but this little piece of drama is now over. Get out of my house," he stormed. "You children have work to do and I want it done right now. Bennett, Thomas, leave now. Children, hit the barn, and I mean right now."

"No, Pete, that's not how it works today," Bennett said, quietly. "Your days of being a tyrant are over. Reverend Thomas, will you take Mims and Jason to live with you until we can find a suitable family for them?"

"Yes, of course, we will, Ray," Thomas said. "What about Skeeter and Jack?"

"I want to stay with Pete," Skeeter said. "I'll be eighteen soon, and I'll leave then, but for now, Pete and I get along just fine."

"You won't have anyone to tattle on," Mims said with a nasty smile on her face. "You'll actually have to do some work instead of bullying little Jason or threatening me."

"You're old enough to make that decision, Skeeter, but I don't recommend it," Bennett said. "Jack, can you hitch up a team and help Mims and Jason get their stuff loaded?"

"You ain't taking one of my teams, Bennett," Pete said.

"Actually, Pete, I am. Jack I'd like you to take the kids and all their belongings to the

Thomas farm and then bring the team and wagon to the bank. I need to talk to you for a spell after," he said, pulling a large cigar from his vest. "Now, kids, get your stuff together."

Jack gave Mims a little squeeze, which Helen Thomas caught immediately, and headed out to the barn. "I'll have the wagon close to the back door here," he said. "Pete, I'm putting my stuff in the wagon, too."

Helen Thomas went upstairs with Mims and Jason to get them packed up. "All of you sleep in this same room? This is horrible."

It took little time to pack and load the little Mims and Jason had, and Jack got everyone settled in and ready to leave. "I'm riding on the seat with you, Jack," Mims announced, plopping down next to him.

12

Jack wheeled the spring wagon down the main street in Fargo and stopped in front of the bank. Ray Bennett was standing near the front door, waiting for him. "You look good up there, Jack," he said with a smile, stepping forward to help tie off the team. "Come in, come in."

They walked into Bennett's large office and got comfortable. "Mims and Jason all taken care of?"

"Reverend Thomas seems to be a pretty nice man," Jack said, "and Mrs. Thomas had sandwiches made before I had everything unloaded."

Bennett was looking at a tall boy, close to the six-foot mark, he figured, with powerful shoulders, a broad chest, and tree trunks for legs. Jack Slater was fifteen years old and was larger than most of the men Bennett dealt with. *If this boy is half as smart as he is big, he'll be going places in this world.*

At his age, there aren't many who could measure up to him.

"Am I right in thinking that you tried to warn Morrison at the Society some time ago?"

"I have written to Maybelle several times but didn't know that Pete tore up the letters until Mr. Walters told me. It just got worse and worse out there, Mr. Bennett. I'm glad we have this chance to talk because I have plans for myself, but I fear I need some help to make them happen."

"I believe you're fifteen now, Jack. You're as big as Pete, it looked like, but you're younger than Skeeter, right?" Bennett was sure that Jack was very close to fifteen, yet the boy was so big, and spoke as a man, not a boy. Jack's voice had become deep and throaty during his beginning adolescence, which made him seem even bigger. "You could hold your own in a pack of grown men, I believe."

"Yup," the boy said, with a smile. "I'm fifteen, well, almost, and I was planning to leave the farm next week when I turn fifteen. I wasn't going to wait until I was sixteen. I'm bigger than most kids my age, I can work like a full-grown man, and I want to go south and find a good farm or ranch to work on."

He always remembered the conversations that he overheard when groups of men were talking. Those conversations usually dealt with either Texas or California, and for Jack, what he heard about Texas made him want to be there. "I want to end up in Texas with a place of my own.

"To do that, I need some money and some supplies. Mr. Morrison will guarantee what I'm about to tell you. When my Pa and Momma were killed our farm had to be sold and that money has been put in a bank and will be available to me when I turn eighteen. I would like to borrow just a little using the account for collateral. Is that possible?"

"How do you know about things like collateral and borrowing, Jack?" *There are grown men running farms right here in Fargo that I have to spend a lot of time explaining the concepts of borrowing and collateral, and this boy already fully understands. I'd rather hire him than bankroll his leaving town.* Bennett sat back in his big chair, looking forward to Jack's answer.

"Momma always made sure I went to school and I brought some good books with me, Mr. Bennett. Pa was very smart, and our farm was a very good one. I have never known how much it sold for, but it should have brought a good price. My Pa believed in using the farm to increase the farm, as he put it.

"Lots of the men that Pa knew wouldn't borrow on their property, but Pa said it was the best way to get ahead. Well, that's what I want to do, too." He reached inside his coat pocket and brought out a couple of sheets of folded paper.

"Here is the list of things I think I would need to make the trip south to Texas. Along with what is on the list, I think I would need some cash money in my pocket as well, just in case I need something along the trail."

"Pete will never know just what he lost by mistreating you," Bennett murmured, taking the papers from Jack. He went over the list a couple of times, made some notations, made a short list of his own, and sat back in his big leather chair. "Ever thought of being a banker, Jack?" he laughed, putting the papers down. "You've got the mind for one, I think."

"No, sir, but I do want to own my own farm or ranch someday soon."

"And you will, son. You will."

It was two days and lots of work, and the residents of Fargo watched young Jack Slater, sitting tall on a fine saddle horse, lead a well-packed mule along the main street, and turn south. Among those waving goodbye, with tears streaming down her lovely face, was Mims Thomas, formerly Mims Jablonski. She wanted to be with him so bad, and knew that she might never see that man again.

The evening before, Jack had ridden to the Thomas farm, several miles north, along the Red River, to say goodbye. "All I know, Mims, is I'm going to end up in Texas, and I don't even know for sure where Texas is," he laughed. They were sitting in rough wood chairs under a large cottonwood tree, sipping hot chocolate made by Mrs. Thomas.

"It's a long way south of here and it's going to be a hard trail, I'm sure."

"Aren't you scared?" Mims asked. "What will you do for food and where will you sleep?"

"I'm bringing some supplies that I bought from Mr. Walters, and I'll buy more along the trail. I will probably eat a lot of rabbit and other small game along the trail. My real worries are possible encounters with Indians and with mean and bad men. Mr. Walters gave me the right address to send you letters. You probably won't be able to send me any cuz I don't know where I'll be, but I will write to you."

It was a long and sad goodbye for both

and Mims cried herself to sleep when Jack finally had to leave. He spent that night in the hotel, wondering just what he would be riding into when he started out early the next morning. The dreams were exciting, he remembered.

He followed well-traveled trails toward Black Hills country. Most in Fargo had heard that that section of the country was going to be opened up to mining and maybe even to homesteading. Troubles with the Sioux Indians were soon to be over, they were told. Everyone read and re-read the horrible news of Colonel Custer and his army, about the massacre of the Seventh Cavalry.

But, following that event, things in the Black Hills had calmed down some. Jack had heard all the stories, but the locations of things didn't always add up. "I can pick up a trail south just before I reach the Black Hills area and make my way to Colorado country," he believed, but certainly didn't know for sure.

The main trail west out of Fargo was originally cut by trappers fifty years ago, and well used by the army, and Jack figured his first few days would be his easiest. He knew he had to learn how to live on the trail, and he had to learn fast. He had never fired a weapon and now he was wearing a Colt Navy revolver and had a repeating rifle in a saddle scabbard. His knife was one he made on the anvil at Pete's, and was sharp as a razor, the same with his ax.

Because of all the talk about Sitting Bull and Crazy Horse, and the Sioux Indians wanting war, Jack rode with a high degree of concentration. "I'm probably too worried," he murmured. "Sounding like Charles and worried that the Indians will eat me." He snickered and enjoyed the early summer weather. "Getting out on the trail early gives me the edge," he said.

He had time to do some serious thinking, something the big boy enjoyed. "I lost my folks back in 1872 and I was just ten years old. I traveled more than half way across this huge land of ours, was forced to live with a miserable old man for five years, and here I am, sittin' on the back of a fine saddle horse trailing a pack mule loaded with everything I own in the world.

"I couldn't have done this last year, even though I wanted to," he murmured. "It was just about a year ago that Custer's army was destroyed by the Sioux, and now, I'm about to ride through Sioux country. Sure wish Charles was with me, now," he laughed, watching some ravens dance through the sky and feeling the warm spring prairie winds blow the grass about.

The first week was a learning experience he would never forget and it was only because of his size and strength, and his capacity to learn that he lived through the week. Jack was good with animals but had spent little time in the saddle, and after the first twenty miles or so that first day, he could feel his knees cramping up and knew he would be in pain sitting down for a few days.

Better get used to it, buster, if you plan on making Texas, he told himself s couple of times that evening. He was out of the organized farming areas heading southwest through open plains and rolling hills. There were lots of little streams and a big river or two that he crossed. Fording the big river was difficult.

His horse and mule had no trouble with a couple of small streams, but the mule was not going to swim the big river. He tried four times, and finally made the right decision to follow along the river, find a proper ford, and not make either animal swim. He locked that knowledge in his head for future use.

He found a small grove of trees on a bank

overlooking a creek and set up his first camp. And discovered his first mistake. He had not included a fire starter on his list of provisions. He had his camp laid out, wood gathered, and needed to find some flint. If he had been another hundred miles or so west, in the foothills of the front-range, flint would have been easy to come by. Not so right here, and he spent hours before coming up with something that would send sparks when he whacked a stone onto his knife or ax.

A pocket full of stones went back to camp with him and it wasn't long before he had a good fire going. The day had been hot but as the sun slowly dipped into the western haze on the plains it cooled off. He watched the sky turn various shades of many colors, and realized that it had turned dark. The end of an eventful day, he thought, stirring the fire.

He ate some smoked meat boiled in his coffee and was getting ready to call it a day when he heard what sounded like someone trying to be quiet walking toward his fire. He pulled his revolver, slipped away from the fire and got behind one of the trees.

"Who's there," he said in the biggest voice he could muster. "Answer me now or die," he said, cocking the big handgun.

"I'm not an enemy," the voice said. "I saw your fire, thought I might find hot coffee and some conversation."

"Come slow to the fire, stranger. Make one wrong move and this old Navy will talk to you, loud and clear." The man stepped out of the shadows of the trees leading a saddle horse. He was wearing canvas pants and a wool blanket-coat over what looked to Jack like buckskins. There was a bedroll tied to the back of the saddle.

"Name's Whitney, Peter Whitney. Sure could use some coffee. Indians stole my mule two days ago and I ain't eat nothin' since. Just drank water," he said, tying off the horse and kneeling down by the fire. "Got a good fire, boy, but I wouldn't build a big fire in this country. Wrong people might see it," he continued. "Where you headed? Looks like you got a full pack, must be headed a long way."

"What do you mean Indians stole your mule," Jack said, stepping out from behind the tree, but keeping that big Navy cocked and ready. "Closest Indians are in the Black Hills."

"Small band of marauding killers, they was," Whitney said. "I was lucky to save my scalp, I was. Sure could go for some coffee, and maybe a small bite of something, if you have it."

"Use the tin cup on the rocks there, and there might be a piece of meat left in the coffee. Where were you heading when you were jumped by them Indians?"

"Goin' to Fargo, get away from the Sioux," he said, wolfing a piece of boiled meat and slurping some coffee. "Had plans to do some minin' in the Blacks, but jist got skee-red, I guess," he said with a little snicker.

Whitney was a skinny little fellow, mostly bald when he pulled his hat off. He had a long sharp nose, his eyes, sunk deep in their sockets, darted about, seemingly to see everything all at once. He had a wide belt that held a large knife. The belt kept the blanket coat closed, and Jack couldn't see if the man wore a sidearm.

"Well, throw out your bed-roll on t'other side of the fire and I think I'll just sleep with this old Navy tonight." It was a lovely spring night, no wind, no clouds, and no cold temperatures to ruin the image. Jack let the cook fire burn down and stretched out under a light blanket.

The rattle of horse hooves woke Jack up with a start and he caught a glimpse of Whitney trying to mount his horse, hold onto Jack's horse, and control Jack's pack mule as well. Jack spring from the coverlet,

Navy in hand, and raced to Whitney's little melee.

"You got about a couple of seconds to live, stranger. Step off that horse now," and he aimed the big revolver at Whitney's chest. Whitney laughed, saying, "You ain't got it in ye to kill a man, boy. Thanks for the coffee," and he started to rein his horse around and put the spurs to it.

There was no hesitation or second thought or deep emotional throb when Jack squeezed off a round, knocking Whitney plumb out of the saddle. He fell to the ground, his hands grasping at the middle of his chest. Jack jumped forward and grabbed the reins of Whitney's horse, his horse, and the mule's lead rope before they bolted for the unknown.

He got the animals quieted down and tied off before he checked on Whitney. "You shot me," Whitney said, his eyes as wide as quarters. "You shot me, boy," he said again.

"Don't guess you'll be stealing horses and mules anymore," Jack said, seeing blood pulse from the man's chest and dribble from the sides of his mouth. In less than ten minutes Whitney died and Jack dug a quick grave for the horse thief. *Everything I've read and everything I've heard said tells me I should feel horrible for taking another man's life,* he thought, filling in the grave. *I don't feel horrible at all. That man came to my camp with the intent of stealing from me. A sneak at best, because a real man would have been open and forward about it. It would have still been stealing, but, well, I don't know if it would have been better or not.*

He had a wry smile on his face as he finished up filling in the grave and walked back to the animals. *I am not a killer,* he said to himself. *I was not going to let that foul man steal everything I have. I'm fully justified,* he thought again. He opened the saddle bags on Whitman's rig and found the man had several twenty-dollar gold pieces in his poke and put them in a sack with the ones he had. He found Whitney's revolver and rifle, took that large knife, and left the man's saddle and bedroll.

He checked all the gear and rigs on the animals, stepped on his horse, which he now called Fargo, and started the long ride toward the Black Hills. "That man thought he was going to take everything I owned," he said to the animals, "and I guess he was wrong."

He vowed not to be quite as friendly to those coming to his camps in the future, but was glad to have a second saddle horse. "Change off each day and neither horse gets

overworked," he smiled, leading his little
train out of camp and back on the trail.

13

On his second day out, he discovered there was considerable traffic on the trail, some heading west, some the other way, out of Indian troubles. Jack kept as much to himself as possible, shunned the few that seemed to want to join up with him, and was surprised at how poorly many were prepared for a long cross country journey.

"Most of these people have already come half way across the continent and seem oblivious to what they are facing." Everyone in Fargo knew about Sitting Bull and Crazy Horse, about the massacre of General Custer and his entire army, and the terrible times that followed. "Do these people know where they're going?"

He was just a couple of days from Deadwood, Dakota Territory, when he met up with the Peter Davis family. One of their wagons threw a steel tire, and Pete was having a miserable time getting it back on the wheel. "Looks like you could use another hand, there," Jack said pulling his little train to a halt at the side of the trail.

"We'll make it," one of the young men said. "Don't need no help from a boy."

"Hold on there," Pete said to the man. "Don't pay Skinny no mind, son. He don't know nothin' anyways. You know something about wagon wheels?"

"Yup," Jack said stepping off Fargo, scowling at the man called Skinny. "You need heat to get that iron tire on there. Build a big fire ring, get that tire red-hot and put it over the wheel. Drench it in cold water and that iron will grab hold like as if you welded it."

"I'll be dad-gummed," Pete said. "I remember seeing that at a blacksmith shop one time. Well, I'll be," he said. "I think I better introduce ourselves, cuz you might just turn out to be somebody to know," he said, spitting a stream of tobacco juice into the weeds. "I'm Peter Davis, this here's my son Jon and my daughter Jessie, and that fool that mouthed off to you is cousin Skinny."

Jack stuck a big hand out to the scarecrow of a man and said, "I'm Jack Slater, heading eventually to Texas. Nice to meet you." *I've never seen so many pine pole thin people in my life,* he thought looking at the bunch. *I wonder when they had a good meal last?*

"Texas," Pete said. "By golly, I sure heard good things about Texas. Well, now, let's do what Jack Slater said and get a nice big fire cookin' so we can roast that iron tire," he said, laughing a bit. His shirt hung on a bony frame, his pants were held up by a length of rope tied off, and his boots probably wore out a year or so ago. Peter Davis was wearing a floppy hat and his stringy gray hair hung down to his shoulders.

Jack was amazed that they had two wagons and four horses, and didn't know how to fix a simple tire coming loose. The Davis family, he saw as he watched them, were all small and wiry in stature. None stood close to six feet, none weighed more than one-twenty-five, and the girl Jessie was almost tiny.

He saw a girl with almost no form, and remembered how Mims, his age but smaller, was nicely filled out at the top and the hips. This girl was a standing pine tree and shorter than Mims.

Jack helped them lay out the fire ring, get a good fire going, and put the iron tire in the flames. He moved the wheel near the fire and asked Pete for a bunch of rags. Pete sent Jessie to gather them up. "When that tire is red hot, Pete, you use some rags for your hands and take hold of it on one side, and I'll do the same thing on the other.

"We'll fit that tire right over the wheel, and Jon, you and Skinny pour a couple of buckets of water on the tire." They all seemed to get the picture, and Jack continued. "Have you been soaking these wheels every chance you get?"

Pete looked at Jon, then Skinny, and said, "Don't reckon I know what you mean."

I'm dealing with idiots. Never soaked a wheel? "Well, when you cross these creeks and rivers, take a few minutes and let your wheels sit in the water. If you're camped near a creek, move the wagon into the water, and make sure the wheels get a good soaking. Keeps those iron tires nice and tight."

"Haven't done that," Jon said. "How come you know this stuff? What makes you so smart?" There was more than a challenge offered, but Jack thought about Skeeter back on the farm and just let it pass.

"Been working on a farm since I was a little boy," Jack said. "Just stuff you learn. Where you heading for?"

Pete seemed to tell Jon and Skinny to let him do the talking, not in so many words, but by way of his eyes and movement of his head. "We're going to Deadwood and maybe down to Lead. They say there's gold to be had. You're going to pass up finding gold to go to Texas?"

"Yup," Jack said. "Hope to get a farm or ranch down that way. I'll be passing through Deadwood then heading south through Colorado country."

"You're welcome to roll with us as far Deadwood, if you like," Pete smiled. "We might lose another tire, you know," and he chuckled, watching Jon and Skinny scowl just a bit. "We do kind of keep to ourselves, though."

The fire was good and hot and the tire turned cherry red in no time. Jessie had a couple of hands full of rags and Pete and Jack had the tire pounded onto the wooden wheel quickly. Jon and Skinny had their buckets ready and Jack gave them the go ahead. Steam billowed when the water splashed on the hot iron. Jack told them to get a couple more buckets and get that iron cooled off fast.

Jon and Skinny did what they were asked, but Jack noticed that Jon Davis gave his father a nasty look as he walked off. *There are a lot of problems with this family,* Jack thought watching the two younger men go for water. *I might want to keep my distance a bit. I surely don't think a one of 'em could swing a pick to go lookin' for gold.* He wanted to snicker but didn't.

The entire operation took less than an hour and the wheel was remounted on the wagon, with the axel greased too. "By golly, I wouldn't have believed that if I hadn't see'd it," Pete said. "Thank you, Jack. Jessie, make sure there's enough of that venison stew so's young Jack Slater can have supper with us."

Jack watched the frail girl head off to the wagons and gave the wagons a good look as well. Much of the canvas was ripped, some roughly mended, some just hanging and frayed. The horses looked weak and the harness needed a lot of work.

These people are lucky to have made it this far, he thought. *They are not only not bright, they must be lazy as well. Pete Davis has dull eyes, even when he's trying to joke some, and Jon is angry at everything. He'll hurt somebody someday, I would bet on that, and that guy they call Skinny is even more dangerous.*

As he was breaking down his packs for the night's camp, he noticed that Jon seemed to take interest in what was being un-packed. *Don't you fret none, Jon. You won't be getting none of this. One man has already died trying.* He did what he could to keep his body between his packs and Jon's eyes. *I'll be more awake than asleep tonight, I think,* he said, stretching out his bedroll.

Pete Davis seemed to believe that all they needed to do was get near the Black Hills and gold would be there to find. "I've heard some really good tales about some of them boys gittin' filthy rich just goin' behind a tree to relieve themselves," he laughed. "Homestead Mine is a big one, and I don't think we want to work for someone else, do we boys?"

Jon and Skinny both nodded in agreement. "No, Pa, we don't. We gonna find gold for us not for somebody else. Skinny here, he's the gold finder." Jack saw the two young men give each other a nod, like they were sharing something that others didn't know.

Jessie brought the iron pot of venison stew to the table and started to ladle it into bowls. Jack was surprised at how little was in the pot. A few small morsels of meat, some wild onions, and lots of mostly clear broth was all he saw in that pot. "Just a bit for me," Jack said. "I had a big dinner up the trail. Sure smells good," he said. *There's enough in that pot for Mims and Jason, not for these four adults. I'll break away from these people in the morning.*

It was a little later that Jack realized that what was in that pot was all they would be getting that night. No biscuits dripping with jam, and none of Mims' fresh pie to set the supper off. *The more I see people on the trail the more I'm sure that I'm going to stick by myself. She's got iron pots, why doesn't she make bread, or at least biscuits? These people are as bare bones as I've ever seen in my life.*

Jack got back to his camp, a little away from the Davis clan, munched on some smoked meat as he lay under his blanket watching the stars move slowly through the pine boughs above him. He figured he would be in Deadwood in two days at the most and would take off at first light. "I sure don't plan on spending two or three days on the trail with the Davis family. That boy Jon's lookin' for some trouble, and I wouldn't trust Skinny for nothing," he murmured, thinking about his day.

"I sure saw some pretty country today, though." He had reached the mountains, with huge slabs of granite soaring to the sky, big trees hiding the rolling hills, and this evening, a high altitude coolness to the air. It brought memories of coming across the country five years ago on that train.

"Mims used to make me read from my journal about that train ride. I need to buy a notebook when I get to Deadwood and start keeping another journal so I can read to her after we get back together." He had a picture of Ephraim come to mind, and that wonderful letter he wrote to him. *I hope I meet that man again. Wise in so many ways, and willing to help a little boy who was lost in sadness.*

It was a night for thinking, for remembering, for wondering about all the tomorrows that he would work his way through. Pictures of Pa and Momma floated through scenes of little Claudine, of feeling Mims close to him, and of scowling and angry Pete Jablonski. More than anything else, pictures of him on a farm.

"I think I was born to live outdoors," he said. "That's why I like the idea of farming, I guess." Sleep came quickly, and within moments, it seemed, dawn was bursting through.

He had a small fire and made coffee, had the animals packed and was ready to hit the trail before anyone in the Davis camp moved. "You're not riding with us, Jack?" old man Davis said, stepping out of the back

148

of one of the wagons. "I thought we were gonna ride into Deadwood together."

"I'm sure we'll meet up again, Pete. Glad I could be of some help to you. You remember what I said about soaking those wheels." He waved and nudged Fargo lightly with his heels. "Those people won't get on the trail much before dinner time," he snickered, setting the animals in a strong pace on the trail to Deadwood.

"Well, Fargo, what do you think, so far? The first person we meet wants to steal everything we've got, and now we meet some true fools. Gonna be a long ride to Texas, my friend." Thoughts like that danced in his head all the way to Deadwood.

14

"Well, here we are boys and Deadwood is a swamp," Jack Slater said to his horses and mule, riding slowly in the gulch that once was filled with deadwood, blow-down from winters, floods, and high wind. "Lots of mud," he mused, riding to a stables at the other end of town.

"Howdy," Jack said to a large man in a leather apron standing near the open doors of a livery.

"Howdy yourself," the man said back. "You look a little trail worn. Where you comin' in from?"

"Came in from Fargo, and looking to head south to Texas," Jack said to the smiling man. "Where's a good place to set up a small camp for a couple of days?"

"Well, son, if it was me doin' it, I wouldn't," he said. "There be a lot of nasty critters in this old camp. They'd clean you out in half a day. Might cost a dollar, but if you put your animals up here, leave your pack with me, I'll guarantee you'll have it all when you get ready to leave for Texas."

Jack gave him a long look, wondering if the man was setting him up to take everything. He saw a large man, heavy in the shoulders and chest, with big strong arms, a square head with bright, dancing eyes, and a generous smile. "I know, I know," the livery man said, "you're wondering if I just want to steal everything, but I'll tell you, I ain't never stole nothin', ever, and never will.

"I'm a fair and honest man, young traveler, and just to prove my point, you can leave your animals and rig with me, and I'll let you throw your bedroll in soft straw right back there, and all of that for two dollars a day. No fires, though, you got to promise me that."

"You got yourself a deal, sir," Jack said, stepping off Fargo. "Name's Jack Slater, soon to be of Texas."

"Howdy to you, Jack Slater. Hiram Biggins here, at your service. Need a tooth pulled, a horse shod, or a broken bone set, I'm your man," and he reared back with a long and happy laugh, Jack joining right in with him.

Jack got his animals all settled in, made

up an area in an open stall for his pack and bedroll, thinking, *Didn't I just leave a place where I slept in an open stall?* and chuckled some, spreading straw. "I could use a good hot meal, Hiram. Where would you go for one?"

"Right over there," Biggins said, pointing across the street and down some. "That's Tom Miller's Bella Union Saloon, and they serve good whiskey and fine victuals, Jack, my friend."

"Thank you," Jack said, still tickled at the way Hiram Biggins talked, and headed across the muddy avenue and onto the boardwalk across the way. It seemed that every other building was a saloon, and some, even in the middle of the day, were jumping with noise, music, and loud voices.

Jack found the Bella Union and, just as Biggins said, had a good meal of roasted buffalo, lots of onions and potatoes, and a piece of pie almost as good as what Mims could make. He spend the next few hours walking about the town, getting the lay of the land, he would say if asked.

He found a general merchandise store and bought two flint strikers, hiding a little embarrassed smile, and a good sharpening steel for his knife and ax. "Sure lots of activity around," he said to the storekeeper.

"Everyday, all day," the man replied. "Some of these folks are here because of the gold, some are here to get away from ravaging injuns, and some are here to create trouble for everyone else." There was no humor in his face or comments. "You think the street's are busy right now, then you don't want to be around when the sun goes down." He took Jack's money, made some change, and kept right on talking.

"See that saloon right down there?" He pointed out the open door and across the street. "That's Nutall's place. Nutall and Mann's Number Ten, they call it, and there was a famous killing in there."

"Somebody got killed right there?" Jack said, amazed by what the man said.

"Yes sir. Wild Bill Hickok himself, shot in the back of the head while playing poker. Right in that saloon. Crazy Jack McCall snuck in and shot the man right in the back of his head, he did.

"You here to go minin'? I hear the Homestead Mine is hiring. Big boy like you could get a job pretty quick."

"Nope, not mining," Jack said. "Traveling south to Texas."

"Best bet, then, is to stay out of them saloons. This town is filled with bad people lookin' to steal anything ain't hammered down."

Jack liked this big man with the heavy black moustache and penetrating eyes. *It wouldn't be hard to call this man a friend,* he thought, gathering up what little he had purchased. "My name's Jack Slater," he said, rather abruptly.

"Nice to meet you, Jack Slater, I'm Seth Bullock. Where you staying, not out at that camp area, I hope?"

"No, Mr. Biggins has me all set up at the stables. He warned me about trying to set up a camp."

"He's a good man, honest as the day is long, and strong as an ox. Tell Hiram you met me, and maybe the three of us can share a meal soon."

Jack headed back to the livery with a broad smile on his face. *After that Davis clan of fools, I've just met two very nice people. I'm glad I didn't ride in with the Davis family,* he thought, watching all the activity along Deadwood's main street.

Jack spent the next two days just watching all the activity that swirled through Deadwood day and night. He talked with a couple of men at the Bella Union that had come north and got some idea of the country he would be moving through. They were cattle drovers, they said, but wanted to get in on the gold strikes in the Black Hills. He learned a lot about Texas, New Mexico, and found out there was a railroad that might take him south faster than his horse.

"I came across the country on a railroad," he said. "I want to see this country I'll be going through at ground level and slow speed."

It was on the third morning as he was leaving a café after a big breakfast that he saw two busted up wagons pulled by limping horses pull through town. *Looks like the Davis clan managed to get here. I wonder how long it'll take Jon or Skinny to get in trouble,* he snickered. He sipped the last of his coffee watching the pitiful little train wend its way through the mud and hubbub of Deadwood.

Jon Davis was driving one wagon with his father sitting next to him, and Jessie was driving the second. *I wonder where that fool Skinny Davis is? Whoa, is Jessie nursing a big black eye? Glad I got away from those fools.*

Jack got back to the stables thinking it would be best if he got out of town as soon as possible. He had bad thoughts about the Davis clan and didn't want to be around them. Hiram Biggins met him at the doors of the livery. "You be in heavy thought, my traveling sir," he said, sucking on a long stemmed pipe that he must have carved himself.

"I think it's time to get the next leg of this journey underway, Mr. Biggins. You've been most kind and generous, and I thank you for that. Shall we settle up my account and I'll get packed and on the road."

"Well, let's see," he said, sending a cloud of smoke into the rarified elements. "Three days at one dollar a day comes to," and he paused, as if counting to himself, but with a wide smile across his broad face, "about three dollars, I do believe."

"Well now, sir," Jack said, "you fed those three animals and gave me a place to bed, you must account for that," Jack said, remembering that Biggins had quoted a higher price before, but he said it with an equally bright smile. The two were almost fencing with each other, and having a grand time doing it.

"Ah, true you be, young friend, I did indeed feed your chargers and accommodate yourself, so, I should add another dollar to that fee. Would four dollars seem right to you?"

"It would, sir, but only if I would be allowed to ask you to join me in having a cold beer together before I leave this fine city."

"So be it," Hiram Biggins bellowed, untying his leather apron and leading Jack Slater down the boardwalk to the Nutall and Mann's #10. "It's always a pleasure to have a good libation with a good fellow."

"Is this really where Wild Bill Hickok was murdered?" Jack asked after they got mugs of beer and found a table. "He was a real hero, wasn't he?"

"Army thought so. I thought he was a pompous ass, myself, but yes, that table right back there. Jack McCall came in the back door, over there," and Biggins pointed it out, "and walked right up to the table and shot Hickok in the back of the head. Terrible, that's what it was, just terrible."

This was the second time that Jack had sat in a saloon and had a cold beer with someone he liked. The first was the day before he left Fargo, and he and Ray Bennett had beers at the Barrel House Saloon. Jack was thinking about Bennett and Biggins, how very different the two men were, yet how much he enjoyed their company. Jack wasn't even aware that anywhere else in the land, except for these frontier areas, he would not be allowed to enjoy a cold beer.

"You're a big boy," Biggins said, "but I have the idea that you're much younger than you appear."

"I probably am. My Pa was very big and I guess I take after him. I'm fifteen, Mr. Biggins, but I've had to act like a grown man for many years, I think." *First, I had to take care of Claudine and little Timmy, then along came Mims and Jason, and now, it's just me,* Jack thought. "It seems I've had responsibilities all my life."

"Well, son, you stay on the straight and narrow, and you're going to have a fine life, I think."

The two large men walked out of the saloon and back toward the stables, talking up a storm, laughing at each other's comments, and enjoying a bright sunny day. "You, Slater," a hard voice said as they neared the livery. "I want to talk to you."

Jack turned and saw Jon Davis walking up behind him. "Hello, Jon. I saw your wagons pull in this morning. Glad you made it."

"Don't give me that glad-hand stuff. Skinny told me what you did to my sister. I'm gonna take it out of your hide, mister." Davis was at least five years older than Jack Slater, but was probably thirty pounds lighter and not half as strong as the younger man. He stood with his legs wide apart and a sneer on his face. "I'm calling you out, boy."

Jack stood on the boardwalk, quietly, thinking about what he had seen when the Davis wagons pulled through Deadwood. He also had memories of Jon Davis standing helplessly while he fixed their wagons.

"I don't know what you're talking about, Jon, but don't ever threaten me. It looked like somebody smacked Jessie a good one when you folks drove through this morning. If you're accusing me, you're wrong. Back off."

A crowd started gathering around, always ready for a good fight or some other kind of excitement, maybe even a killing. Hadn't been one since just after sunrise. Neither man was packing, so that meant it would be fists, feet, and maybe knives. One of those stepping out onto the street was Seth Bullock, owner of the mercantile and hardware business.

"You tried to rape her and hit her in the face with your fist, Jack Slater and I'm going to skin you, boy," Jon Davis said, swinging a big fist at jack.

Jack was half again bigger than Davis, simply caught Davis's hand, twisted it around, hearing the arm bone break, and pushed the man into the mud. "I never

159

touched your filthy sister, would never lower myself to that, and if you ever swing on me again, you won't see another day."

Jack still stood on the boardwalk, his legs spread some, his shoulders tensed and fists closed. Hiram Biggins saw a man completely in charge of the situation, and backed off just a step or two. "I take it you know this man, Jack?" he asked, keeping an eye on the crowd in case Jon Davis had backup.

"Met the family on the trail a couple of days ago. This is what you get when you try to help scum. They had wheel trouble and I fixed them up, and this fool has been looking for trouble from the minute he laid eyes on me."

Davis was whimpering, holding his broken arm, and squalling loud enough to keep the attention of the crowd. "He raped my sister and now tried to kill me," he howled, getting the crowd riled up pretty good.

Jack stepped down off the boardwalk, glanced about at the crowd and kneeled down next to Jon. In a voice loud enough for the crowd to pick up, he said, "I never touched your sister, Davis, and all I did was defend myself from your stupid attack. Is that why Skinny wasn't in the wagons this morning? Was it Skinny that attacked your sister, his own cousin? Is that why you want to blame me? You better hide back in the sewer you came from, scum-boy, and not threaten me again."

Jack stood back up, tall and proud, not a whimpering little boy in the dirt and mud, looked at the crowd and said, "I tried to help these people just five days ago, and this is how they respond." He turned back to Jon. "You are a foul mouthed fool, Jon Davis. Crawl back in your hole."

He turned and with Biggins started back to the stables. Was it because of what he said that the crowd didn't get rowdy? Or was it because he was a friend of Hiram Biggins? Whatever it was, the crowd ignored the whimpering Jon Davis, and drifted away from the scene.

"That could have turned nasty, friend Jack," Biggins said. "Maybe it would be a good idea for you to get out of town today. There are some people, you know, that you simply can't help. I would take this as a good lesson, my friend."

"I think you're right, Mr. Biggins, very right indeed. I'll pack up the mule and be on my way. Thank you for all your kindnesses, sir. I'll not forget my few days here."

Jack was putting his pack together in the barn when he heard crowd noises outside. As he walked toward the big open doors he was joined by Biggins. "Something else going on?" he asked the large man. "Seems like these excitements happen regular in Deadwood."

"They do, my boy, they do."

They found a crowd gathered in the middle of the street and as they walked up, Jack recognized the voice of Peter Davis, screaming that his daughter had been raped and beaten and the man that did it was named Jack Slater. Jack bristled at the comments, pushed and shoved his way through the crowd and slammed a fist into the man's face. "You ever say something like about me again, and I'll horsewhip you until there ain't a piece of meat on your bones," he bellowed. Davis was wallowing in the mud, unable to regain his footing.

The crowd seemed about half believing the old man and half believing Jack until Seth Bullock stepped onto the street and stood next to Jack. "You people know me and you better listen to what I'm about to say, here," he snarled, that massive moustache of his bristling with every word.

Bullock had dark eyes, and strong face, and big voice, and most in Deadwood knew he had been a lawman, was being talked up and down the street about being Deadwood's lawman, and knew he didn't take nonsense from anyone. "This here young man's been in town for several days, is a friend of Biggins, and I watched Davis's wagons pull through town this morning.

"That girl was beat up just before getting to town, blood still fresh on her face, so this big boy here didn't have nothing to do with it. Now go on back to your saloon tables and get away from the front of my store." He shot a plume of tobacco juice toward one of the men's boots, getting some chuckles from the crowd, and most started wandering away from the scene.

"Follow me into the store for a minute, Mr. Slater," Bullock said, then turned to Davis, still sitting in the mud. "Better get your people out of town, mister. Don't need your kind around here." Davis's jaw was already starting to swell and discolor, and he was mud from top to bottom.

"Now, Slater, what's your story," he said, sitting in a large well-crafted rocking chair near a wood stove. "Sit, son, and tell me what you're doing in Deadwood." Bullock saw a big boy about to be a man, with good morals and respectful too, toward his elders. "First, tell me how old you are, then why you're here."

"Well, sir," Jack said, taking a bent cane chair, also near the stove, "I'm fifteen and

163

I'm on my way to Texas. I made Deadwood a stop for supplies. That Davis clan is dangerous, Mr. Bullock, and stupid ignorant, not just ignorant."

Bullock chuckled at that and agreed with the comment. "I like that," he said. "Stupid ignorant. I gotta remember that. What's in Texas, son? And you said you're just fifteen? I would of bet you were closer to eighteen. You are one big boy."

"I'm going to buy a farm or ranch when I get to Texas. I've been on farms all my life and I really like being on a farm. I'm good with animals, I work good with wood and iron, and I've heard a lot of people talk good about farming and ranching in Texas."

"I guess you've never been there, eh?" he said, getting a nod back from Jack. "That's one big bunch of country down there. Been in the nations but never deep into Texas, myself. Do have some friends down there, though. It's good cattle country, where the buff used to run, but they look at water like miners look at gold."

Jack snickered at that, got up and poured the two of them some coffee that had been heating on the wood stove. "I've worked grains and hogs and I like the idea of having cattle, but I don't know much about raising a herd of them. I know I can learn.

164

"Thank you for stepping into that crowd out there. I don't know what might have happened if you hadn't."

"That Davis was telling lies on you, Jack, I just couldn't let that pass. How you getting to Texas? Do you know anyone there?"

"Thought I'd go south through Colorado from here, then maybe south from Santa Fé, I'd work my way east into Texas. Don't know a soul down there, but I meet people easy. I've read a lot about Texas. Railroads are opening up a lot of territory, so I figure I'll find a place without much trouble."

Bullock was looking through some papers he had on a desk near the stove, found what he wanted and sat back down. "Man I knew a few years ago, was a ranger, Texas Ranger, named Stoney Pearson. Stoney's a lot like me, done law work and enjoy it.

"Stoney had the right idea when he put his cattle ranch together. He said, you got to get that cattle to market, and today, the best way to do that is with a railroad. Now here's what I'm leading up to. They've built a big railroad from the east coast and another one from the west coast, and those two railroads have joined up."

Bullock took a long drink of coffee and continued. "Now, if I was a young man like you and I wanted to have a farm and raise

165

cattle, I'd want to be near a railroad where I could get my crops and steers to the big markets. Do you understand what I'm saying?"

"Yes sir, I think I do. You're trying to say that maybe I should find out more about this big railroad and find a place near where they are."

"That's exactly what I'm saying. You're big and strong, young and willing to learn, Jack Slater. I'd say, travel south from Deadwood until you meet up with the Union Pacific Railroad, and follow their rails west until you come to the spot that strikes you as being a home place for the Slater brand.

"When you think you might be pulling out, Mr. Slater?"

"I was packing the mule when that ruckus started out on the street. I'll head out as soon as I finish," Jack said. "Got food and provisions, and Mr. Biggins gave me some good maps on getting south to the Denver area. Probably just follow the railroad from there," he laughed. "I've had Texas on my mind, just because of all the things I've heard, but I like what you've been saying. This new railroad would have to go across the Rocky Mountains and there would be good open country on the other side of those massive hills, and I might find good land at a reasonable price.

"Yes sir, I'm glad we've had this talk."

"You have a good ride, Slater. You put a couple of years on you and I betcha you'll be running a fine ranch. You keep in touch, Jack," he said, offering his big hand.

"I surely will do that, Mr. Bullock, I surely will. Thank you again for what you did, and if the Davis clan sticks around here, keep a close watch on them. Jon and Skinny are trouble from the first word." Jack shook hands with the store owner and headed up the boardwalk for the Biggins' livery. *I've got two things I have to do before I can leave Deadwood,* he thought, sitting down next to his pack. *I need to finish that letter to Mims and get it sent off and I need to memorize this map of how to find Denver or that railroad. My new home is waiting for me, I believe,* he snickered.

15

Jack shook hands with Biggins, stepped into the saddle and with his pack mule and second saddle horse, made his way out of Deadwood, Dakota Territory. *It may be Wichita Falls, Texas, it may be anywhere else that looks good, but we're going to find us a new home, boys,* he chuckled to the animals, chewing a tough piece of Biggins' elk jerky and thinking of Mims' apple pie. "A new home, that's where I'm heading," he snickered to his animals.

After the several days of good food and little work, the horses and mule stepped out right fancy, Jack thought, enjoying riding through mountain country on a good trail. He found few on the trail but it apparently was well used. He overtook one wagon that held a small family headed for a large mine, not too far distant.

"Been looking forward to this for some time," the man said, driving a matched team of mules. "Goin' to Lead in Colorado country. I worked some in the coal mines back in Kentuck, and working gold's just gotta be better."

He was skinny as a rail, his wife just a bare skeleton, and the two little girls in the back of the wagon looked like they ate once a week at most. Jack rode with them for an hour or so, and finally let his animals step out at a good fast walk. "Since I left Fargo I have run into so many people that just don't seem to eat. All of them remind of poor little Jason never knowing if he was gonna get fed or not." He remembered telling Mims that if he ever had a family he would never ever use food as a means of punishment.

As dusk came on, Jack started looking around for a good spot to spend his first night on this new trail. Off the main trail by half a mile or so, he saw a stand of fir and pine with a small stream not far off, and went cross-country to the spot. "It's too late in the day to start a fire," he murmured, thinking Indians on the one hand, and two-legged varmints on the other. "You boys have good grass and water and I'll have myself a cold supper of elk meat and biscuits." He snickered remembering meals of cold meat and biscuits in the barn back at Jablonski's. "Won't be as good as Mims's biscuits, and the meat ain't home growed beef, but it's all mine, and I ain't sneaking it from mean Pete," he laughed.

He was stretched out under his red wool blanket watching billions of stars twinkle in the clear sky, thinking about what he would be doing during the next weeks or months, looking for a new home. He had wonderful thoughts of Mims dancing through those dreams, and realized that once again, he was absolutely alone in the world. "I wonder if this isn't my true future, always being alone and thinking about being with others? When Mama and Pa were gone, I was alone in New York surrounded by thousands, but alone.

"On the train, I was with all those people and all that time, even with Claudine, even with Ephraim, I was alone. I never felt a part of Pete Jablonski's, even though I was close to Mims, but I was always alone."

The period of melancholy eased into dreams of a large farm, and he could see waves of grain and corn dancing in a prairie wind, see cattle grazing on acres of green grass, and could picture a large, at least two-story home, smoke curling from the rock chimney. His dream burst with the frightened braying of his mule, and as he tried to shake off his sleep, he felt a crushing blow to his head, and then nothing.

"Biggins, you in there? Come here, quick." Seth Bullock had run to the livery from his store. Biggins came out from the back of the large barn at a trot.

"What's got your tail twisted, Mr. Bullock? Got an animal hurt or sick?"

"No, look," Bullock said, pointing at a man trailing a mule. "That's Jack Slater's mule, sure as I'm standing here. Who is that on the horse? Sure ain't Jack."

"That's the one Jack called Skinny Davis. That's the fool that Jack said tried to rape his own cousin, the rape that they tried to blame on Jack."

"Something's wrong, then, Biggins. Help me get my horse saddled, I gotta go find Jack. While I'm gone, see what you can find out around here about why Skinny Davis would have Jack's mule."

Bullock had been a lawman in the past, before moving to Deadwood and opening his mercantile store, and he smelled a crime. *I liked that boy the minute he started talking to me. If something's happened to him, I'll see to it somebody gets hurt real bad.*

Bullock was on the trail out of Deadwood within ten minutes. "Not much activity on

171

the road this morning," he said, putting his horse into a comfortable trot. "I'll back track Davis's trail. Oh, I hope that boy's not dead. I liked his stuff, the stuff of a full growed man, and he's still a boy." The trail left by the horse and mule was easy to follow in the dusty trail that led toward the mountains, and Bullock found himself more than just anxious as the hours passed.

"There," he exclaimed, seeing the trail move off into the high grass and toward a stand of tall trees and a small stream. "Let's go nice and slow," he said to his horse, easing him into the grass and a slow walk toward Jack's camp. He saw the trail that Jack cut the evening before with his three animals, and the trail out that Skinny made coming out. In less than twenty minutes, Bullock rode into the remains of Jack Slater's camp and saw the crumpled boy lying in a pool of blood.

Bullock feared the worst and leaped from his horse, and ran to the boy, kneeling down at his side. Jack moaned slightly when Bullock touched his shoulder, and Bullock eased the boy back onto his blanket. "That's one nasty bash on the head, Jack. You just lie still here and I'll get you cleaned up."

Bullock found Jack's coffee pot and ran to the stream filling it with icy cold water and dashed back to Jack's side. It took little time to cleanse the wound and get some clean bandage cloth tied on. The cold water also brought Jack around, and despite the pain in his head, he was able to talk to Bullock.

"The last thing I remember was my mule kicking up a fuss," Jack said as he tried his best to sit up, feeling waves of nausea and dizziness sweep through. Bullock took his time and told Jack about seeing Skinny Davis ride through Deadwood leading Jack's mule.

"I never saw anyone, Mr. Bullock, just heard that old mule howling and stomping around. I wonder why Skinny would do this? Why only take my mule, when I have two fine saddle horses? And why ride right through town?"

"There's a whole lot more questions that we're gonna find answers to Jack," Bullock said. "He didn't take the horses thinking they would be known, but figured no one would pay any attention to the mule, but that doesn't answer the main question. Why attack you in the first place? And then, why not take your pack?" Bullock busied himself for the next half hour building a small fire, making a pot of coffee, and frying up some elk meat and a couple of wild onions.

"Here, eat this and let's drink up this coffee, and if you feel up to it, we'll ride back to Deadwood and take old Skinny Davis down, along with his whimpering cousin Pete. That family's just about got me riled, now boy, and I hope you're about as riled as you are big."

They laughed, even though you could see the pain in Jack's eyes, and drained that coffee, ate up the meat and onions, and Jack managed to get to his feet, wobbled to old Fargo, and got him saddled and bridled. "This is gonna hurt, Mr. Bullock."

"I hope it hurts enough to make you really angry, young Mr. Slater, cuz we're gonna start a war when we get back to Deadwood." All the time he was talking, Jack was watching the big man's eyes.

When I'm full growed I hope I am about half the man this Seth Bullock is, he thought, settling himself deep into the saddle of his horse. They had fixed the pack onto the second saddle horse that decided maybe a little bucking show was in order. It took a full ten minutes to get that horse convinced it should be a good-natured pack animal.

Biggins put a sign up on the barn door that said he would be back in a few, saddled a horse, and rode out toward where the Davis family had their camp set up. There were several different groups camped along a stream where good grass grew, and Biggins tried to give the impression he was just passing through. It didn't take much for him to spot the miserable little camp that Pete Davis had set up. He saw Jon, with the broken arm, saw scrawny Jessie screaming at Skinny, and watched Pete swing an open hand and knock her to the ground.

"Keep it in the family," Biggins chuckled to himself, letting his horse continue on the main trail around the encampment. "Inbreeding and many generations of ignorance all wrapped up and on display," he muttered. "I wonder why that fool Skinny had Jack's mule, and I wonder just where Jack Slater might be? Seth Bullock's got himself all riled up, and from what I know of his background, he'll be hell on hooves when he gets back to town. Got a lot of law-enforcement in his history, that man does. We do need some of that in Deadwood," he chuckled, nudging his horse into a lope and heading back to the livery stables to await Bullock's return. "I'm gonna have to talk to him about that when he gets back. Yes we do need some law in this old town."

"What you hittin' me for?" Jessie wailed. "It was Skinny tried to do me, and it's Skinny

175

that stole that mule, and you got no call to be hittin' me," she bawled, tears streaming across high cheekbones that were covered in bruises. Tears came from blackened eyes. "What happened to this idea of robbing the mines south of here? How come you big strong men got yourself all whupped by a boy?" She kicked some dirt toward Pete Davis and he whopped her again, but this time with a doubled up fist, knocking her to the ground, putting a large lump on her jaw bone.

"Shut up, Jessie," Davis snarled, and turned on Skinny. "Just what have you done, now, boy? Is that Jack Slater's mule? Cuz if it is, that means you done something really stupid. Are you gonna bring every lawman in the territory to our little camp?"

"Ain't nobody knows it's Slater's mule but us, Cousin Pete, and Slater's dead as all that wood in the gulch down there. 'Sides, ol' Jon there kinda wanted that boy dead, didn't he? He made both you and Jon look kinda foolish out there on the street, you know. You should be thankin' me, Pete," he said, puffing himself up some, never seeing the big fist coming that knocked him back about five feet and plunked him down in the dirt.

"You are one stupid fool, Skinny," Pete

snarled. "You get rid of that mule just as soon as you can. You got anything else that belongs to Slater? This whole town already hates us cuz of you trying to stick it to Jessie and then you and Jon tryin' to blame the Slater boy, and now you gone and kilt the boy and stole his mule.

"Now, you get rid of the that mule, and I mean, now." He was towering over Skinny Davis, kicked dirt in his face, and stormed off to his wagon, found a bottle of whiskey and took it down considerable, cussing the whole time. "Jessie, quit your crying and fix something to eat. Something good, this time."

Jessie watched Skinny and Jon wander off toward the creek, punching each other in the shoulder and laughing. "I'm gonna find some dude in this town and move in with him and be away from these miserable fools," she muttered.

"How'd you kill him?" Jon asked, as the two wandered away from camp. "Did he put up a fight?"

"Naw, no fight at all. I just snuck up behind him and whacked him with a rock. He just rolled over and gave it up," Skinny laughed. "Easiest thing I ever done, killing that boy. How's your arm?" He gave him a little punch to the shoulder and danced out of the way of a counter-punch.

"You really got Pa angry this time, Skinny. Probably should have left the mule behind. I'd take him to the livery, if I was you, and sell him. Might get five for him. Ain't nobody but us knows he ain't yours, an' they ain't nothin' on him says he's Slater's. Five dollars is good money, Skinny."

"You want to ride in with me? Let's eat, then we can ride in. We won't tell Pete what we're doin' and that way, we can keep the five dollars. Maybe buy our own bottle an' not have to always ask for a drink," Skinny laughed, punching Jon on the shoulder again.

Despite making good time on the trail back to Deadwood, it was late in the day when Bullock and Slater rode up to Biggins' old barn. The stable operator was inside working on some business papers when they rode in. "I was startin' to think bad thoughts, Bullock. Sure glad I was wrong. Jack, boy, are you okay? You look like the leavings of a bad war," he laughed, looking at Jack's bloody and bandaged head.

"You ain't gonna like what I've got to tell you," Biggins continued. "That fool Skinny Davis and his cousin Jon showed up at the livery several hours ago with your mule,

Jack, wantin' to sell it to me. Can you even believe that?" He shook his head in disgust, and walked back toward one of the stalls. "Got him right here for you."

Biggins motioned for Bullock and Jack to come into his little office, pulled chairs out for them, and settled behind his desk. "Need to talk serious for a few minutes, Seth." He reached over to the old stove and grabbed the coffee pot. He pulled three cups off the shelf and poured the cups full, and put the pot back on the stove.

"Want a little sweetener, Seth, I'm gonna have some," he said, pulling a bottle from a desk drawer. "None for you, Jack," he laughed. "What we've seen the last several days is happening every day, it seems, and we gotta do something about this.

"Girls gettin' raped, people gettin' the tar beat out of 'em, old Wild Bill Hickock gettin' his brains blowed out over at the Number Ten. Seth, you've carried a badge, and right now, Deadwood could sure do with you carrying one again."

"I know," Bullock said, quietly, taking a long drink of hot coffee. "Been talking to others around town and I've told most of them that we need a town marshal. I've already told them that I would do it, but I need to continue running my store, too. So

179

far, that's agreeable to most of them. What about you, Hiram? Would a part time town marshal work for you?"

Biggins thumped the desk and gave forth a mighty "Yes Sir!" back to Bullock. "I gave that stupid little Skinny Davis five dollars for the mule, which I guess makes me guilty of buying stolen property, but I'd be willing to bet that fool boy is still over at Nutall and Mann's right now, if we should happen to venture that way," and he snickered a little bit, pouring just a bit more amber dynamite into his and Bullock's cups.

It was probably a good thing that Skinny Davis and his cousin weren't in the saloon, but the group that was there grabbed Bullock and Biggins and had them join in a discussion to change the atmosphere in Deadwood. "Too many dead people, too much lawlessness, and we need a change now," is how Nutall put it.

16

Bullock actually took the job of Sheriff of Deadwood the very next day, and with his new position decided to visit the Davis camp just outside the town. Slater was being cared for at the doctor's little hospital in the back of his offices, and felt a full recovery would follow along. Seth Bullock was a tall and heavy man, carried a huge moustache and had penetrating eyes that could stare most men down. He had his new badge pinned on his coat and rode alone through the streets, nodding greetings to his many friends.

"You Pete Davis?" he asked, stepping off his big horse, giving the man a hard look. Davis saw the badge immediately, recognized the big man that had tormented him in town just a couple of days ago, and felt his knees go weak.

"I am," Davis stammered. "What do you want?"

"Right now I want your son, Jon, and his cousin, Skinny. Bring them to me now."

"I'm not sure where they are. What do you want with them?"

"Get 'em, Davis or I'll arrest you instead. Maybe I will anyway. Get 'em."

Davis felt shivers scream up his spine, wasn't sure he could walk, and wanted to run faster than a horse. He tried to stammer something when Jessie stuck her head out of one of the wagons and hollered that Skinny and Jon were going to hightail it out of the back of the wagon.

Bullock took the extra second or two to slam a heavy right fist into Davis's jaw, sending the little man tumbling in the dust, and sprinted to the back of Jessie's wagon in time to meet Skinny and Jon. "Hello, boys," he smiled, using a thumb to flash his new Sheriff's badge in their faces. "Don't make me shoot you, no matter how much I want to. Find your horses and saddle up. You're under arrest."

After each Davis saddled up, Bullock handcuffed them to each other so they had to ride side by side into town, him following right behind. He made it a little parade through town to a building that overnight became the jail and Sheriff's Office. Bullock saw to it that a few onlookers got quite a show as the two Davis boys, cuffed together, tried to dismount. They ended up sitting in the dirt listening to some good-natured hoorahs.

He got the two inside and sitting in chairs opposite him and spoke to them across a big oak desk. "You sold a mule yesterday to Hiram Biggins at the stables, am I right?"

The two started talking immediately. Skinny said he found the mule along the banks of the creek near their camp and Jon said he bought the mule from a feller that was down and out.

"You were seen bringing the mule into town yesterday morning, Skinny, and that mule belongs to Jack Slater. You're under arrest for stealing the mule and for attempted murder."

"That boy ain't dead?" Skinny said, too slow to stop himself. "I was sure . . ." and his voice trailed off.

"No, Skinny, you didn't kill him," Bullock said with a menacing scowl, "but you did come close. Jon Davis, you're under arrest for aiding and abetting Skinny and for possession of stolen property. We'll have your little trial as soon as we get ourselves a judge." He motioned the two toward the back and into quickly made cells, using another set of handcuffs to attach them to a ring bolted to the rock wall.

"Don't be trying anything stupid because I really would like to shoot both of you right where you stand."

He walked up the street to find someone he could trust to sit in the office and keep and eye on the two boys, grabbed old Eli Perkins and hired him as a deputy and sent him back to the office. "Take good care of 'em Eli, shoot 'em if they need to be shot," and he continued up the street to Tom Miller's Bella Union Saloon for a cold beer and a chat with Hiram Biggins.

"There he be," Biggins said in a big voice when Bullock walked in. "Deadwood's first sheriff. You get those Davis boys?"

"Yup, I did. Let's take a table Hiram. Get me a cold beer and keep 'em coming, Tom," he said to Miller, taking a table near the back wall. "I got a dreadful taste in my mouth."

After they were settled and the bad taste was washed away, Biggins told the sheriff what he had seen when he visited the Davis camp. "That old man bashed that girl twice, Seth, once with what I thought was his doubled up fist. Some of the people that seem to be wanting to call Deadwood home simply aren't the kind I want for neighbors."

"Guess we can't pick our neighbors,

sometimes, Hiram. I got Jon and Skinny locked up and sent word that we need a judge. We don't want these boys let go like they let Jack McCall go.

"Do you have all of Jack's personal belongings in from where he got attacked? According to the doc he'll be ready to ride out in just a couple of days."

"I saw him this morning, and he's chewing his way out, I think. Said the headaches are about gone, that he isn't sick to his stomach anymore, and how are his animals? He's just about barn-bound, Seth," he laughed. "He'll be on the road as soon as the doc clears him."

"That boy's got a lot of spunk in him. I wish I was young enough to ride with him or he was old enough to work for me here in Deadwood. What a deputy he'd make. These old drunks would think twice before kicking off their shenanigans, or shooting up the neighborhood. Make sure I know when he's ready to leave, Hiram. I want to make sure I can say goodbye to that boy."

"Thanks for all you've done, Doc. I feel fine and I'll do as you say about taking it easy for the next few days. I'll ride slow and rest every chance I get. Besides, I feel a little weak, so that will come natural, I think."

Jack was shaking hands with the doc and ready to head to the livery to pack up and leave Deadwood. *I don't think I want to stay another day in this dirty little town. Only three people I like are the doc, Seth Bullock, and Hiram Biggins. Follow the railroad, that's what I'll do, just like Bullock said.*

It was a quick walk down the street, past Bullock's store, which he knew he would remember for many years. Glancing about, Jack remembered having good meals at the Bella Union and cold beer at Nutall's place. He knew he would never forget seeing the gambling table where Hickok was murdered. He was wearing a little smile when he walked into the barn and spotted Biggins hammering a piece of red-hot iron.

"Mornin' Mr. Biggins. My animals in good enough condition to make a couple of hundred miles before sunset?"

Biggins laughed, setting the hot iron in some cold water. "Keep it under fifty miles and they'll be fine. I doubt you would be though." He took Jack's offered hand and gave it a strong shake.

"Doc made me promise to go nice and slow for the first few days. I want to thank you again for all you've done for me. I would have been a canary to a cat if you hadn't kept me out the places I shouldn't go. I'll go get packed," he said, turning away before Biggins could see the tears welling in his eyes.

Biggins hightailed it up the street to alert Bullock that Jack was packing up. The two hurried back to the barn before Jack was finished getting all the animals ready. "So, Mr. Slater, you're gonna try again to leave old Deadwood," Sheriff Bullock said, helping Jack lift part of the pack onto the mule's back. "You have a long and safe journey, my friend. You're welcome to come back for a visit anytime."

"I value yours and Mr. Biggins' friendship, Mr. Bullock, and I'll miss you very much. Thank you for everything," he said, walking the horses and mule to the front of the barn. There were strong handshakes all around and Jack Slater stepped into Fargo's saddle and rode out on the south trail. "So long, my friends," he whispered, nudging the little pack train into a strong trot, tears streaming down his young face.

All I've done for the last month or so is say goodbye to good friends, he thought, not daring to turn and see Deadwood slowly fade from view. *I'm going to find my little farm and ranch in good country with good water, and I won't leave friends again. I don't want to always be alone.*

It was three hours before he stopped alongside a creek to rest the animals and himself, let them drink and graze for half an hour, and he was back on the trail. "Tomorrow or the next day, I should be somewhere near where that railroad will be coming through. Just follow the rails, Bullock said, and ride to the top of the Rocky Mountains and down into good ranching country. Sure made it sound easy," he snickered, giving Fargo a little nudge.

All thoughts of the crazy and dangerous Davis family were out of his head, and only thoughts of a farm, a ranch, and Mims were front and center, and he rode with a broad smile. His visions of how his farm would be had their start in New York where water was plentiful, and the ground was good.

Those visions were layered with good thoughts from his years in Fargo, Dakota Territory, where again, there was plentiful water, and the ground was excellent. He had visions of wheat waving in the wind, of corn climbing for the clouds, and hogs and cattle getting fat on good food.

I wonder what I'll find on the other side of those high mountains. I should have been afraid when I was put on that train and headed west with all those kids, but I wasn't, and I should have been afraid when I walked away from Pete Jablonski, but I wasn't.

I'm sitting in what was Indian country just a couple of years ago, close to where General Custer lost his entire army, looking to find some railroad tracks to follow somewhere, and I should be afraid. I'm not afraid, I'm excited, he almost wanted to bellow that out to the world.

17

Jack made camp that first night alongside another creek that offered good water for the stock and with plentiful grass where they could be hobbled. After a quick supper and a full pot of coffee, Jack could feel every mile he had covered. "That doc was right, telling me not to over-do." He stripped and eased his aching body into the cold water of the creek, grimacing as he knew he was going to freeze to death in snow melt.

He sat near a small fire, wrapped in a wool blanket, letting the warmth build. Ever so slowly his muscles came back to life. Jack pulled a map that Hiram Biggins had drawn for him, and studied it carefully. It was pretty rough and of course not to scale, but he now had a better idea of what he would be doing for the next several days. "It looks like this trail that I'm on will take me to Cheyenne, which is still Dakota Territory, and Biggins said he thought the railroad coming from the east would pass right through there."

He could feel every muscle in his body as he got up to put some more wood on the fire. "Biggins and Bullock kept telling everybody how big and strong I am. They wouldn't say that if they could feel what I feel right now," he snickered, huddling back down into the warmth of the wool folds of the blanket. *Look at these beautiful trees cascading down the mountains, huge pines and fir, spruce and cedar, and mixed in with all that is mountain mahogany, oak, and who knows what.* The sight brought back memories of Fargo and the Jablonski farm.

"The only trees I ever saw, for miles and miles in every direction," he said, as if he was talking to someone, "were those that had been planted by someone. Even coming across the great plains on that train, the trees were either right around a farm house or planted as a wind screen, and look at where I am right now. Huge trees running wild like crazy people, up and down the mountains, across the valleys, even making the creeks and streams change course so they can grow," he laughed.

"And the colors," he sighed, "all muted greens and blues and browns and tans and yellows, and mostly, beautiful." He threw some more wood on the fire and laid back on the blanket, watching as evening turned to deep night, saw the night hawks and bats feasting on bugs, heard coyotes way off in the distance, and just close enough to prick the skin along his backbone, a wolf began his night song.

Jack Slater read the Fargo newspaper every time he was able to get into town and remembered reading about the Union Pacific building a road that would have a terminus at Cheyenne. "It was that army general," he muttered, trying to remember back several years. "Dodge, that was his name, and he became the boss of that railroad, or something like that. Imagine, a railroad that starts at the Atlantic coast and goes all the way to the Pacific Ocean.

"I'm gonna be riding right alongside those rails. Old Mr. Bullock was sure right to tell me to follow the railroad."

He folded the map and tucked it away and let his mind wander around some. "I can't just ride in somewhere and try to settle down," he realized with a start. "I'm fifteen-years-old. I can't get my money until I'm eighteen. Probably can't even buy land or homestead it until I'm eighteen." He spent a few restless hours worrying about what that meant to his immediate future, and then told himself that it didn't matter what he was thinking anyway, there wasn't anything he could do about any of it. Bullock and Biggins would have said something about 'welcome to maturity, Jack Slater.'

It was a full four days on the trail before he rode into Cheyenne, the bustling little western town reminded Jack too much of Deadwood. There were more saloons and gambling parlors than there were other types of businesses combined, and he saw loud, boisterous crowds of men about on the streets, and rode straight through without stopping. *My supplies are fine and I wouldn't want to leave these animals tied off without me standing right with them. It wasn't this way in Fargo,* he was thinking. *I wonder what makes places like Deadwood and Cheyenne different than Fargo?*

It came to him slowly, that Deadwood was built on gold fever, the people that came to that area didn't come to settle for the rest of their lives, they came from a burning desire to get rich overnight. *Fargo was built on farming, on families, on a desire for permanence. That's why I didn't fit in, in Deadwood, why I don't want to stop here.*

It wasn't hard to find the railroad, most of Cheyenne was built around the tracks and railroad buildings. General Dodge had laid out the plans over the Laramie Mountains back about ten years ago. Cheyenne, Jack realized, was a terminus for the railroad, and like Deadwood, the people weren't looking for a new home, just a good job or in some cases, easy pickin's.

Jack followed the rails for several miles west, right up into those nearby mountains. It was a good camp that night, well off the trail and tucked into a fortress of big trees and brush. "The idea of spending some time in that town certainly ended quickly," he chuckled, getting his animals set up for the night. "It's time for some serious planning, Jack Slater," he said as he put together a small fire pit and prepared supper. "I don't know a single person within a hundred miles of where I'm sitting," he said, "and I've got two and half years before I can claim any of my money and build my new home.

"So, what am I going to do?"

It was close to middle of the next day that Jack got his answer. He had been riding slowly along, following the rails, when he saw a single rider coming toward him. He pulled up and moved his animals off to the side, loosened the rifle in its scabbard, and made sure his sidearm was handy. The rider was moving at a comfortable trot and pulled up twenty feet or so from Jack.

"Howdy," he said. "Would you be Herb Reynolds?"

"Howdy yourself," Jack answered. "No, I'm Jack Slater. I haven't seen anyone on the trail this morning. Something I can help you with?"

"Just darn it all. My name's Henry Rupert and Reynolds was supposed to be here yesterday. Where are you heading Slater?"

Jack kind of smiled a little when his answer was a simple, "West, Mr. Rupert."

"Everyone's heading west, son, and I don't blame 'em. I've got a cattle ranch about twenty miles back that way," he said, pointing toward a couple of high peaks that it appeared the railroad would run around. "Do you want a job, Slater? Pay's two dollars a day and found. We'll even put your two extra animals to work and care and feed 'em.

"I won't sugar coat nothin', sir, it's hard work, long hours, and little rest, but it's honest work and you'll be proud to know that you will help build a fine cattle ranch in a wild and good country."

Jack felt he could listen to this Henry Rupert talk all day. He was tall and thin, wore a full red beard that was a curled and tangled raven's nest, his red hair flowed out from his slouch hat in every direction, his green eyes sparkled when he spoke, and his hands, large and gnarly never seemed to be at peace.

"I've never done much cattle work, Mr. Rupert. I've always been on a farm, but I sure would like to have a job. I've helped raise hogs and some cattle, but mostly worked grain, like wheat and corn. I'm good with mending equipment, though, both leather for harness and tack, and I can work iron on a forge."

His mind was working at the speed of a wild mustang, thinking that there would be no better way to spend the next couple of years than tramping these mountains and let Mr. Rupert pay his way to a good farm with sweet water. *He might just be buying my little farm for me.* He almost chuckled at the thought.

"You look big and strong and I'm thinking you're a fast learner. Ride with me back to the ranch and I'll spell it all out for you. Even if Reynolds shows up with some more people, as of this minute you are on the job, making your first two dollars," he said, turning his horse around and nudging it back the way he came. Jack rode right up along-

side, and the two shook hands, guarantee-
ing the deal.

Jack caught his breath when they rode
across a high ridge and he was able to look
down on a long valley, cut along the very
south edge by the railroad, with miles of
valley floor spread north and about five to
ten miles wide. There were obvious streams
pouring out of the high mountains to the
west, and Jack saw several thousand acres of
high mountain grass, dotted here and there
with groups of cattle.

"There's your new home, Jack Slater,"
Rupert said, gesturing with both arms
spread wide to take in the entire valley.

"That whole valley is yours?" Jack asked.
"Besides cattle, what else do you raise or
grow?"

"When you have cattle on grass like that,
you don't need much else," he laughed. "We
do grow just about everything else we need,
though. I ride into Cheyenne twice a year
for stuff we can't grow."

Jack laughed at that, remembering how
Pete Jablonski would get so upset because
he had to ride into Fargo every couple of
weeks. "Better make sure your list is right,
it's a long wait if you forget something," he
chuckled.

They worked their way down off the high ridge and rode quietly through the tall grass, sage, rabbit brush, and other high mountain valley vegetation. There were glorious stands of huge trees on the surrounding mountains, and the breeze moving through the valley, coming from the southwest, was almost sweet to taste. "How many head are you running, Mr. Rupert?"

"Call me Henry, Jack. I am your boss, I am the guy that will pay you, but we should also be friends, I think. Right now I've got three hundred cows and twenty five bulls, and I'll hold back as many heifers as I can over the next few years, to build a strong herd. Right now, with the calves and all, about seven hundred or so, total.

"Cheyenne is buying most of what I'm raising right now, and there's always a market in Deadwood. I expect a lot of growth in this area, and I've got some fine tasting beef to offer all those new people. I've had a hard time keeping people. First, the railroad hired away my cowboys, then the lure of Cheyenne took the rest.

"There's a lot of talk about this part of the country becoming Wyoming Territory, and Cheyenne is being talked up about being its capitol. Right now, my beef don't get shipped much further than Cheyenne and

Deadwood, but with the railroad, the whole country's my market," he laughed.

They crossed three nice full streams getting across and up the valley to the home ranch along the west side near the edge of the valley. "I saw some nice trout in those streams, Henry. I might have to learn how to fish again. My pa and I did some fishing when I was much younger."

"You'll like old Growls Like Bear, then. He's a fishin' fool, but probably not the way your pa taught you." He was laughing, picturing Growls Like Bear crawling on his belly through the tall grass, right up to a stream, and shooting the trout with his arrows.

The home ranch was laid out such that one didn't have to do much walking to get from one point to another. There was a bunkhouse that would accommodate as many as twelve men, which surprised Jack. "You have had big crews, Henry?" he asked, looking at the bunks lined up along the walls.

"Anticipating, Jack," he said, a wry grin on his face. "Right now, you and Bear are the crew. That's why I said it would be hard work with long hours."

The corrals separated the bunkhouse from the barn, which was mainly used for hay

199

storage, and across from that group was the main house, a single story mountain cabin. Henry Rupert wasn't married, but was in the market, as he put it. Showing Jack through the main house, he said, "I'll probably have to advertise for a good wife cuz I sure can't find one in Cheyenne. Those are wicked women in that foul town."

Jack spent the next several minutes thinking of Mims, fresh biscuits, and apple pie. His reverie was blasted apart when Henry asked if Jack carried a sidearm. "I have a fine Colt's revolver, but I carry it in my saddlebag most of the time." The question caught Jack off-guard and he didn't really understand why it would be asked. "Is there a dangerous something I should be aware of, Henry?"

"I'm afraid there is. Cheyenne is more that just rowdy, Jack, there are several groups that are known cattle rustlers and thieves. They know that I don't have a large crew, heck, I haven't even had a crew for a couple of months now, and I know I've lost some prime steers.

"I want you and Growls Like Bear to be armed at all times when you're out on the range moving the cattle. I know you have a rifle, I saw that on your saddle, so with all three of us armed with pistols and rifles, we might keep those poachers off the place."

The tour continued right up to suppertime when Jack got one more little surprise. "We eat our meals together, right here in the kitchen of the big house. This is Evangelina (Oak Blossom) Contreras, my cook and housekeeper," Henry said, introducing the young Indian girl to Jack.

"Evangelina came to live with me after her father was killed in a raid on Fort Russell a few years ago. Pablo Contreras was married to a lovely Shoshone woman and lived with the tribe, became a valued member, strong warrior, and a dear friend I will always miss. She was just ten when her father was killed in the raid, and her mother died of a broken heart."

Jack Slater was looking into enormous brown eyes set in a friendly face. Evangelina's high cheekbones, strong jaw line, and smiling mouth held him speechless for several seconds. She was almost frail, he thought, more along the lines of Claudine, certainly not strong and healthy like Mims. *She's beautiful.* He finally snapped out of it and said, almost tentatively, "Hi." Henry was laughing hard, watching he boy try his best to gather himself up and not be rude.

"You two must be almost the same age, I think," he said. "Well, let's see what Oak

Blossom has for us this evening. Did you ring the bell for Bear?" he asked.

"He's washing up now, Henry. Hi, yourself, Jack Slater. I'm glad to meet you," and she extended her hand. Jack grasped long, thin fingers that he found were nice and strong, and didn't want to let go. She smiled and walked into the large kitchen dining area. Unlike Jablonski's, this kitchen had the feeling of a home, of natural warmth and friendliness, and Jack felt like he wanted to be there.

The table, already set for four, would hold ten or more, easily. It was hand-hewn oak, built by Henry years ago, and comfortably worn some. The chairs were more bench like, but for individuals, not groups, with strong legs and sturdy, straight backs. Growls Like Bear came in from outside as Jack and Henry entered from the living room.

"Bear, say hello to Jack Slater, our new man. Jack, this is Growls Like Bear, a man you will spend many hard hours working with," he chuckled.

"Hello, Growls Like Bear," Jack said, sticking his hand out.

"Unh, yup, hello," the big Indian said in a deep growl, but smiling as he took Jack's hand and shook it heartily. "Let's eat."

Evangelina brought a cast iron kettle of beans to the table, then a platter of fried beefsteaks, and another large kettle that had a loaf of bread steaming away. He was surprised when Henry said a short prayer before he served up bowls of beans and plates full of steaks and hot bread.

This is what I was hoping for when I got off the train so many years ago in Fargo. I work for Henry Rupert and he treats all of us as family. I was supposed to be family and Pete Jablonski treated us all as just workers. Amazing.

Talk consisted of the day's activities, the fact that Reynolds did not show up with a crew, but Jack Slater did, and what might be on tap for tomorrow. There was lots of humor at the table, and Jack had his first real family meal since the night before his parents were killed, almost six years ago.

It was a pleasant night and Jack found himself alone in the large bunkhouse, wrapped in his own blanket, sleeping on a bed for only the second time since leaving Fargo. The first time was at the doctor's place, and he figured that didn't count. *I have at least two years before I can get my money, and I think I've found someplace to enjoy those two years. I'm in a comfortable bed, and for the first time in many years, I*

203

don't feel alone. As the sun came up, he was still smiling.

18

Work on the Bar HR was much different than any work Jack had done on either his parent's farm or in Fargo. The only fences were holding pens near the home place, and some of those were simply piles of brush used to keep something out or something in. He spent most of every day on horseback, and he was alone many hours at a time. It took a few days before he became slightly adept at throwing a lasso, learned fast how to brand, doctor, and castrate, and discovered Growls Like Bear didn't talk much, but when he did, it was either pure humor or pure education.

Jack learned fast to never leave the home place without a heavy coat and slicker tied onto the back of his saddle. He was caught in a late summer thunderstorm while miles from the home ranch, and in that high mountain valley, the rain was icy cold and the wind threatened to freeze him solid.

Summer storms in Fargo were pleasant compared to high-country storms.

"You're a mess, Jack Slater," Evangelina laughed when he rode back late that afternoon. "Get some dry clothes on and I'll have some coffee waiting for you." She was still snickering when she went into the house. Jack was so cold he almost couldn't get out of the saddle. Maybe she was smiling at him, he hoped, not laughing at him.

Growls Like Bear said something along the lines of, "I told you so," when they sat down for a big roast beef supper. "These storms boil in," the big Indian said, "and sometimes will leave as much as two or three inches of hail on the ground." Henry and Oak Blossom shook their heads in agreement, and Jack promised to never leave out again without his Mackinaw and a slicker.

"Winter time, Jack, you'll want some heavy gloves and a heavy buffalo coat," Henry said. "How're you coming with that little roan? Should be a fine horse."

"He's got spirit, Henry," Jack said, and Bear laughed loud at the comment.

"Spirit enough to put Jack in the mud twice this afternoon," he said.

"He did that," Jack said, not wanting to smile, but couldn't hold it in. "He's fast, has good stamina, and wants to learn, Henry. Old Fargo is a farm horse, but Blue is definitely a cow horse."

"Did you bring those apples in your saddle bags, Jack? They are delicious. Where did you find them?" Evangelina walked over to the big wood stove and opened the oven door, letting the kitchen fill with the aroma of freshly baked apple pie.

"There's a whole bunch of wild apple trees up along the banks of Third Creek, and the trees are drooping with apples. Maybe we ought to take the wagon up one day soon and bring back a barrel or two, Henry."

"I vote for that," Bear said, staring at one of the pies that Evangelina put on the table. "Maybe tomorrow morning, Henry." Amid the laughter, there was general agreement, and planning was soon underway.

Jack was more and more aware of just how attractive Evangelina was, and went out of his way to help her at every chance. She in turn offered him help as well, made sure he had snacks for the saddlebags, and was full of smiles often. To Henry it seemed that each wanted to say or do something and were afraid to.

Evangelina drove the wagon and Henry,

Bear, and Jack rode their horses off the home place early in the morning. Oak Blossom had two big baskets full of food for dinner, and they planned to make a day of it. Jack wondered what Pete Jablonski would think of such a thing as this. *He was just an angry old man and little Jason paid the price for that. This is special right now, very special.*

It took a couple of hours to reach the apple orchard and several hours to fill the barrels with ripe apples. "You ate more than you put in the barrels, Bear," Henry laughed as they gathered up for the return to the home place.

"Jack ate more than me," Bear growled through a last bite of apple. "He is really getting big, Henry. He's taller than me but I'm heavier. I hope he stays with us for a long time." Jack realized right from the start that there was a special bond between the big Indian and Rupert, almost as if they were related. Growls Like Bear had said he would protect the older man with his life if it ever came to that.

"You're right, Bear. He's a good hand and is getting better."

Back at the ranch and following supper Henry asked Bear and Jack to stay at the table for a few minutes. "It's coming fall and we have to start thinking about bringing the cattle in closer to here. Some of those steers are coming close to their prime, and those scoundrels in Cheyenne will be looking to rustle up a bunch. Let's get working on bringing the northern herd down first, then those along eastern rim, and the southern last."

"This will be your first drive, Jack, so pay close attention to what Growls Like Bear tells you. Moving a herd of cattle can be stressful on the animals, and we're only moving them twenty or thirty miles, so it's best if we just let them move at their own pace. We may have to give 'em a nudge, some," he snickered, "but we don't need to get 'em all riled up and nervous."

They had a big breakfast the next morning and helped Evangelina get the wagon loaded with bedrolls, kitchen stuff, food, and everything else that would be needed for the next several days. Jack was like a bull hefting the heaviest objects into the wagon, doing his best to see to it that Evangelina saw his strength, giving her smiles at every opportunity, and often getting big smiles back.

That boy's in love, Rupert smiled, watching Jack heft a barrel of something into the wagon. *Maybe I won't lose him down the line if she falls as hard as he has,* he snickered.

Jack was excited and Bear spent several hours telling him what seemed to work best on bringing in the herd. "Of course, the first thing we have to do is find the critters," Bear chuckled. "They can hide a thousand pounds of prime steer behind the smallest bush you've ever seen, or tuck into a drainage ditch that's not even two feet deep. We'll ride out from camp and do circles, Jack, bringing in what we find. Don't want to leave any behind if we can help it.

"Then we'll bring the herd back to the home place. There should be about five hundred head scattered all over the north end of this valley, so it'll take us a few days to get this first group brought in."

Henry led them to an area with plentiful grass and good water, and everyone pitched in getting camp set up. A couple of fire pits were laid out for Oak Blossom and tents and lean-tos were erected, with bedrolls in. Jack found it more and more difficult to keep his eyes off the young girl called Oak Blossom and sometimes Evangelina. "That's pretty heavy, Evangelina, let me help," he said, taking a large cast iron kettle from her.

"Don't want to wreck that pretty back," he said, then turned crimson, thinking about what he said. "I didn't mean anything," he stammered, catching a smile and giggle from her. She let him take the kettle and didn't say anything. "A person can really hurt their muscles picking heavy things up wrong," he finally said.

"Thank you, Jack," she said, giving him a generous smile. "I'll try to be careful."

He found Blue, had his pockets filled with biscuits and jerky and joined Henry and Bear. They started their first circle, with Henry going furthest north, Bear taking the east side, and Jack going west.

"This'll be a short circle today, but after today, we need to spread as far as possible. These steers don't really want to come home, leave all this good grass," Henry joked.

Jack rode southeast out of camp, planning to make his circle around east, north, and back southwest into the holding basin. He began gathering a few animals right away, and found he needed to bring them in and then go back out. It was on his second go around that he spotted some men walking their horses in the trees, a couple of miles off. "I hope this isn't trouble brewin' up for us," he murmured.

As he continued gathering, he kept an eye on the men, finally decided there were at least five of them, and they were watching him as closely as he was watching them.

"I'm gonna take these critters on down and let Henry and Bear know about these guys. They are far too interested in what I'm doing. Come on Blue, let's get these guys down to the camp."

He had twelve head moving along at a steady walk, not pushing them hard, when he saw dust along his right side and spotted two riders loping at an angle toward him. Some movement on his left caught his eye, and he saw another rider, coming toward him at about the same angle. *This isn't going to be a friendly encounter,* he thought, and took his eye off the cattle, and started looking for someplace to plant himself.

He rode Blue into some Juniper bushes, dismounted and tied him off, and with rifle in hand moved through the bushes to a pile of rocks. He got down into the rocks as low as possible as the two riders came up on him. "That's about far enough," he shouted, keeping his rifle at the ready. "Who are you and what do you want."

"Just some neighborly talk, boy," a large man with a full black beard snickered, pulling his revolver and shooting at Jack. Jack was ready for the move and ducked behind the rock before the bullet slammed into it. He rolled to his right, had the man in his sights and shot him right out of the saddle.

Rupert told him about this possibility but he wasn't really prepared for men to simply ride up to him and try to kill him. *I'm alone and in a very dangerous position right now. Think, Jack, make this work.*

He heard a bullet whine past his head, from the other side just before he heard the rifle report, rolled again, found his target, and fired. *I got you, buster. There were five men in those trees, I only know where three of them are, and two have been hit.* He rolled again, got tucked behind the rocks and listened for the slightest sound. It came from where the cattle were.

"They're going for the cattle, Blue," he said, and at the same time saw the second man from his right mount and ride hard toward him. He had the rifle up and felt terrible pain in his face. He pulled the trigger of the gun but couldn't see his target.

The rustler's bullet hit the rock Jack was using as a shield, splattering gravel into his face, partially blinding him. Jack wiped the blood from his eyes, jacked another round into the chamber, and ran for Blue. He jerked the lead rope free and mounted Blue with a leap onto the saddle. Blue bolted from the juniper bushes and Jack saw two men riding hard toward his little group of cattle.

Jack heard a bullet pass close to his head, turned Blue hard to the left, pulled the rifle up, aimed quickly, and fired. Blood still flowed on his face and he couldn't tell if his shot hit anything or not. Jack turned back toward the men trying to get his herd, when he saw dust down in the valley. *Sure hope that's Henry or Bear, but even if it is, they're a long way off.* Jack was riding at a hard trot, reloading the rifle, and watching the two outlaws try to gather his cattle.

The gunshots, the two riders pushing too hard, and the cattle became nervous, ready to scatter at a full run, as Jack got his rifle loaded and ready. He bailed off Blue, got behind a bush, kneeled, and shot one rider off his horse. The other jumped off his horse and scrambled into some bushes. *Hope he doesn't know where I am,* Jack thought, moving closer to the man. *There were five in those trees and I think I've hit at least three of them,* and tried to wipe more blood from his eyes.

"Give it up, mister. Your friends are down and out, and you're surrounded and outnumbered," Jack yelled across the fifty or sixty feet separating the two. "It's over," he yelled again. "Come on out with empty hands held in plain sight."

He was answered by a gunshot aimed at

214

where he had been, and Jack moved again, as quietly as he could, to an angle that gave him a good view of the gunman. The man held a revolver and was looking at where Jack had been. Jack took careful aim, fired, and watched the man's head explode, his body flung back onto the ground.

"I don't know if any of those men that I hit are still alive, and worse, I don't know where any of them might be." He mounted Blue, knew this one was a goner, and rode quietly around the small herd of cattle, getting them quieted down, looking carefully for bodies, or wounded men with weapons. He knew what a perfect target he was, perched up high on Blue's back, and with the cattle put together, stepped back off the horse.

It took Growls Like Bear another twenty minutes to get to the scene, while Jack took that time to keep the cattle into a small group and held them. It wasn't until Bear arrived and Jack sat down on the ground that what happened was fully understood. "This is the second time I've killed someone who was trying to steal from me," he said, so softly Bear almost didn't hear. Tears were trying to flow and Jack fought them back, finding his knuckles covered in blood when he wiped them away.

"You've been shot?" growled the Indian, rushing to Jack's side. "Here, let me see," and he pulled Jack's hand away from his face. Blood leaked from half a dozen spots on Jack's face, with pieces of rock still in some of the wounds. "Missed your eyes, Jack. You're one lucky boy." Bear spent half an hour cleaning him up, and the two spotted more dust in the valley. "Henry coming at a high gallop, I think."

The two men, pistols in hand, spent the next several minutes walking through the grass and brush, trying to locate all five men. "I know I counted five in those trees up there, Bear," Jack said, "and we can only locate four people, so far." That missing man could still be alive, could be aiming a rifle at one of them at that moment, and fear could be seen in Jack's eyes.

"We know one of the four we found is badly wounded, and can't hurt us, but where is that fifth man?" Jack was pacing near a stand of juniper brush when he heard the distinctive click of a revolver hammer being cocked. He dove to the ground and fired his own revolver twice into the bushes. There was a return shot that plowed through the dirt right next to Jack, and the next shot, from Bear's rifle, ended the game.

The man in the brush was still alive but in

no condition to continue the fight. "So, now we have all five," Jack said, watching Henry Rupert rein his lathered horse to a stop near Growls Like Bear. "Cattle are safe, Boss," Jack said, "and two of the outlaws are still alive."

"Where are they?" Rupert asked. "We need to get you back to camp and get those cuts tended to. Let's you and me take these steers in, and Bear, get what you can from the dead men so they can be identified, and bring the wounded into camp. That so-called sheriff in Cheyenne will want to know who the dead are, and maybe these jaspers will live long enough to hang."

Rupert wanted to simply put bullets in their heads, but he also wanted other potential thieves in Cheyenne to know his people were ready to kill rustlers. "Good job, Jack, good job."

Evangelina was more like a wildcat than an Oak Blossom when Jack and Henry rode in and she saw Jack's face. She was cooing and humming, working so softly he almost felt no pain. She had him sitting and was cleaning his wounds before Henry even got out of the saddle. "Don't worry, Jack," Rupert laughed, "I'll take care of your horse."

Evangelina was fast and thorough, removed chunks of rock and grit, and he felt her soft fingers cleaning all the wounds. He looked right into her big soft brown eyes, and wanted to feel her close to him, wanted to hold her, and knew he simply couldn't. She cooed and made little sounds as she got all the cuts closed up, all the bleeding stopped, and stepped back to look deep into Jack's eyes as well.

"Thank you," he said, taking her hand. She let him hold it for several long moments, then took it back.

"You be careful, Jack," she said, letting her eyes continue to bore deep into his. "I don't want you to get hurt," and she got up fast and slipped away. Jack was back at work within half and hour, but still carrying the image of a beautiful young girl tending his wounds. He was able to look straight into her wonderful and big brown eyes as she doctored his cuts and scrapes. He offered as many smiles as he could manage.

He remembered how she cooed and smiled back at him, getting out chunks of rock and grit that had been blown into his face by the ricocheting bullet. She said, "You're lucky that pieces of the bullet didn't hit you. You might have some small scars, but that will just prove that you are big and strong, a ferocious warrior to be feared," and those thoughts were burned into his memory.

"Help me make a quick count on what we've moved down so far, Jack, and maybe Bear will be back by then. It's these kinds of problems that make me even more determined to have a bigger crew. If there had been two of you up there, or three, those jaspers wouldn't have tried to steal that bunch.

"Now, because of all this, we're gonna have to make some big changes in our roundup. We'll talk about that at supper." Jack and Henry spent the next two hours riding through the cattle that had been brought to the holding area, then broke off when Bear rode in with the three dead men, two wounded, and five horses.

"Those horses are now part of the Rupert remuda, by God," he said, and there was no smile. "Let's get those three in the ground, and Oak Blossom see if you can do anything for the two wounded."

19

It was a solemn supper, despite the beautiful early fall evening, a brisk breeze brought cascades of bright leaves floating to the ground in their camping area, and Jack thought there might even be frost on his blankets in the morning. "I'm going to have to call a halt to our early roundup in order to take the wounded rustlers into Cheyenne, along with their companions' belongings. Bear, you and Jack drive the three hundred cattle on down to the home pastures and when I get back, we'll continue."

Rupert was ready to chew iron and spit nails, and worried that a delay like this could put a lot of his cattle in jeopardy. He thought there should be five hundred head up north, and they had only brought down three hundred. There would be another three hundred at the south end of the valley, and he had to go to Cheyenne to deliver two men that caused the problem. Rupert would not leave some prime beef to starve to death in deep snow during the long winter.

"It wasn't that long ago, Henry, and we would have just shot or hung these two."

"I know, Bear, but times, they are a-changing. If I take Evangelina and the wagon back to the home ranch and then go on to Cheyenne with the wagon and wounded, and Oak Blossom rides back out to take care of camp, would you and Jack be able to bring in more head?"

"You'll be gone for at least four days, Henry. That would be a lot of lost time, and with winter right around the corner, we have to get these cattle into home pasture. Evangelina can just stay, she doesn't need to ride in with you in the morning, and Jack and I can keep right on bringing in the herd. We'll probably be getting ready to move them when you get back."

That's what I wanted to hear," Rupert said. "Did you recognize any of the dead men? I sure don't seem to know the two you brought back."

"I never seen any of 'em before. When you're in Cheyenne, hire us a couple of dudes, boss. Jack's a workin' fool, and two more like him, this old spread will sing a song or two."

"I like your thinking, Bear. Gonna be cold tonight. See you in the morning." He checked on the two tied-up prisoners, made sure the ropes were tight, covered them with blankets, gave 'em a good cussin' out, and found his bed roll. "One problem after another," he murmured, watching the stars until sleep came.

Bear and Jack lifted the wounded outlaws into the back of the wagon after feeding them and watched Rupert head off toward Cheyenne. "One of those boys give the boss some trouble and they'll find his busted up body alongside the road, I think," Bear laughed. "Let's work together Jack. Make a big circle to the north, bring 'em in, have a bite, and make another big circle to the east.

"We should be able to clear out this section in three days and start the herd south, before Henry gets back."

"He's gonna have to stick to the trail, Bear, and that'll surely slow him down. That one feller that was shot in the side, he didn't look very good."

"Yeah, your bullet did a lot a bad things to that bad man," Bear chuckled. "If he does live, he won't be rustling cows anymore. Hope Henry can pick up a couple of men while he's there."

Jack realized just how little he knew during this first day working a circle right alongside Growls Like Bear, and determined to learn everything he could from the big Indian. "Where did you learn all these little tricks of yours in gathering cattle?" he asked, sitting at the table with Oak Blossom and Bear.

"Growls Like Bear was raised on a ranch in The Territories, and is far more a white cowboy than a red Indian," Oak Blossom giggled, ducking from a friendly swat aimed by Bear.

"And you, my dear, are more Mexican than Shoshone," and the two of them laughed, and took gentle pokes at each other. Jack could see genuine affection in the way they treated each other. Oak Blossom's eyes sparkled and her smile lit up the table. *I think if she smiled like that at me I would just fall right out of this chair. She was so tender, working on my cuts, and so careful not to hurt me. I sure would like to know her better.*

Bear drained a cup of coffee, poured more for everyone, and told Jack why he's a fine cowhand. "After a big fight between my people and the army, a couple of cowboys, just following a trail, found me hiding in the bushes. They figured I was probably

223

about two-years-old, and they became my parents, my teachers, my best friends in the world.

"You're working for one of 'em right now. Henry's partner, Sparky McNaughton, died several years ago in a fight with rustlers. I was born an Indian but I was raised a white man, and I've been a cattleman from my first time in the saddle."

"So, Growls Like Bear is the name that Henry gave you?" Jack's eyes were wide and he wanted to know everything. "You're just like me, but much luckier," he said. "My folks were killed and I rode a train all the way to Fargo to be a part of a farm family, but the man treated the children like slaves, not family."

"I prefer just to be called Bear, but Henry stuck me with the growls part, I guess because of my big voice, and part because I wasn't always well behaved," he chuckled. "Henry, simply has a huge heart, is the most honest man I've ever known, and will help anyone who treats him fairly. I would have died under that sagebrush if they hadn't found me that day."

"You give me one more little piece of trouble, yahoo, and I'll just leave you by the side of the road," Henry snapped, slapping the outlaw across the side of his head with a big doubled up fist. "I don't give a star's twinkle if your side hurts, it would do me fine if you just rolled over and died, so shut your filthy mouth or I'll shut it for you."

The outlaw scowled at Rupert but kept his mouth shut. He and his partner, both still trussed up in the back of the wagon were only given water since they left the cow camp, and that was the day before. The man that Rupert called Boy, had been shot in the side, had bled considerably, and was in great pain, which he spent lots of time talking about.

"We'll be in Cheyenne sometime today, I think, and you can complain to the sheriff all you want," Rupert said, getting back on the wagon. "You tried to steal my cattle and you got yourself all shot up. Don't be cryin' to me." He nursed the team into a trot, working them so at least one wheel would hit every rock he saw, making that old wagon bump and jump constantly.

They pulled into Cheyenne late that second day and Rupert drove straight to the sheriff's office, jumped down and tied off the team. He found a deputy, the sheriff was across the way, and they brought the two injured rustlers into the jail. "I'll get the sheriff," the deputy said. "Be right back."

Sheriff Tom Richards was tall and broad, and wasn't inclined to do much more than hire deputies to do the actual work of keeping the peace. "So, what's this all about, Henry?"

"These two, and three others that didn't live through the encounter, tried to run off with a bunch of my cattle, Tom. I'll sign the papers and be on my way back. Worst time of the year for this stuff. If they live, hang 'em."

"They'll get a trial, then we'll hang them, Henry." Richards found some papers and offered them to Rupert. "Rex, lock these fools up, find the doc, and get back here fast. Ginny has my supper cookin' at the café. You headin' right back, Henry?"

"Gonna try to find a hand or two and leave out in the morning. Spread the word that rustlers die when they come after my cattle, Tom," he said, shook hands with the rotund sheriff, and headed for the livery with the wagon. He found a café that smelled fine from the outside and ventured into Matilda's Fine Food and Rooms. *Food's not as good as Evangelina's, but Matty is a fine woman. She's too nice a lady to live in Cheyenne.*

The fine food was pork chops, mashed potatoes and gravy, and a slab of peach pie, along with a pot or two of strong, long-boiled coffee. "Any of your regulars lookin' for ranch work, Matty?"

"Got a couple of boys talking about work but don't want to work for the railroad, and that's about all we offer in this town. Should be in for supper shortly. They're big boys, so should be about right for you. Saw you dropping off two that looked hurt. Something go wrong?"

"Yup, it did. Those two you saw tried to rustle up some prime beef and ran into my new hand, who did-in their three companions. We're right in the middle of fall roundup and I should not be here."

The door of the café opened and two long, lanky cowboys came in and headed for a table. "Come over here, boys," Matty said, indicating Henry's table. "Want you to meet somebody." She waited until they got to the table and did the introductions.

"This long skinny one is called Slim Boyle, and coming in from somewhere south of here, and his partner's Roddy Simmons. Boys, this is Henry Rupert, of the Rocking R, and he might be looking for a couple of hands. Sit down and I'll get your supper started."

Rupert was looking at the genuine deal, he figured, both boys underweight but strong as iron, big shoulders and chests, skinny hips, and long legs. "You looking for cattle work?" he asked, shaking hands with both.

"Sure are, Mr. Rupert. We come up from Nebraska country, thinking this was all cattle country, but it ain't. You hiring?"

"Dollar fifty a day and found. Have your own gear? Horses?"

"We each got two horses, Mr. Rupert." Slim was doing all the talking, so far. "We got ropes and bedrolls and lean-tos."

"Meet me in front of the livery at five tomorrow morning, and we'll head out. I had to come to town with the team and wagon so it'll be a slow ride back. I'll tell you all about the Rocking R. We're in high country, winter's comin' our way fast. You got cold country clothes? If not, better rustle some up."

"Old Roddy got robbed the other night, Mr. Rupert, and he lost most of his money and most of his kit. Could you front him some, to get him started?"

"Jackson's Feed Store is still open, Roddy, and I have a line over there. Get set up, and I'll front it. Just tell him you're working for Rupert, and he'll set you up. What happened?"

"Comin' back from looking for a job north of here the other night," Roddy slowly drawled out in a way deep south accent, "and got jumped by three fellers took just about everything. Left me my horse and boots, and took just about everything else."

"This town's known for that, Roddy. Get set up at Jackson's and we'll figure things out when the time comes. Be ready to move in the morning," Rupert said, nodding to the boys as he stood up, and headed for the livery to sleep in the bed of the wagon and save a buck or two.

20

There were no more major problems with the fall roundup, and Henry figured he had slightly more than 800 head on winter pasture. Slim Boyle and Roddy Simmons were fine hands, and Jack continued to learn the ways of the cowboy.

Slim Boyle had a quick temper and took it out on his horses or whatever inanimate object might be handy, and Jack found it difficult to work with the man. He was braiding some leather for a new head-stall he was making when Boyle got himself tangled up in the leather thongs, and gave them a mighty kick.

"Hey, Boyle, I'm working on this. You want to kick something, make it something you own, or something that just might kick back."

"You ain't old enough to talk to me that way, boy," he answered, starting to swagger away.

Jack stood up slowly, put his work down on the bench he had been sitting on, and said, "I'm old enough to teach you some manners. You about ruined a morning's work there, Boyle. An apology just might be in order." Jack had his legs slightly spread, his head lowered just a bit, and his body as taught and ready as a rattler watching a ground squirrel.

Boyle took one step toward Jack, threw a mighty right cross that Jack stepped back from, chuckling at Boyle's effort. "I'm impressed," he laughed, and planted a hard left that came straight out of his shoulder, knocking the southern gentleman to the dirt. Surprising to Jack, Boyle didn't try to get up, and Jack grabbed his leather work and tools and headed back to the bunkhouse. *Ain't much of a man,* he chortled, putting his things away.

It was quiet at supper that night, nobody wanting to ask about the black eye and split lip plastered on Slim Boyle's face. Evangelina looked at Jack, got a little nod back, and giggled softly, but not softly enough.

Boyle slammed his fist onto the table and stormed out of the kitchen, glaring at everyone first. "Don't think that man likes us much, tonight," Rupert said, chuckling a bit and giving Jack a look. "You responsible for that?"

"Man has no manners or respect for others," is all Jack said, and the matter was dropped until after supper.

"We need to talk, Jack," Evangelina said quietly, taking Jack by the hand and leading him out the back door. "Let's sit on the porch for a minute or two." They walked around to the north side of the wide porch and sat on one of the benches. She kept ahold of Jack's hand with both of hers.

"Boyle's been pestering me some, Jack, and I'm not liking it at all. Keep an eye on him, Jack. He's not a good person and I'm afraid of him." She let him put his arm around her shoulders and pull her close to him. "That feels good, Jack."

"I won't let any man ever hurt you, Evangelina," he whispered. She turned her face up toward his and very slowly their lips came together. It was electrifying, Jack wrote in his journal later that night.

Snow came early in the high country and it was Jack's turn to do some teaching. "We have a lot of stuff around here that needs some serious mending," Jack said one morning after a hearty breakfast. He had cadged a forge together, found hammers and tongs, and enough busted up equipment that he had scrap iron to work with. Jack's forge was red-hot for more than a week as he managed to either fix or build new pieces of equipment for the ranch.

"Ain't never done nothin' like this before," Roddy Simmons said late one afternoon. "I didn't know you could just put two pieces of iron together and make it one. If I ever get back to Mississippi I'll surely surprise people doin' it." Roddy was a year or two older than Jack and had worked cattle from the time he was old enough to throw a rope.

"You never worked on a farm, though, eh?" Jack asked. "I've mostly lived on farms, growing wheat and corn, taters and beans. Up 'till I met Henry, I never worked cattle. Sure do like it, though."

"My daddy did some plowing, and my uncles did too, but I lit out when I could and started working cattle. Ain't goin' back unless I can buy some land. Don't want to spend the rest of my life working for somebody. Old Slim, that's all he wants, just a job that keeps him fed and warm," and the two laughed a bit.

"I guess you know that Slim and I ain't the best of friends," Jack said, "but that man sure knows his way around cattle. I've learned a lot working with him."

233

"He's good with cattle but he sure ain't good with horses. That man's right mean when it comes to the way he treats his horses. I've told him more times than I can count what a mean old dog he is. He ain't never forgive you for blackin' his eye, you know," Roddy laughed.

"Man just ain't got no manners," Jack murmured, again.

Winter days were short and cold, storms blasted through the mountains, wind tore things apart, cattle got stranded in drifts or foundered in mud when warm spells created their own problems. Jack, Henry, Bear, and the new hands worked together to keep the ranch together, and one morning Henry called for Jack and Bear to join him in his little office.

"This has been a good winter with lots of snow for summer water and green grass," he smiled, settling behind his old scarred desk. "We'll be seeing a lot of our spring calves born while there's still snow on the ground and the mud will be measured in yards, I'm a thinkin'.

"You've spent a lot of time farming, Jack, and the way you've taken to working cattle, I gotta believe you know good ground. Do we have ground that would grow something we could use for feed during the winter? I lose cattle every year to these cold and icy winters because they can't find feed. You boys have moved that herd all over this part of the valley this winter, and we still lost a number of head.

"Well, anyway, here's what I'm leading up to. Bear, I want you to be cow boss, and Jack, I want you to run the home ranch. You'll still get plenty of saddle time during calving, branding, and driving the herds to summer pasture, but it's obvious we haven't been taking care of the home ranch.

"You're gonna need a couple of people, so before the calving starts, spend a couple of days in Cheyenne and pick up two farm hands, and get whatever farm equipment you'll need, along with seed. Probably get a couple of mules, too, I think."

The only thing that man didn't offer me was part ownership of the ranch, Jack smiled to himself, heading out to the barn. He had planned on talking to Rupert about growing feed, as well as market produce. "The market for beef is well known in Cheyenne and surrounding country." He had heard rumors of men and families coming in from the east and homesteading some of the range in the area for produce farming and figured it would be good for Rupert to get a head start on the idea.

He also knew that most of the ranchers within fifty miles of Cheyenne would be opposed to the homesteaders and their fields of crops and their fences. He was sure Henry Rupert would be among those. But the idea of growing winter feed was something Jack was sure Rupert would favor.

For the next several weeks, Jack drew up plans for the farming section, knew the bottomland in the valley would grow anything as long as it was a short season crop. He and Henry rode through where Jack wanted to plow and plant, spent lots of time discussing what would be needed, how much it would cost, and when he should leave for Cheyenne.

"Best if you take off in the next couple of days, Jack. Ride your horse and buy a large wagon and mules to carry back what you'll need. Do you think two farm hands is enough?" Henry Rupert had never given thought to real farming, beyond Evangelina's kitchen garden, and had no idea what he would need.

"Two good men would be perfect, Henry, and I'm sure we'll have to teach them right from the start. If Slim and Roddy are examples of what's available in Cheyenne. They're fine ranch hands but neither one knows a thing about farming. I'll probably end up with a couple of busted up railroad hands," he laughed.

Jack had Fargo saddled and was tying his bedroll to the back of the saddle when Evangelina came into the barn. "What happened to you?" he asked, seeing tears running down her cheeks, then seeing the rips in her blouse. She ran to him and threw her arms around him, crying, sobbing actually, and burying her face in his shoulder. Jack held her close, felt each sob wrack her body, and gently rubbed her back with his big hands.

The winter had been good for the two of them, offering lots of time to get to know each other, to discover how much in common they had, and how much fun their differences could be. Jack felt very close to the woman and knew she felt the same way. She clung to him now, sobbing, and he was ready to destroy whatever it was that had her so frightened.

It was a full five minutes before he was able to calm the girl enough for her to talk to him. "Let's sit down over here," Jack said, leading her to some old wooden boxes sitting near one of the barn walls. She sat as close to him as she could get, held his hand in a grip that would have hurt someone else.

She blubbered, "Slim," a couple of times and Jack's back and shoulders tightened, his fists slowly formed, and he started to get up. "No," she said. "Listen to me. I went out to get water from the well and Slim tried to," and she choked up, tears pouring down her face.

"What did Slim do, Oak Blossom? Tell me, and I'll take care of the problem. I'm your friend, and I'll never hurt you. Tell me what happened."

She let go of his hands and threw her arms around his neck, holding him so tight he thought he wouldn't be able to keep breathing. "He tried to make me go into the bushes at the side of the house. He tried to touch me," she wailed, holding Jack even tighter.

Jack's temper boiled and he knew that Slim Boyle was probably a dead man, and held the girl close to him. "I'll take care of you," he whispered, gently rubbing her back, swaying some, rocking back and forth. "Let's get you in the house and cleaned up, and in fresh clothes. I'll take care of Slim Boyle." She pulled her face back from Jack's shoulder and their lips came together for long moments.

"I'll take care of you, forever," he whis-

238

pered. They walked slowly toward the house, Oak Blossom's arms still around Jack's neck, his arm around her waist. She was sobbing when they walked into the kitchen and found Henry sitting at the table with a cup of coffee. "What's this, now?" he said, jumping to his feet. "Evangelina, what on earth?"

"Go get cleaned up," Jack said, "and I'll talk to Henry." Impulsively, she gave Jack a kiss on the cheek, slowly let go of the man's neck, and still whimpering, ran upstairs to her room to change.

"We have a problem, Henry," Jack said, pouring a cup of coffee for himself and sitting down across from the older man. "Slim got rough with Evangelina, in the worst way. I'm going to calm down, finish this cup of coffee, and then find him, Henry. I'm going to kill him, Mr. Rupert."

Henry got up and walked to the door and howled for Bear, came back and sat down. "He deserves that, but let's let Bear handle the situation. Evanglina has been in love with you from the day you rode onto this ranch, Jack. You cannot kill that man and then hang for murder. I won't stand for it.

"Bear will know what to do. You walk back to the barn, get on your horse, and ride to Cheyenne, buy what we need, hire two or more people, and hurry back home. This is your home, Jack, and I won't allow you to ruin your life with a murder rap." The two men stood up and shook hands, and Jack, still coiled like a rattler, marched to the barn.

I know he's right, but I want to kill that man. And then he realized what Henry had said. *Evangelina loves me? Oh, my.* The first thirty miles out from the Rocking R were miles Jack would never remember. Only the fact that Oak Blossom loved him ran wild through his mind for the rest of the day. Sitting in a grove of big trees near a burbling creek that night, and Jack only saw Evangelina, dancing to him, smiling at him, kissing him gently.

It was a bright sun and the snorting of Fargo that woke him up. "Could have slept the day away with the dreams I had," he smiled, saddling the big horse for the ride into town. He munched on a couple of cold biscuits and drank some water once on the trail, and the pictures continued to roll through his mind. It was the rowdy streets of Cheyenne that brought him back to his senses.

"Matilda's, Henry said," he muttered, spotting the café, and riding on past it to the stables to put Fargo up and make arrangements to sleep in the stall with him. He found a large wagon and bought it, and had the livery owner checking to find a working team of mules. He left the stables and headed for Jackson's Feed and Mercantile.

He didn't get to Matilda's café for another couple of hours, exhausted from the ride and all the dickering with the stableman and Mr. Jackson. "All I want ma'am," Jack said, falling into his chair, "is a big platter filled with pork chops, biscuits, and a gallon of gravy."

Matty laughed loud saying that Jack was big enough that he could probably eat that much and more. "How about we start you off with a regular dinner and go from there, young man."

"That will be a fine start," he smiled. "Know of any good men looking for honest work?"

"Been two or three coming in for breakfast saying they're looking. Usually get here around six or so. Come in tomorrow and I'll point them out for you. You tell that Henry Rupert that it's all good and fine for him to send his man to town, but it isn't all good and fine for me when he don't come in," and the laughter flowed through the warm dining room.

So, Henry's got himself a gal friend here in town, Jack chuckled to himself. *I'll sure give him the dickens on that when I get back.*

It took two days to put everything together, and even so, Jackson didn't have all the seed and equipment that he needed. "I'll send word when everything gets here, Jack," the old man said. "We have trains coming through from California and from the east every day, so it won't be a long wait."

Matty had steered him to three men looking for work, two of whom had lots of farm in their background. The third one, Jack figured, would replace Slim Boyle. *That man should bless Henry Rupert for not letting me kill him. I better not ever see that man again.*

"Where'd you come up with the name Tooky," Jack asked the man who swore he was one of the finest cattleman that lived. "Tooky Chalmers, you'll have fun trying to prove that to Growls Like Bear, our cow boss."

"My pa gave it to me. Whenever something was missing, he'd tell Ma that 'he took it,' which became Tooky got it. Hated that name but it stuck, and I guess now, I wouldn't even answer to my real name."

Jack and Tooky became fast friends within hours and Jack looked forward to watching the man work cattle. He certainly enjoyed watching the man with his horse. "You have a real feel for that horse."

"Man ain't whole less'n he's got a good horse under him," is all the answer Jack needed to hear.

Richard Smith and his son Sam were rather quiet when Jack talked with them about helping put together a farming operation at the Rocking R, and it didn't take long for him to discover why. "Sam and I went to town to pick up a load of supplies when the storm came through. Twisters, Mr. Slater, mean, black, twisters, came through the farm and destroyed everything. Never even able to find my wife's body," Richard said, doing his best to hold back tears.

"Me and Sam just decided to leave it burning and come west. We'll stay for one or two cycles, Mr. Slater, maybe move on to California or Oregon, but you'll get your money's worth from us."

Jack had Smith and his son, about twelve years old, but big and strong, ride the wagon and drive the mules. He rode Fargo along with Tooky on his saddle horse. Smith had his two saddle horses and Tooky's extra, trailing along behind the wagon, which was loaded with everyone's personal belongings

243

and new and used farm equipment. It was a long slow ride back to the Rocking R.

"It's alright, Evi," Jack said, holding Evangelina as close as possible. "I'm home and Boyle is gone. He can't ever hurt you again." Jack found Bear as soon as the group rode into the home ranch and Bear told him the story.

"That coyote was as yellow as a dog and I gave him a beating he'll never forget. I wanted to kill him, Jack, just like you wanted to, but Henry's words kept coming back to me. 'It would be murder, Bear,' he said, and told me he said the same to you, so I did the next best thing," he laughed. "I made him wish I had killed him. You should have seen him, trying to get on that nag he called a cow horse, all bruised and stiff and sore. I kicked him twice, right in the butt, before he climbed on," and Jack and Bear were hugging each other, laughing.

"I had to leave, Evi, because I would have killed the man. He's gone, and you're safe." They were standing on the veranda of the big house and Henry walked out after hearing all the horses riding in.

"You've got quite a group here, Jack, and welcome home, boy." Jack had everyone gather 'round and introduced Henry, who then welcomed them to the Rocking R. "I'm not one of your mean old bosses, but I am the boss," and that brought friendly snickers. "I want you to call me Henry, I'll treat you with respect as long as you treat me the same.

"We eat at sunrise, if you're in the saddle, dinner is in your saddlebags, otherwise in the house, and supper is served when the day's work is done." He motioned Bear to come up on the porch with him and Jack.

"This is Bear and he's the cow boss, you know the ranch boss, Jack, and this lovely lady is Evangelina, and you better treat her right cuz she fixes your meals. That's enough speechafyin' for today. Put your stuff away, get settled, and you'll hear the bell calling you for supper.

"Jack, you and Bear come in the house with me."

21

Smith and his son, Sam, were exactly what Jack had wanted and late spring found the Rocking R growing wheat, rye, and other grasses that could be cut and stored for winter use. There were other changes taking place in that section of the world, and some of those bothered Henry Rupert no end. "We've been grazing our cattle on these ranges for a long time, Jack, and now, it seems, the government is giving away a lot of that land to dirt farmers.

"Now I'm not certain that what they are doing is wrong, but now it looks like we're gonna be fightin' fences every time we need to move our herds. Some of those boys north and east of us, the biggest ranches in this area, are talking about getting rough with the farmers. That is wrong, I do believe."

"There's gonna be lots of changes, Henry, and you'll have to make some adjustments in the way the ranch is operated. With the railroad, with slaughter facilities close by, people will be eating Rocking R beef more than a thousand miles from here, maybe even more," Jack laughed. "This is an actual territory now, Wyoming Territory, and that miserable Cheyenne is the capitol. Watch the do-gooders clean up that town," and they both laughed at that.

"What are we gonna do to protect the range we have?" Henry asked, getting serious again. The problems developing in the north of the territory bothered him more than he was willing to admit. "What if somebody comes onto that north range of ours and fences it off? My God, Jack, think about that."

"I have been, Henry, and I think you ought to do what those that would fence it off might do. File a claim on the property. You'd have to make sure it was all legal, probably spend at least a week in Cheyenne to get it done, but you would own it, be responsible for it, and you could keep trespassers off it." He sat back a bit, and chuckled, "Of course you might have to spend some of that money of yours."

Henry scowled, then chuckled along with Jack. "By golly I'm glad I stumbled into you, Jack Slater. I rode out through what you and the Smith's plowed and planted, and that green sure is pretty."

"It is that. At this altitude, and short growing season, I'm sure we'll get at least two cuttings a year, and once in awhile, three. Your cattle won't starve in the winters, Henry. Those three little spring fed streams that flow through the bottom land will keep that grass growing good."

Wyoming's cattle industry had been growing every year, and those ranches on the eastern or front ranges had been wintering cattle right on the range, but in the interior, at the higher elevations, winter loss was a problem that Rupert had fought for years. "Graze the cattle right on the stubble," Jack said, "and they will fertilize the fields for next year. When the snow is just too deep, we'll supplement with what we cut all summer long."

Rupert was able to file claims on three sections north of the home ranch and already owned two at that site. It was the following fall, again at gathering time, that trouble came to the long lush valley. This time in the guise of an organized cattle rustling gang. They were led by a skinny man who liked to call himself Mad Dog, and they left a trail of dead men and missing cattle behind them wherever they went.

The railroad line was about ten miles south of the main ranch and Henry had built large corrals and loading facilities near a watering stop. He was able to hold as many as 500 head in the corrals and loaded the boxcars of every train that came through following the fall gather. Jack had made two more trips to Cheyenne and Rupert now had a full complement of ten cowboys along with Bear and Jack.

"Did you get a good look at those jaspers watching us, Bear?" Henry asked the second night out. "I don't like the stories I've heard about this Mad Dog fool."

"Seems like they're staking us out, Henry. I've called a meeting of all hands, and we'll figure out how to handle those fools. Tooky and the new hands are good with the cattle, I just hope they're half as good as Jack with a rifle."

"Something else you and me got to discuss, Bear. Jack'll be coming eighteen next spring, and we're gonna lose him, and probably Evangelina too. He's bound to find him his own place, and he's been talking about the Ruby Valley in Nevada. What can we do to make him not want to leave here?"

"Tie Oak Blossom to a tree and forbid her to leave," Bear laughed. "He'll stay," and they spent several minutes guffawing over the picture they saw. "That boy's in love, Henry."

"She gives it right back. When are you talking to the men?"

"Figure right after supper, we'll get serious about the Mad Dog and these fellers shadowing us. Jack got caught alone last year, you remember, we don't want that to happen again. Nobody rides alone on this gather, and everybody'll carry rifles, not just side arms."

"That's good, Bear. I'll be at the fire with you. Make sure these boys understand just how mean this so-called Mad Dog is."

Bear gave a good talk with the group of cowboys and the plan was that nobody would ride alone, and circles would be kept short, even if it added a day or two to the gather. Everybody paired up with Bear taking the least experienced, Henry taking young Sam Smith and staying on the valley floor to maintain the herd as it developed.

"Mind if I ride with you, Jack?" Tooky asked, pouring a quick half-cup of coffee before leaving out.

"I'd like that, Tooky. I'd sure like to get a good look at these men that have been giving us the big eye the last few days. I wonder how many there are?"

"It seems like they ride in groups of three, Jack. Never seen more than three at a time, but Henry and Bear said the same thing. There might be ten or twelve of them. If they came hard once we get the herd put together, they could run off with 500 head, and that would be a rustler's dream."

"We won't let that happen," Jack said, and the two rode out to the eastern flank of the valley to begin their first circle. They spotted two or three groups of three men during the day, as they brought group after group of fine cattle into the valley. It was a long day in the saddle, breaking cattle out of timber, out of ravines, off escarpments, and even out of deep mud along creeks and streams.

"I don't think there's cow left in our area, Jack," Tooky said as they rode into camp, smelling roast venison wafting in the early evening breeze. "Somebody shot a deer, and I'm gonna eat half of it," he laughed.

"Only if you can eat faster than me," Jack laughed, jumping from Blue and pulling his tack. "Get these horses taken care of quick tonight." He spotted Henry and Sam riding in from herd duty. "We better have a couple of night hawks tonight, Henry, instead of just one. I think we've pretty much cleared these hills."

"I already got 'em out there, Jack. We can start moving the herd south in the morning, I think. If that is a thievin' gang out there, tonight would be when they would hit. Scatter the herd, shoot us up some, and take what they can find. That's how I'd do it."

"Sounds like the voice of experience," Bear snickered, understanding that Henry Rupert may have started his herd with some beef that wasn't properly branded. He got a scowl and a strong harrumph back, and snickered some more.

"Anyway," Bear continued, "I think we need two night hawks, and three wouldn't hurt, and we need someone here in camp to stay up and awake tonight. Considering there ain't very many of us, that means we'll be moving the herd in the morning after a night of very little sleep.

"I'll take the first shift after supper, Jack you relieve me, and Tooky, you relieve Jack. That'll keep camp safe. Roddy, you and Richard Smith ride herd and I'll have two men relieve you sometime after midnight."

Bear was interrupted by the clanging of chimes as Evangelina called out her wonderful "Come and get it boys or I'll feed it to the dogs." The scene that followed was similar to a stampede and when the dust settled there weren't nothing left but bones from that sweet side of venison.

The night came on fast and because so many of the men would be doing guard duty at some point during the night, those that could hit their bedrolls right away. Henry and Jack saddled up and took a long quiet ride far out and around the herd, coming back into camp several hours later.

"Never saw a flicker, Henry. You?"

"Nope. Making cold camps, and probably moving slowly down onto the valley floor. If they hit tonight, it'll be late, after midnight, I'd bet. You relieving Bear?"

"Yup, and I'll bet he stays up with me."

"Then, Jack my boy, there'll be three of us around that fire."

"Might be best if you stay by the fire and me and Bear ride out to join the night hawks."

"Best idea yet," Henry said, climbing down from his horse. "Yup, me and a pot of coffee and a warm fire. Evangelina is pretty good with that scatter gun of hers, so I might just invite her to sit with me."

22

There was no moon to guide the way for anyone, bandit, nighthawk, cow, or horse, and Jack Slater rolled out from his bedroll, pulled a heavy point blanket around his shoulders, and tripped his way to the fire. "Black as sin tonight, Bear," he said, grabbing the coffee the big Indian offered. "Heard anything moving around?"

"I'm thinkin' it's too quiet, Jack. Cattle are quiet, though, so nothing's getting them all riled up. Maybe we're just spookin' ourselves," he chuckled. Henry emerged from the darkness and poured some coffee, nodding at the two.

"You boys make sure you get your night eyes on before you ride too far from camp," he said. Too often, after sitting around the fire sucking down hot coffee, one's eyes don't adjust to darkness quickly, and more than one cowpoke has gotten lost for a few minutes just trying to find his horse.

Sam Smith walked up to the fire, wiping sleep from his eyes. "Pa doesn't want me out there riding with the herd, but there ain't no reason I can't help keep watch here at the fire."

"You're right, Sam, glad to have you with us," Henry said. "I think this boy is gonna be as big as you when he gets his growin' in, Jack. You're twelve, Sam? Didn't you tell me you were twelve when you made that long train ride from New York to Fargo?"

"No, I was ten, but Sam is gonna be a big boy. We were working with some of the harness and those heavy wagon wheels the other day, and he was a big help. Want some coffee, Sam?"

He took the coffee and stood with his back to the fire, feeling the heat up and down his long body. "Pa's out with the herd. Are you going out there? Are we gonna be attacked?" Sam's eyes were large, he was frightened, but didn't want to let these men know that.

"We'll be going out in just a couple of minutes, Sam," Bear said, splashing the last few drops of his coffee into the fire. "As dark as it is, I don't know if they'll try something tonight or not. It's best that we believe they're gonna, though," he chuckled. "Do you have a weapon of some kind? Heck, do you even know how to shoot one?"

255

"I don't have a gun, but Pa has taught me how to shoot. I'm pretty good with a rifle, but that pistol of his is awful big and heavy. It's hard to shoot. Pa has both with him tonight."

"Henry, if you have an extra rifle for this boy, it might help if those fools do strike tonight. We better head out there, Jack," Bear said, starting off toward the horses.

"Pour yourself another coffee, Sam, and put some more wood on the fire while I rustle you up a rifle or something."

He wasn't gone a minute when Evangelina came to fire. "Hello, Sam. Where is everyone. I thought Henry, Bear, and Jack would be here?"

"Bear and Jack just left to ride the herd and Henry is getting me a rifle. I'm going to help keep watch with you and Henry."

"That's good," she said. "Maybe we can get to know each other a little better. Your Pa and Jack keep you pretty busy. How is your reading coming?"

"Jack's a good teacher, Evie, but some of those words sure are big that he wants me to know. I'm gettin' better though."

Henry came back to the fire with an old breech loader and spent the next half hour or so going over the workings of the weapon until he was sure the boy could handle it safely. "It's gonna be very dark for several more hours, and if we do get attacked by those men, don't just start shooting. Make very sure you know what you're shooting at, because some of our men may be trying to get back here to the fire."

"I will, Mr. Rupert. I'll make very sure," Sam said, cradling the rifle as if he'd had one in his hands for years and years. "Pa always wanted me to shoot the squirrels in the head so's not to ruin good meat."

"Evening, Richard," Bear said, riding up alongside Richard Smith on the northeast edge of the herd. "See or hear anything?"

"Nothing, Bear. Strange, but not even any coyotes or wolves singing to us tonight."

Bear tensed up at that comment thinking that men moving through the high grass and brush would keep the predators at bay. "Better make sure your weapons are primed and charged, Richard. We've been hearing those wolves for a week now, and coyotes are always sneaking around. Pass the word on to the other riders," he said, turning to face away from the herd.

The only thing Bear could see were billions of stars twinkling their hello to him from deep in the black sky. Jack rode up alongside him. "No wolves, no movement of any kind, Bear. They're moving in on us, but coming from just where? And how many are there? We have been seeing groups of three or four all week, but just how many are there all together?"

"What did that fool sheriff say when you were in town? Did he give you any numbers?"

"I got the feeling he was talking about eight, maybe ten men. If that's the case, we should be able to run their butts right out of the territory."

"I've noticed that you've been working quite a bit with young Sam. He's gonna be a good farmer, I think, but I don't know about being a cattleman."

Jack smiled at that comment. "You had that same thought about me a couple of years ago, Bear," hearing Bear chortle a bit. "Sam reminds me of myself, I guess, lost most of his family, lost his home, doesn't know what's gonna happen next. I guess I have been doing my best to make sure he knows as much about this old world as it is possible, so he can find his place in it.

"I've found my place, and it's on a cattle ranch that does some farming."

"You'll be eighteen pretty soon, Jack. Are you still planning to move on west. I guarantee Henry will make you an equal partner with us if you stay." It was the first time that Jack had understood that Bear was more than just Henry's adopted son, but an equal partner in the ranch. "I'm pretty sure Oak Blossom would like that," he snickered.

"I would like that too," Jack whispered. "Which reminds me, Growls Like Bear, I understand that Henry gave you your name. Did he also name Oak Blossom?"

"Why do you ask?" Bear was chuckling when he said this, almost laughing.

"Because, it dawned on me just the other day, oak trees don't blossom. No Indian would give that name." If there were men riding through the pitch black of this late night, they were serenaded by a growly bear laughing loud, accompanied by his side-kick.

The cow boss and ranch boss rode back and forth, meeting the other herd riders, listening hard, not seeing or hearing anything, hour after long hour. It was after four when the first indications of a new day started appearing on the eastern horizon. "Probably didn't hit us during the night because they couldn't see any better than we could," Bear snarled, as he slowly was able to make out bushes and trees, mountains in the distance, and cows and calves, milling about.

The night air exploded with gunshots, but not coming toward the herd from crazed rustlers, but rather from the camp. "They're hitting the camp," Bear howled, spurring his pony into a full gallop toward the fire, a good half mile away. "Stay with the herd, Richard, Simmons," he yelled, and waving his arms, screamed, "Jack, you follow me." Bear was riding like a madman, reins in one hand, revolver in the other, screaming vile words at the top of his lungs.

Jack's Blue was faster and he too was riding like banshees were following, and they slid their horses into camp finding four riders circling the tents and fire pit, shooting aimlessly at anything and everything. Jack reined up some sixty feet or so from the melee, pulled that fine shooting rifle of his and promptly knocked two riders off their horses.

Bear rode ride into the four, firing his single action Colt until it was empty, killing one rider, and shooting the horse out from under another. Jack and Bear were dismounted and making sure those on the ground were either dead or out of the action, and moved toward the tents, fearing the absolute worst.

They were feet from Henry's tent when a voice behind them yelled, "We're over here.

Come help." It was Henry, calling from behind a stand of Jack Pines. "Oak Blossom and Sam have been hit, hurry."

Jack rushed to Evangelina's side, and heard the whimpers as he fell to his knees, saw blood pouring from two horrible wounds to the middle of her chest. He held her close, cradled her in his powerful arms, and felt her life flow softly away. Anger, loss, fear, came in crashing waves, cascading through him, his young body wracked in sobs. He rocked slowly, back and forth, back and forth, finally letting her back down onto the blood soaked ground, and screamed his loss to the world.

His mourning period was cut short by gunshots near the herd, and moans from the outlaws that were shot. "Stay with Henry," he shouted to Bear, raced to his horse, mounted with a leap from several feet away, and felt the power of Blue hitting full gallop in two strides. Tooky and Richard Smith were in a serious gunfight with the rest of the Mad Dog gang when Jack rode into the fray, that rifle barking death with every lunge of the big horse.

Jack found only three men firing at Tooky and Smith, and bailed from Blue, taking a kneeling position, and dropping two of the outlaws immediately. The third preferred living and threw out his handgun, giving it up. Jack walked up to the man and his jaw dropped, his eyes widened, and anger at a level he had never felt surged through his body. He swung the butt of the rifle up and then drove it forward into the middle of Jon Davis's face, sending the skinny little man to the ground with a face full of hamburger.

"So you've graduated from stealing a man's mule to stealing a man's herd. You are gonna hang, Jon Davis and if I find Skinny or your father, they'll hang with you."

"You know this outlaw?" Tooky asked, walking up at the end of Jack's speech, his weapon cocked and ready for anything else that might happen.

"His whole rotten family," Jack snarled. "Where's Pete and Skinny?" he bellowed, kicking Jon in the face. He levered a round into the rifle's chamber, laid the end of the barrel between Jon's legs and said, again, "Where?"

Davis screamed "No!" and tried to squirm away from that horrible vision, but couldn't. A little prod that took his breath away and almost made him vomit, brought the answer Jack wanted.

"Pa and Skinny are in the trees to the east, waiting for us to bring the herd," he moaned, and Jack slowly withdrew the rifle, with a bare smile on his face.

"I never thought I'd see this fool family again," he said, letting the hammer down on the rifle. "Their people are incredibly foul, Tooky, and not a one of them can be trusted. Skinny tried to rape his cousin, Jon here helped him try to kill me and steal my mule, the father taught them how to act like sewer rats.

"I'm going to kill you, Jon, but not just yet. You're going to watch me kill Pete and Skinny first, then I'm going to kill you." He took a long breath, finally letting his anger settle back to the boiling point, down from pure steam, and told Tooky and Smith what happened at the camp site.

"Evie is dead, shot in the chest twice. Sam is okay, Richard. He got nicked, but nothing at all serious. And he did well, firing that ancient smoke stack three times, he said, and I think that Henry's been hit, but will live, for sure. Tooky, ride around the herd quietly, get the cattle calmed down, see if you can find the rest of our crew, find out if anyone's been wounded, and see if any of the scum rustlers are alive.

"Leave a man or two with the herd, and then help Richard bring the bodies and wounded into camp." He got a big nod from

Tooky, mounted Blue and rode back to the torn up camp at a fast trot. All he could think about was Evangelina, gone, murdered by people he should have killed two years ago.

"We thought we knew what we were going to do for the rest of our lives, and she's gone, just gone. It's time for me to go, too, I think. I can't stay here, not now, not without Evie." He was soon to be eighteen, he was soon to have enough money to establish himself somewhere, and after all, he remembered, isn't that what he was aiming for all along?

Jack Slater snickered, almost sarcastically, to himself. "Well, Sheriff Bullock, I'll still be following the rails, won't I?"

He saw Henry limping near the fire pit, and then saw Bear carrying Evangelina's body, wrapped tightly in a point blanket, off into the pine trees. His heart was knotted as was every muscle in his body as he walked up to Bear.

"Sam said they took special aim at her, Jack. One laughed, he said, when he shot her." Tears poured from his eyes, and sobs bawled from his soul, as the big Indian laid the body into some soft pine needles. "This was a senseless attack, Jack. This was open murder. They didn't have to do this to steal the herd."

"They did it because they could," Jack murmured, kneeling down next to his Evie. He pulled the edge of the blanket back and looked for the last time into her beautiful face, leaned down and kissed her forehead, as gently as a butterfly would land. He didn't feel even slightly gentle.

"I need to see those we killed and wounded. One of the men we found at the herd is someone I know from Deadwood, Bear. He said there are still others in the trees to our east, waiting for these men to bring them our cattle."

He touched where Evangelina's shoulder would be under the blanket, folded it back over her face, stood, and walked to the fire, where Henry and Sam had the three bodies laid out and one wounded man moaning and leaning up against a rock. "How bad is it, Henry?" Jack asked, taking a cup of boiling coffee from the older man.

"I'll live," he muttered. "Hit me in the calf, just above the boot. Any higher and I wouldn't have a knee, so I guess I'm very lucky. Might have nicked a bone in there, but I'll be fine. Bullet went all the way through.

"How's the herd?"

"Herd's fine and nobody hurt. Do you

remember me telling you about that foul family I met in Deadwood? Well, I just met them again. Smith will be bringing Jon Davis into camp in a bit, and his father Pete and cousin Skinny are up in the pines, on one of those ridges, east of us, waiting for Jon to bring our cattle to him."

"You think they knew you were here? You caused them some grief as I recall."

"Not half as much as I plan to cause," Jack whispered. "No, I don't think they had any idea I might be here. They're just stupid, mean, ugly people, Henry, looking for the easy buck.

"After we get ourselves all straightened out around here, I'd like to take Bear and find Davis and his family."

"I think you need to," is all Henry said. Henry had felt loss in his past, could feel his heart fighting back at the loss of Evangelina. "She was my daughter, Jack, just as Bear is my son. She had every intention of being your wife and I so wanted those grandchildren you two were to bring.

"Yes, Jack, you need to ride into those mountains to our east and reap vengeance, horrible, screaming vengeance."

Jack could remember Henry pleading with Bear not to kill Slim Boyle, pleading with him not to kill Slim Boyle, "It would be murder," Henry had said, but now, this wouldn't be murder, this would be retribution, and Pete Davis would die hard, very hard.

23

Roddy Simmons, Tooky Chalmers, Richard Smith, Jack, and Bear rode out well before sunrise the following morning, picking up the trail Jon Davis left when he and the other outlaws descended on the herd. They hadn't tried to hide their movements in any way, and Jack picked up the smoke smell as soon as they neared the outlaw camp. "Seems they might be pretty sure of themselves," Bear said. "No back trail guards, smoky fire anyone could follow."

"If I hadn't heard from my people before this, I would have been long gone," Jack whispered to Bear as the men dismounted and moved slowly toward Davis's camp. The men spread out wide and slowly advanced right up close. Jack spotted a night guard slumped up against a tree, sound asleep.

Bear slipped up to the man and with one quick move broke his neck with very little noise. He dragged the body into the brush and Jack recognized Skinny Davis immediately. "That's the cousin," he said. They counted four horses and moved them back into the wood and tied them off with their horses. Tooky brought fresh wood and got the fire going, even made a fresh pot of coffee.

All five of Rupert's men sat around the fire, weapons drawn and cocked, each with a fresh cup of coffee, and waited for the gangsters to come out from their tents and bed rolls.

"Surprise," Jack said when Pete Davis walked out of his tent, pulling suspenders up and over his shoulders.

Pete made a move for a weapon, but there was no weapon and Bear slammed him in the head with the stock of his rifle. This brought the other two outlaws out, and each was thumped hard. "Might's well enjoy this coffee," Jack laughed, "before we tie these fine gentlemen to their horses."

"Why not just drag 'em back," Bear said, and he wasn't trying to be funny.

Tooky and Roddy tied the men's hands to the saddle horns, flopped Skinny's body across the saddle of his horse, and all the weapons were gathered. "Roddy, why don't you stay here, go through everything, just in case they have something else planned, and

269

then burn everything. No sign of the Davis clan should exist." Roddy smiled his okay, and the group rode back to camp.

Jack wanted to kill Pete Davis, rip his arms off and beat him to death with the stubs, wanted to run a knife right up his middle, spill his guts all over the ground, and rub Davis's face in the foul intestines, and took pleasure in just thinking about it.

"It's a shame we have to take these vermin into Cheyenne," Jack said as they neared the Rupert camp. "I would love to march these fools right down the main street in Deadwood and fling them in the mud in front of Sheriff Seth Bullock's office, and then join Hiram Biggins for the hanging."

Bear was still chuckling when he jerked Pete Davis off his horse and pushed him down next to his son, Jon. He grabbed Skinny's body off the horse and tossed it to the ground in front of the Davis's. "Looks like only three of these mangy dogs are left alive, Henry. I guess that means another trip into Cheyenne."

"Maybe, maybe not," the rough old rancher said, rubbing the bandage wrapped around his leg, just below the knee. He limped over and stood in front of Pete Davis. "You are responsible for my daughter's death," he snarled, pulling his old Colt, cocking the hammer back, and pointing it at Davis's left eye.

"Better not," Bear whispered, "you talked me down just a while ago, Henry. It's my turn."

"What say you, Jack?" Rupert said.

Jack walked over and put his hand out, asking with that gesture for Henry to hand him his weapon. Henry looked at him, nodded, and slipped the heavy iron back into its leather. "I got a better idea," Jack said, jerking Davis to his feet. "I heard in Cheyenne that this ignorant fool strutted around calling himself Mad Dog," and he slapped Davis across the side of the head. "Mad dogs need to be put away," he said, and untied the ropes wrapped around the outlaw.

"You get by me, you're a free man, Mad Dog," Jack said, handing Bear his rifle, pulling his Colt Army and giving it to him as well. "Just you and me, Mad Dog," he snarled, and smashed the skinny little fool right in the mouth.

Davis's eyes flared with hatred as he stumbled backward from the blow, tasting blood from split lips. He caught his balance and dove toward Jack, and the very big, almost eighteen-year-old man, side-stepped the rush and blasted the man with a huge fist on the side of his head, putting him face down in the rocks.

Davis came to his feet with a large boulder that he flung at Jack, turned and tried to run for the horses. Jack took three long steps, grabbed Davis by the back of his shirt, spun him around and drove a fist into his groin. "You got a knife handy, Bear?" Jack asked, dragging the coughing, choking Davis back toward the fire.

Bear didn't say a word, just handed Jack a large skinning knife. Jack felt its heft, nodded with a smile, and handed the knife to Davis. "Like I said, Mad Dog, you get by me, you're free," and he stepped back and pulled his own massive Bowie from its belt scabbard.

"No," Davis cried. "No, you'll kill me," he whimpered, dropping the knife. Bear picked it up, cleaned the dirt off, and handed it back to Davis, chuckling some more as he did so.

Jack had death written deep in every crease of his young face as he advanced on Davis. "You're right, Mad Dog, I'm gonna kill you," and he slashed out with the big knife, slicing away a large part of Davis's shirt, and cutting deep into the man's skinny chest. Davis screamed, dropped the knife, and tried to run, but Jack leaped on him, driving the knife deep into his back, then slicing up, and severing every attachment connected to Davis's black heart. His scream of pain stopped at the same time his heart did.

"Jon Davis, I'm going to be there when you hang," he said, wiping blood and tissue from his knife and slipping it into its scabbard. "Your father was a murdering fool who wouldn't ever stand up for himself. Your cousin tried to rape your sister and you gave him your friendship.

"I'm taking you and that injured coward over there to Cheyenne to hang, and maybe you'll live long enough to feel the rope."

No one saw Jack for the next two days. Bear told Henry Rupert that the boy was sitting next to the grave they dug for Evangelina, rocking back and forth, singing songs that they had sung together in the evenings. "He's telling her stories, and telling her that those responsible are paying and will pay."

"He needs to come back to camp and get these fools sent off to Cheyenne," Henry said. "Maybe tomorrow would be soon enough."

"Looks like Jack, Henry," Bear said, pointing at some dust about two miles out. "He's not alone, either." The wagon, piled high with personal belongings, some furniture, and other stuff, pulled to a stop in front of the home ranch house, Jack waving hello to the two men.

He'd been gone for almost two weeks, taking his prisoners into Cheyenne and getting a long shopping list filled. Henry and Bear, along with the cowboy crew brought the herd into the home ranch pastures, gathered the cattle on the south range and had it pastured as well.

"Bout time he got back," Henry growled to Bear's delight.

"Brought a friend, Henry," Jack said, stepping off the wagon and walking around to help Matty off. "Said she needed to talk to you about something," and he chuckled long and deep, seeing first amazement, then a big smile from the older man.

"Now, just hold on there. Just hold on," he said, but limped off the porch to greet the lady.

"Jack told me all about what happened, Henry, and so, I am here to keep all you big strong men fed, and to nurse your brittle old bones, and maybe just make myself a new life."

Bear grabbed Jack by the shoulder and

aimed him toward the bunkhouse. "Time for you and me to disappear, my friend." They sent Sam back to help unload the wagon, and saddled up and lit out for the winter pastures to check the animals.

"You can't just close your business and move out here, Matilda." He was saying this, but wanted to hug her close and welcome her to the Rocking R. "What are you thinking?"

"I'm thinking I should have done this a long time ago, Henry Rupert. Young Mary-Ellen has wanted to buy that café of mine for a long time, and, well, when Jack told me about poor Evangelina, I just made up my mind. I've wanted to be with you for a long time and I think you feel the same. We're getting older, and we need each other." The strong language and firm jaw line was all Henry saw as Sam Smith started moving things from the wagon.

"Come along, Henry, let's help get this stuff put away. It's time to start thinking about supper for all these cowboys you have working out here."

"So that injured boy didn't make it to Cheyenne," Bear said. "I didn't think he would. You let Jon live? Here again, I didn't

275

think you would."

"He died dumb just the same as he lived. The sheriff's deputy, shot him dead the second day he was in jail. Deputy took him his dinner and Davis kicked the tray out of his hands and made a grab for the man.

"That deputy is even bigger 'en you, Bear, and he ripped Jon's arm right out of the socket, and was so angry, he pulled his gun and shot him, twice. Sheriff and judge chewed him out some, but I bought him dinner a couple of times."

"Any other excitements in Cheyenne?" Bear asked. "They won't like you for taking Matty out."

"That was a surprise, but that's one woman you don't much argue with. She sold that place in one day and we were on the road the next. I did meet a man that might just change my life, though. His name is Valley Paddock, an old railroad man who just named a town in honor of his mother, and is now the postmaster there. Isn't that something?

"I never thought you could do something like that, but he swore with his hand raised that he wasn't fooling. Told me about good land available, good grass, and close enough to the railroad facilities that shipping would be even easier than here. I'm going to start making the arrangements to have my money transferred to Elko, Nevada, and come spring, Paddock is going to sell me a quarter section of land, and I'll be a resident of Skelton, Nevada."

"I know that's been your plan the whole time, but I always hoped you'd change your mind and stay here with us."

"I think I may have done that if Evie hadn't been killed, Bear. We talked about it a lot, and Henry was talking about helping us set up our own place adjacent to the Rocking R," and he choked up a bit, thinking about just how much he had lost when those rustlers attacked the camp.

"I would have a difficult time staying, Bear. But I'll work through calving, help Smith get the plowing and planting started for spring, and then ride for Elko. Probably just hop a train," he chuckled, giving Bear a little friendly punch to the shoulder.

"Gonna miss you, boy."

24

Jack worked through the brutal Wyoming winter, penning letters to Maybelle in New York, to Mims in Fargo, and to Valley Paddock in Skelton. He sent a long letter to Seth Bullock in Deadwood and covered it with a letter to Hiram Biggins. One night, with the wind screaming its anger through the dancing pines outside the bunkhouse, he found himself almost dreaming about what was going to happen in his life.

"I've always felt as if I am alone, but I'm not, really. I've been writing all these letters and all of these people are right here with me, I've not really left them, nor they left me, we're just separated for the time being. It's only Evie that is truly gone, but, she isn't either, is she? I'll always have Evie right here, in my heart."

A clattering of boots on the bunkhouse porch woke him from his reverie, and Bear and Sam Smith came barreling through the door, both of them covered in snow, their noses bright red from the cold, and laughing up a storm.

"This little skunk just got our Christmas dinner for us," Bear laughed. "Come look, Jack, and help us get him in the abattoir. Biggest elk I've seen in years. Come on," he yelped, "Come on."

Jack found his heavy bear skin coat and gloves, and followed the two out into the storm. "You two have been hunting in this storm? Bear, the wind is howling faster than those trains can run, trees are crashing from the weight of the snow, and you two have been up in the woods?"

"This big boy is just like you," Bear laughed. "He got off his horse, leveled that old muzzle loader he's been nursing, and dropped this," he said, as they walked up to a pack horse struggling under the weight of half of a massive Colorado Elk. A second pack horse was in equal jeopardy of collapse. "Just look at how big that animal is."

It took several hours to get the animal in the slaughter house, hung, and skinned. "Pa knows how to mount horns and I bet Henry would like these horns hanging in his house," Sam said and they chopped them from the head.

"I think it would be better if they hung in

the bunkhouse," Jack said. "For the next hundred years, every cowboy that works at the Rocking R will know that Sam Smith, bad man Sam Smith brought that elk down." They were laughing and joking all the way to the ranch house to get Henry and Matty to come see.

"Your winter feed saved us from a pretty heavy loss, Jack," Henry said one early spring morning. They were in the large winter pastures, checking for early calving, looking over the herd in general. "Guess you'll be leaving us pretty soon, eh?"

"I got notification from the bank in New York and the bank in Elko that my money has been transferred, and according to Paddock, he has a hold on a hundred and sixty acres of bottom land right along the western front of the Ruby Mountains, not too far south of Elko.

"I'll never be able to tell you how much you mean to me, Henry Rupert, and how much the Rocking R means. I don't know if I'm really a cattleman yet, but I'm not afraid of making this move, and a lot of what you and Bear have taught me will be part of the Rafter S in Skelton."

The entire Rocking R crew was gathered

around the loading pens next to the railroad tracks on a cold blustery April morning, watching a big steam engine slowly come to a stop for water, wood, and one passenger. "You keep in touch, Jack Slater," Henry said, vigorously shaking the big man's hand. "Just like Bear and Evangelina, you are my son, and I'll miss you."

There were hugs, there was crying, there were promises made, and with an angry blow of the whistle, for the third time, mind you, Jack Slater finally broke free and stepped onto the boarding platform as the train jerked into motion. He stood there for a full ten minutes, until finally, the porter forced him to come into the passenger car.

He settled into his room, put belongings away, and sat down in front of the large window. *How many times have I done this? It seems like I've spent many hours sitting in front of this very window, watching a world go by, seeing parts of this country that so many others have not seen.*

My whole world is changing again, and it's only been eight years since I lost my Mama and Pa, lost a way of life that I loved, and look where I'm going. Henry called me a good man, and I have to make sure I live up to that. I am a man now, not a little boy, and I make my rules, I'm responsible for whatever is in my future.

This feels good, hearing and feeling the rail car moving along. I've travelled thousands of miles on these long thin steel highways. It feels like home, and I know, once again I'm going to a new home. This will be my last big move, I am going home, and the gentle swaying of the train put the big man into a deep, comfortable sleep.

A gentle knock on the door and the porter announced dinner would be served in half an hour. "I've slept the day away," Jack chuckled, washing the sleep from his eyes, dressing in clean clothes for the trip to the dining car. *I won't be having supper with Claudine,* he thought, moving through the cars, *and I wonder where old Ephraim Clairidge might be. So many wonderful memories associated with trains.*

After supper he called the car porter into his stateroom and asked if he knew a man named Ephraim Clairidge. "Well, yes sir, I do indeed know Mr. Clairidge," the porter said. Jack spent the next half hour writing a long letter to Ephraim and asked the porter to see to it that the wonderful old man got it. He also took the time to pull that old worn out letter, now several years old from his luggage and read it again.

■ ■ ■ ■

Two days later, he watched as the train slowly made its way into Elko and was amazed at the activity so early in the morning. *There he is, just like he said he would.* Valley P. Paddock was on the Elko station platform waiting for Jack's arrival. Jack spent the night wondering if this strange man would be there, or would Jack find himself in the wilds of frontier Nevada without knowing a soul.

"I'm finding it hard sometimes to take people at their word," he wrote in a long letter to Mims. "I've been lied to and double-dealt just often enough that trust is something that is no longer simply handed out. And when I say something like that, I then remember men like Ray Bennett at the Fargo Bank, Hiram Biggins and Seth Bullock in Deadwood, and of course, Henry Rupert."

Jack Slater jumped off the train and joined Paddock on the platform. "Well, my young friend, I'm glad you had a safe journey, and welcome to Nevada." Paddock was a large, exuberant man, not quite as tall as Jack's six feet and three, but probably twenty pounds heavier. "I brought a nice sized wagon for your gear, not knowing what you might be bringing in with you. Let's get it loaded and then get you over to the bank.

"Mr. Feemster is anxious to meet you, his newest depositor," Paddock chuckled.

"I wonder, sir," Jack said, "if we couldn't find some breakfast first. The train arrived before the dining car opened and I haven't even had a cup of coffee."

"My goodness, where are my manners. Of course, Jack, of course. Let's load the wagon, and we'll head right over to the Drover's Hotel, get you some good food, get you checked in, and then go to the bank."

Jack was polishing off some pork chops, mashed potatoes and gravy, and sourdough biscuits while Valley had coffee and a roll. "Tell me about this property you have lined up for me. It sounds wonderful, but coming from Salt Lake City to here, I didn't see a lot of fine farm land."

Paddock chuckled at that, thinking of the salt flats, Montello water stop, and great flat areas of sagebrush covered desert. "Skelton is about fifteen or twenty miles south of here, Jack, right at the base of the Ruby Mountains that will provide you with fine water. You rode past the Rubies coming to Elko, they would have been on your left, looking out of the train. They are high mountains, and plains that stretch out to the west are well watered, good land for cattle, sheep, and grasses."

"It would have been during the night, I guess, Valley. I sure don't remember any big high mountain range."

"Well, they are there and you'll live with their bounty, believe me. It will take us today and tomorrow to get all the various legal things done, get your banking squared away, get your property recorded and on the tax rolls, and then, we will need to arrange for ranch and farm equipment."

"I didn't even ask," Jack said, "is there even a house of some kind on the property?"

"There's a nice stone cabin, a storage and equipment shed, stables, and a few corrals. The only thing missing is the Lord of the Manor, and I'll be delivering him in the next few days," the big man laughed. Jack laughed right along with him, thinking, Lord of the Manor?

"What would make someone give up such a fine piece of property?" Jack asked, remembering that Henry Rupert had voiced the same question. Rupert said something about fine pieces of property aren't simply sold off and at reasonable prices.

"Man had a problem with John Barley

Corn on the one hand, and wasn't very good at robbing banks on the other hand," Paddock laughed. "The judge had him hauled off to Carson City, gave the property to his wife who in turn told me to sell it quick so she could get as far away from Nevada as possible."

Paddock reached inside his coat and produced a couple of sheets of paper. "This is an inventory of buildings and ranch equipment," he said, handing Jack one of the sheets, "and this is an inventory of what is inside the house. As you can see, there are things missing from these lists."

Jack studied the lists and said, "It looks like I'll need to spend a few dollars in the next day or two," he chuckled.

"Jack, this is Aaron Feemster, manager of the Elko Bank. Aaron, meet Jack Slater, now of Skelton, Nevada. You two have a lot to talk about. I'll make our arrangements at the Drover's Hotel," Paddock said and left the two men.

Feemster gave Jack a warm welcome, ushering him into his rather plush office and inviting him to sit in a large, heavily uphol-stered wingback chair. "It's a pleasure to meet you, Mr. Slater. I must say you're younger than I anticipated. Cigar?"

"No, thank you, sir," Jack said remembering one he had lit up after finding it on the train ride to Chicago. "I'm eighteen, Mr. Feemster and been on my own for many years now. I believe you found all my papers in order?" Jack was looking at a thin, pale man of about fifty, mostly bald and with a pencil thin moustache that was almost white.

"Your papers are in fine order, it's just unusual to find a man as young as you having accounts of this size. I don't want to pry, after all it is your money, your account, and all is in good order."

He wants the whole story, and guess what, Mr. Feemster, you ain't getting it, Jack thought, looking at the little man. *I need to be very aware from this moment on, I think. I wonder if I can even slightly trust this man? Everything better be in order.*

Feemster had several packets of papers in front of him and started itemizing each packet and handing it to Jack. The account from New York surprised him since he had not heard a figure mentioned in all this time. "Your parent's farm sold for eight thousand dollars and in the eight years since the sale, that figure has increased to twelve thousand and nine hundred dollars.

"You authorized a payment of one thousand dollars to Raymond Bennett at the Fargo Bank, and that has been made. The receipt is in the packet here. And you have authorized a payment of two thousand dollars to Valley B. Paddock for the purchase of property in the Skelton Valley area, again, the receipt is in the packet. At this moment, Mr. Slater, you have a balance of nine thousand and nine hundred sixty two dollars.

"Did you want to make a withdrawal for traveling money?"

"No, Mr. Feemster, that won't be necessary." Jack had more cash than he really wanted to be carrying, since Henry Rupert paid him off in cash, not a note. "What I need to do is make a deposit. When I left the Rocking R I was paid in cash." He found his wallet on the inside pocket of his heavy coat and counted out seven hundred dollars, leaving him another eight hundred with which to purchase what he would need for his ranch.

"I think you're off to a fine start, Mr. Slater," Feemster said, handing him a receipt for the deposit. "I hope we do business for many years."

Jack headed down the block toward the Drover's Hotel wondering just how safe his money was going to be. "I'm not sure I really trust that gentleman," he murmured, looking up and down the main street of Elko. It was a booming little community, a ranching town, he thought, as opposed to Fargo, which was a farming town.

He was analyzing the towns he has known since coming west. *Fargo was set up to be a major stop for the railroad and supply the necessities of the farming community while Deadwood was a wild mining town with no roots of any kind, and then there was Cheyenne, a town in flux. Part mining, part railroad, and part ranching, and then they made it the capitol of Wyoming. It'll take Cheyenne a few years to figure out what it wants to be.*

He was enjoying the walk through Elko, feeling the brisk spring air and watching the people. He remembered being slightly anxious on the streets of Deadwood, almost frightened on the streets in Cheyenne, and felt alone but not the least bit anxious in Elko.

"How much I've learned in these last few years," he said. "These men on horses are cowboys not farmers, and when I met Henry, I was a farmer. I've got farmer in my blood, but I'm also a good cattleman now. I'm now completely on my own again, and that means I have to be smart.

"No more meetings with people like Pete

Davis and that horrid family, hopefully meetings with people like Seth Bullock and Mr. Biggins. And be wary, Jack, be aware," he snickered, walking into the Drover's.

"We have adjoining rooms on the second floor, Jack," Valley said when Jack walked into the hotel. "How did your meeting go with old Feemster. He has the only bank in town or many people would do business elsewhere, I think."

"A bit slippery, is he?"

"I don't know if I'd go that far," Valley chuckled. "He talks too much, and other people tend to know your business, if you get my point."

"You just backed up my initial thinking, Valley. I'll keep my business close to my vest. He did ask some rather personal questions. Where are we off to now?"

"Let's go make you legal with the county, get all that out of the way, then we'll take in the sounds and sights of greater downtown Elko, cattle capitol of the Great State of Nevada." Jack found himself liking Valley Paddock more and more, chuckling as he was thinking it.

"Did you put things in the rooms?"

"All taken care of, sir," Paddock said. "Did you want to go to your room before we continue?"

They walked through the lobby of The Drover's, and Jack took it all in, the gas lights, plush carpeting, an ornate barroom off to the side with access to the street as well. The stairway was broad, with carved bannister and newel posts, curving gently as it climbed to the second floor.

Their rooms were half-way down a broad, well-lit hallway and Jack walked into a nicely appointed room that featured a large bed, table and chairs, and a window that looked out onto Elko's main street. He heard a train whistle and realized that the rails were on the other side of the hotel. *Glad our rooms are on this side,* he chuckled, putting some of his things away in the closet and bureau of drawers.

25

Paddock and Jack spent the rest of the morning taking care of all the legal things that needed to be done at the Elko County Courthouse, and they returned to the Drover's Hotel for something to eat. Paddock seemed to know just about everyone they met on the street and at the courthouse.

"I guess you've been in this area for a long time, Valley. You have introduced me to more people than I've ever met in my life."

Paddock laughed and reminded Jack that he worked in the railroad office here in Elko before he moved to what is now known as Skelton. "The town was called Hooten Station and sometimes The Meadows, but when I moved in I became the postmaster and named the area Skelton after my mother.

"There are some fine ranches in the valley, and fine people, but there is also a nasty crowd, gamblers, thieves, drunkards, that I would gladly see run out of town. We don't have enough money to hire a town marshal, though."

"I saw that in Deadwood, and it took a few murders and a few people getting the stuffings knocked out of them before they finally elected a sheriff. Hope I'm not moving into an outlaw's nest, Mr. Paddock."

"No, it isn't that bad, just irksome, Jack. Nobody in their right mind would bother someone your size," he laughed. "Let's go check on some hardware, shall we?" Paddock had it in the back of his mind, ever since he met Jack Slater in Cheyenne, of trying to hire the large man as a part time town marshal. He remembered how the sheriff told him about the first gunfight Slater had gotten into, and now, how he had helped wipe out a murderous cattle rustling gang.

That boy could do us a lot of good in Skelton. He's awfully sincere about that ranch, though. Maybe just being around will be enough to chase those yahoos out of town. Along with the Skelton Post Office, Paddock also had a small mercantile shop, and dabbled in real estate. He wanted a safe and friendly town.

■ ■ ■ ■

They walked down the street, seeing shops filled with merchandise from California, the mid-west, and the east coast. "Elko's quite the town, Jack. Biggest town between Sacramento and Salt Lake City, right now. There's a lot of cattle shipped through here."

"Hope some of it will be mine, soon," Jack said. "That's a nice saddle shop," he said, stepping inside. "Look at this one, Valley, it's beautiful. Those boys in Wyoming kept talking about the Spanish influence moving through the west from California. This is what they were talking about."

"You know your saddles, young man," one of the men working in the saddle shop said. "This is made by a man named G.S. Garcia in California. There are a number of us here in Elko that would love to talk this man into moving here. We might get lucky someday," he sighed.

"I'm Jack Slater, just in from Wyoming and moving to Skelton, and I think you just sold a saddle, sir," Jack said. They spent the next several minutes working out the details, and Jack and Valley walked on down Commercial Street. "That is one fine saddle, Valley, one fine saddle."

"Here's the hardware store, Jack. They'll have just about everything on your list." They walked into a large, two story building crammed with everything a rancher or farmer would ever want in life.

"Good afternoon, Jeremy," Paddock said, walking toward the back where two men were working. "I want you to meet the newest resident of Skelton. Say hello to Jack Slater.

"Jack, this is Jeremy Hazelton, one of the best businessmen in Elko."

"Glad to meet you, Mr. Slater. And," he brought the other man, actually a boy of about 12 up to him, "this is my son, Percival. Percy, say hello to Mr. Slater. Percy will be running this store before long, and he'll be about as big a man as you are, Slater," and the laughter rang through the large building.

Hands were grasped and shaken around and Jack's eyes roamed through the vast amount of merchandise that was being offered. "You have just about everything a man would ever need or want, I think, Mr. Hazelton."

They spent several hours at Hazelton's emporium as Jack bought most of the material he thought he would need to get started at his new home. "We'll have a slab or two of Elko's good beef for supper, Jack, get everything loaded in the morning, and make the short drive to Skelton."

"I didn't think we could do it all in one day, Valley, but it looks like we did. I'll fill in the holes with stuff from your store. A slab of beef this big would suit me fine," he laughed, walking into his hotel room. "I'll get cleaned up and meet you downstairs in the saloon for a cold glass of beer before supper."

The barroom was filling with the late afternoon, early evening crowd, a mix of store and shop owners and workers, cattlemen off the ranches, and railroad people. Gas lamps hung in profusion, flashing their brilliance, aided some by crystals hanging on the edges. There was a long, ornate bar with no less than four barmen working the crowd, pouring the finest liquor available, and probably gallons of locally brewed beer.

Jack spotted Valley Paddock standing at the bar talking with two men dressed in suits, and one in full cowboy getup, including chaps and spurs, as if he just rode in from herd duty. "Evening, Valley," he said, stepping up to the bar. He signaled one of the barmen for a beer, and nodded to the others.

"Evening, Jack. Some more fine people I want you to meet," he snickered, taking a nice pull on a snifter of what might have been Kentucky's finest. Gentlemen, this is the newest resident of Skelton, Nevada, Jack Slater. Jack, meet Bill Vierra, who is Elko Superintendent for the railroad, Ted Wilson, owner of the Block S Ranch, some north of here, and his ranch manager, Slim Hendricks."

Hands were shaken around and Jack quipped, "I've met about two thousand people so far today, so if I'm not right on top of remembering your names, please forgive me."

Wilson jabbed him lightly in the ribs. "Only two thousand? Valley, you're slipping." He turned back to Jack. "Understand you've been working for Henry Rupert in Wyoming. He's one of the best. That huge Indian still with him?"

"Growls Like a Bear is the cow boss and Henry's got a nice operation going. Too many people moving onto open range, though. Henry's bought up about all he can handle, so he'll have a fine herd for many more years."

"We have a meeting, gentlemen," Vierra

said, and the three stood, shook hands all around and walked toward a meeting room off to the side of the barroom. "Have a good evening, and Jack, it was a pleasure. Hope to see more of you in Elko."

"That's a nice group," Jack said.

"Bill Vierra and Ted Wilson might just end up on the board of directors for the Elko Bank after this meeting they're attending tonight. They are part of the crowd that's tired of hearing their stories blathered about by Feemster. Either that or there might just be a new banking enterprise opening up in Elko."

"Both Vierra and Wilson look like strong-minded fellers," Jack said. "Slim Hendricks is a cowboy. How does he fit in?"

"He owns half of Wilson's ranch," Paddock, chuckled, softly but with narrowed and gleeful eyes. Jack chuckled right along with him.

"He seems kind of young to be Wilson's partner," Jack said.

"Hendricks' father was Wilson's partner and Slim inherited his half and some other fine properties in the county. He's not quite as bright as his father and Ted Wilson pretty much takes care of him."

"Better have a hefty breakfast, Jack," Valley

Paddock said as they slid into chairs in the café. "It's a long ride to Skelton after we get a ton of material in that wagon."

"Mr. Hazelton is shipping most of what I bought because, as he put it, it might take a day or two to find some of it. We just need to pick up the saddle and other tack, and the supplies that I'll need right away. That'll make a much lighter load for that team and get us on the road faster.

"For some reason, Valley, I keep forgetting to ask you if there is any stock on the place. Any animals at all?"

"There's a couple of pretty worn out horses, maybe a steer or heifer or two that got left behind, some chickens and barn cats, and that's about it. There are two outfits in the valley that produce some fine stock horses, and I'd recommend one of them before buying one here in town.

"You'll want to build your herd to your standards, so it's best that there aren't many cattle on the property."

They were on the road before ten that morning, which was clear and cold, but there was no biting wind and the day promised a bit of warmth as it wore on. The road to Skelton cuts off the road that leads to a large canyon in the Ruby Mountains, and travels south along the western edge of that majestic range.

26

The sagebrush was high and thick, trees were sentinels at every water source, elms, cottonwood, various pines, spruce, cedar, and fir, and the land rose and fell mostly because of flowing streams of pure water pouring out of those mountains. "Is this all snow melt, Valley?"

"From now till maybe July it will be mostly snow melt, but the streams and creeks run all year, fed by thousands of mountain springs. Just south of Skelton is Harrison Pass, where more than one wagon train suffered long delays in their attempts to get to the California gold fields. And further south, there are some fine mines producing gold and silver today.

"Hamilton and another mountain town, Eureka are a little further south."

The team of heavy ranch horses pulled the wagon through the country with little trouble, forded many creeks and streams and needed little direction from Paddock. Jack sat tall on the seat and took in everything his eyes could glom onto. He remembered he had come from a lush Atlantic Coast farm, to a fine prairie farm, through good ranch country in the Rocky Mountains, and was seeing more lush ranch country. *This is going to be just fine. This country should be prime for cattle, sheep and hogs.*

He was deep in thought when it finally dawned on him that there was no way he could operate a one hundred sixty acre cattle ranch alone. "By golly, Valley, I'm going to need to hire at least two men, I think. Are there people available for hire in Skelton."

'There are, Jack, but you'll want to be cautious. Remember what I told you about the outlaw element in our town. I wouldn't be too quick on hiring, until you get to know your way around."

They rode through Skelton with Valley Paddock waving at just about everyone, and Jack seeing his new hometown for the first time. He saw just a few buildings, one owned by Paddock stood out from the rest. It was not the wild and crazy scene that he found in Deadwood or Cheyenne, and that pleased him. *This is the permanence that I saw back east and particularly in Fargo. This is home to these people, not just a stop along the way.*

The road south forked a couple of miles out of town, and Paddock drove on the west fork another five miles, coming to some gently rolling folds in the country, crossed a stream and on the right stood a small cabin, back several hundred yards from the roadway.

"There she is," Paddock proclaimed, waving his arms in a broad sweep that took in some fine cattle country. There were several locust and cottonwood trees near the cabin and Jack spotted some apple trees off to the north of the cabin. He also saw the remains of the home garden and was pleased to see a small stand of corn stalks.

The outbuildings were in good shape, fences for corrals and holding pens seemed to be standing straight, and as they drew nearer, he saw chickens fluttering about, and a couple of horses munching hay in one of the corrals.

"Is somebody staying here, Valley?" he asked, hoping that some decision had not been made about that.

"One of my boys from the store has been coming out and making sure there was water and feed for the few animals left on the place. No, Jack, I can see that in your eyes. No, I would not hire someone without your consent. One of those horses out there is mine, since I knew we would be coming here with the wagon.

"There is considerable feed cut and stacked in the barn, and you'll see the fields that have been planted for cutting grasses for winter feed. I'll help get you unloaded, and then I'll have to get back to Skelton. I haven't been in my store for several days now. Hope those boys haven't given the store away," he laughed.

The wagon was unloaded and Valley Paddock was on his way back to town in less than two hours and Jack took his time looking at everything. "This is all mine," he whispered to himself, a smile as wide as the valley he was standing in spread across his broad face. He walked to the house and pulled a ring of keys hanging from his suspenders, found the one for the door, and slowly turned it, hearing the distinctive click, and walked into his new home for the first time.

The first thing he saw was the large rock fireplace that dominated one wall, and windows on the south side of the building.

He learned that in Fargo, when Mims showed him how to set his bedroll near a south window and it would be warmed all day and ready for him at night.

There was a large wood cook stove in the kitchen, plenty of cupboards and shelves, and a heavy home made table that looked like it may have been hewn from oak. He found there was water available right in the kitchen from a hand pump, fed from a well or springs right under the house. The wood box was filled and there was kindling cut as well. He had already seen that a fire had been laid in the fireplace and gave a mental thank you to Valley Paddock for the thought.

His bedroom was large and roomy with more south facing windows. "Good thing I bought that bedstead," he commented, not seeing one. It took the rest of the day for him to get everything in the house and generally, at least put away or in the rooms where it belonged. As evening shadows approached, he lit the fires, lit a couple of lamps, and sat in a large chair he had found at Hazelton's store, and contemplated just where he was and what he was doing.

I'm in my home, sitting before my fire, about to cook supper on my stove in my kitchen. I've never been able to say that. I'm home. His thoughts drifted to Oak Blossom and to

Mims, he remembered how Maybelle had been such a help when he was found on the streets. The bad days with Pete Jablonski never entered his mind, but he did want to try and get another note to old Ephraim if he could.

He found simple pleasure in stoking up the fireplace and kitchen stove before snuffing out the lamps and climbing into bed. His dreams were filled with herds of fine cattle, each one of those animals wearing a Rafter S brand. He would have stock horses even better than Blue, and a cow boss as knowledgeable as Bear. There was a woman in most of the dreams, but he didn't know who she was.

The sky had a touch of light to it when he stirred the fires, got a pot of coffee going, and ventured out to feed what little stock he had. He was back in minutes with half a dozen fresh eggs in his hat and a big smile on his face. *Breakfast provided by my own ranch,* he chuckled.

He saddled one of the horses he found in the corral and rode out to make a grand tour of his new ranch. That brand new G.S. Garcia saddle got its first ride and Jack found it to be as good a ride as it was pretty. "I don't think you're as old and tired as you want me to think you are," Jack snickered, getting a couple of sidesteps and crow-hops from the buckskin dun. He nudged with his knees and felt immediate response, did a couple of loping figure eights, noticing the quick lead changes, and good response.

"You're just a little bit more than the old dopey I was told about," Jack smiled, and rode off across some rich grazing land in search of corner posts, and an inventory of what this ranch was all about. That little dun ate up the miles and didn't lather up or quit at any time during the long morning.

There was fine grazing throughout the property, he found twenty acres set aside for cutting winter feed, there were at least two natural springs and a couple of streams that wandered through, heading north to join the Humboldt River, he expected. At every opportunity, Jack found himself looking to the east at the towering granite peaks of the Ruby Mountains.

"You and me are gonna be in those mountains soon," he said to the dun. "I thought I was in heaven when I was in the Rockies, but I was obviously wrong. I hope Henry Rupert and Bear get a chance to visit me someday. They have to see this."

It was two weeks before Jack found a chance

to ride off the property and visit Skelton. He had a pretty good shopping list with him and brought the wagon and team. His first stop was Paddock's Mercantile and a visit with Valley. "Ah, our new resident rancher comes to town, eh?" Paddock laughed as Jack walked in. "It's good to see you, Jack," he said, coming from behind the counter to shake his hand.

"And you, my friend," Jack answered. "Thought I better pick up some stuff and see just what your town has to offer. Also, Mr. Postmaster, sir, I have some letters to send off. How often does mail come through?"

"Once that railroad got punched through, we have incoming mail on every train, and I have a rider bring it to Skelton every day. Your letters will go back to Elko with that rider and be on the next train east.

"Let's see that list of yours, and while Pete or Juanito get started on it, we can take a walk through our little town."

"I'd like that," Jack said handing him his list. "Is there a livestock sale yard here or will I have to go to Elko?" It was late in spring, but Jack wanted to get started building his herd, and figured, even so, he wouldn't have anything to sell for two years. He needed to get a good line of heifers and some strong bulls on the property soon.

"I'm hoping to get some feeders also," Jack said. "I wouldn't argue about a little income along the way," he chuckled.

"You'll need to go to Elko for that, Jack." Paddock was a merchant, not a rancher, and didn't go into any detail. Jack left it at that, planning a trip to Elko in the near future.

They walked out of the large store and onto the main street of Skelton. Paddock's place was toward the south end of the small town and they turned north. Paddock spread his arms wide, something Jack noted that he did often. "You can see why this place used to be called The Meadows. Just look at that," he said, gesturing at a grand view of grazing land undulating from the base of the Ruby Mountains west almost as far as the eye could see.

"I'm very glad we met, Valley. I feel as if I'm really home." They found themselves at the blacksmith shop and Paddock introduced Jack to Jesse Winthrop, standing near the street in his leather apron.

"Nice to meet you, Jesse," Jack said. He was looking at a stocky man, maybe five nine and one eighty or so with thinning auburn hair, a bulbous nose, and gleaming brown eyes.

"Jack Slater, eh?" he said, offering a big,

thick fingered hand. "Welcome to our little village. You bought the Fairly place, eh?"

Paddock answered him with the affirmative. "Jack was in Wyoming and looking to move to Nevada and I knew Fairly's wife was looking to get out."

"She was at that," Winthrop said. "That could be some fine property, Mr. Slater. That fool Fairly didn't know enough to get his boots on the right feet," he coughed and laughed at the same time.

Jack was impressed with the blacksmith shop and said so. "You're familiar, I take it, with the tools of the trade," Winthrop said.

"I'm self taught, certainly not a craftsman, sir, but yes, I do some iron work. I grew up on a farm where the owner did not take care of his equipment and found myself mending everything, wood, metal, and leather," he laughed.

"Aye, laddie, I understand how that is. I'm a smithy like my father, grandfather, and great grandfather before me. Some of these tools are more than one hundred years old," he said, pride spread across his face, his eyes even brighter than usual.

"It was a pleasure meeting you, sir," Jack said as they started back down the main street of Skelton. "I hope to see more of you and your fine shop."

"Are you up for a cold beer before we get your wagon loaded up, Jack?" Paddock asked with a sly little grin. Jack snickered at the man and nodded, letting Paddock direct them into a small building across the street from Winthrop's shop. The building looked like it may have been a carpenter's shop or something similar, with large doors that opened onto the main street, large enough to drive a wagon right in if they were both flung open.

It was a simple saloon, the bar being only about twelve feet long, two tables took up space along with a large pot belly stove that was burning hot. "This is Jose Torres, our fine keeper of the ale. Jose, meet Jack Slater, just moved to the area from Wyoming."

They shook hands and Jose poured large mugs of beer. "This is good country, Jack, and the water makes some fine beer," the middle aged Mexican said. He stood about five six and weighed one twenty at the most, wore a massive black moustache, had big bushy eyebrows, and his brown eyes seemed bright and curious.

He was going to say more when the door was flung open and a large man barreled in, fuming with anger. "Lookin' for you, Paddock," he growled, muscling his way between Valley and Jack. "Who do you think

311

you are telling my boy I ain't got no credit in your foul emporium? I ought to knock you into the next county," he said, giving every appearance of doing just that.

Jack grabbed the man's arm, spun him around, and pushed him hard, back toward one of the tables. "That's enough of that," Jack said. "You have something to say to Mr. Paddock, you say it like a gentleman." Jack stood as tall as he could, several inches above the intruder, had his legs slightly spread for balance, fists knotted into clubs, and eyes narrowed in a frightening scowl.

"Don't you be pushin' me, boy. I'll whup on you like the dirty dog you are," and he lunged at Jack. Jack used the man's attack and spun him around, slamming his back into the edge of the bar, letting the man bounce forward, and put one of his big fists into the man's groin.

Jack wouldn't let the man crumple onto the floor, but straightened him up and smashed a fist into the man's face, flattening an already flat nose and splashing blood on both of them. As the big man staggered back, another fist flew forward, clipping the man's jaw and sending him crashing into one of the tables, knocking it over, breaking at least one chair.

The man stood up, slowly, and pulled a

large knife from his boot, and came toward Jack, very slowly, very aggressively waving the shiny blade. "You're mine, dog," he snarled, slashing savagely with the knife. Jack danced out of the way, and as the back swing of that knife came toward him, he stepped forward and drove a knee into an already painful groin.

Knife man dropped the blade, puked up his guts, howling in pain, doubled over, gasping for breath. Jack kicked the knife out of the way and slammed his two grasped hands onto the back of the man's neck, dropping him into his own vomit. Jack walked over and picked up the knife, and stepped back to the bar. "Friend of yours, Valley?"

"No one has ever bested Clint Bayliss," Jose Torres said, almost in awe. "You can drink here anytime you want, Jack Slater." Torres's eyes were wide, his mouth still open, and he was shaking his head in wonder. "Bayliss is the worst, meanest man I've ever met and you beat him. He would have hurt you, Mr. Paddock."

Torres picked up the knife and felt the keenness of the blade, and slipped it onto a little shelf under the bar. "I think you have done this town a nice little favor, Mr. Slater. Word will travel fast about Mr. Bayliss getting stomped good."

"I'm afraid you're right, Jose, and Jack, I'm afraid you just made yourself a serious enemy. Bayliss is part of the crowd I told you about. You'll need to be ready to protect yourself from now on. Bayliss has some mean friends and they have no rules.

"Do you have weapons you can carry?"

"I have a rifle in my saddle scabbard and I usually carry a revolver in one of my saddle bags. I know many men wear their hand guns, but I never have."

"I think, my friend, it's time you start doing so." Paddock downed his mug of beer and motioned goodbye to Torres, and they walked out onto the street, leaving the beaten man on the floor of the saloon. "Bayliss is big, but you're much bigger. The problem is, he has friends, and he is a sneaky, shoot 'em in the back, type of person.

"I have a rig at the store I'll show you. You can carry your pistol slightly under your left arm and still get it out fast. And, still be able to do your work."

"I'll give it a try, Valley. Tell me about Bayliss, his friends, and why you let them get away with this nonsense. Why don't you run 'em out of town, or better, why doesn't the sheriff do something?"

27

Jack wasn't happy with the story that Valley Paddock told about Clinton Bayliss and his friends, and mulled it over ten times on the ride back to the ranch. The wagon was filled with essentials such as flour, sugar, coffee, and salt, a few items he needed for the ranch, and a couple of special things for himself.

"Valley told me the sheriff doesn't have a deputy named for this district, and that seems strange to me. This is a big county, I understand that, but with the problems that Bayliss and his little gang create, there'd be plenty to keep a deputy busy." Jack often had trouble seeing, or maybe wanting to see, the bad side of people.

He walked right into Pete Davis's problems and it wasn't until Skinny almost killed him that he saw the real trouble in the family, and he let that man into his camp, fed him, made him warm, and almost lost his entire kit. But he did learn from those encounters, he picked up other concepts from the likes of Seth Bullock and Hiram Biggins.

I wonder if the sheriff might have personal reasons for not keeping Bayliss and company under control? Valley Paddock didn't seem to question the sheriff's motives, but I think I just might have to do some checking. On horseback, the ride from Skelton to the ranch would have been quick, but with the wagon and team, it took long enough for Jack to do some serious planning.

"I'm going to Elko in a couple of days to buy some cattle, and I think I'll just do some checking on our fine sheriff while I'm there. I don't like the idea of people riding rough over other people just because they can. I've seen enough of that in Deadwood and Cheyenne, and I don't want to see it in Skelton." His muttering kept up for a few minutes longer, and at least once he had to chuckle.

That was brought on by thoughts of the Jablonski farm. *I do tend to meddle when I think someone is being taken advantage of. It didn't start on old Pete's farm, it started on the train west and I was only ten. Maybe I should just mind my own business once in a while.*

The ride out and across the meadows to the ranch was filled with eastern Nevada's beauty, high granite peaks, still covered in snow, waving tall grass and lush sage taller than a man, and rolling meadows stretching for miles to the west. He had a smile plastered on his wide face driving the team into the ranch.

"One man did this to you?" Joe Temple chuckled, as Clint Bayliss finished washing up. "The great Clint Bayliss, down for the count? You must be losing your touch, old man."

Bayliss reached into his boot and the knife wasn't there. "Don't you talk to me like that, Temple, I'll kill you like the dog you are," and he swung a mighty roundhouse right that Temple knocked away with a flick.

"Don't push your luck, Clint. You got your butt whacked, lost your knife in the process, and if you ever swing at me again, you'll find yourself helping the flowers to grow. We got some work to do, and I don't have time to pamper you. Get over it or get out."

Temple and Bayliss joined Lefty Roberts at Roberts' barn on the outskirts of Skelton. "Toby got himself jailed in Eureka, boys, so he won't be with us today or for some time, I guess," Lefty said. He produced a bottle of whiskey, took a good pull for himself and passed it to Temple.

"What happened to you," Lefty said, looking at Bayliss. "Find an old griz to mate with or something?"

"Got his butt whipped," Temple said. Bayliss took the bottle from Temple and almost emptied it with one swallow. Temple looked around and asked, "Where's Primm? He do something stupid too?"

"Whupped? Clint Bayliss got whupped?" Lefty Roberts howled, and took the bottle back for the last nip. He watched Bayliss tighten up like a length of coiled steel, saw the eyes narrow down, and decided not to pursue the humor any further. "Primm should be here shortly.

"Let's talk about this mine job you think you have planned, Joe. The Hamilton Mines are producing well right now and they are getting the payroll delivered from the bank in Elko every week. That delivery comes right through Skelton, and Primm says it's lightly guarded, sometimes just one man on the wagon with the driver."

Joe Temple lived in Elko, not Skelton, and was known as a card player, seldom got in any kind of trouble, enjoyed a game or two with the banker and some of Elko's business community. It was during a recent game that Aaron Feemster let it out that Hamilton's payroll was sent in cash every week from his bank. It took very little prodding from Temple to get most of the details.

Sonny Primm worked as a woodcutter for the Hamilton Mine and knew all the dates that the payroll would be shipped. He strode into the barn, took one look at Bayliss and started to say something, when Lefty cut him off with a scowl. "Payroll should be coming through tomorrow, according to Flanders. Want to tell me what this is all about?" he asked, nodding toward Bayliss.

"Got his butt whupped," Temple laughed. "Lost his knife in the fight, too."

"That's just about enough of your mouth, Temple," Bayliss exploded. "I'll tell you what happened, and I'll tell you what's gonna happen. Some cowboy bought Fairly's place, stole it from Fairly's cheatin' wife, and blindsided me. That's what happened, and I'm gonna kill him next time I see him."

"You'll have to buy a new knife," Temple prodded, "and from what I hear, you ain't got no credit at Paddock's."

Bayliss exploded and jumped across the old table the boys were sitting around, and took Temple to the barn floor, desperately trying to get his fingers wrapped around the smaller man's throat. Temple twisted and

319

turned with more strength than Bayliss expected and got free of the big man's hands.

He jumped to his feet first and kicked Bayliss in the head, then went to stomp on his neck when Sonny Primm grabbed him. Bayliss managed to get to his feet, still groggy from the kick, and was going to swing on Temple when Lefty stepped in and held him up.

"If we're gonna kill ourselves off, we'll just forget pulling off the Hamilton job, eh?" Lefty Roberts found his chair and sat back down at the table. "We can find that cowboy and take care of him later, let's talk about making some money here."

Joe Temple sat down across the table from Clint Bayliss and the two spent the next ten minutes in a stare-down contest. Sonny Primm outlined the time the payroll should roll through Skelton and where they should intercept the wagon. "So the wagon leaves Elko early Thursday morning," Lefty said, "and we'll need to be in place and ready to hit 'em sometime after noon.

"If we bust 'em somewhere near Harrison Pass Road, and we ride off in different directions after, that dumb sheriff won't know what to do," and that eased the tension and even brought a smile to Temple's face.

"Paddock said the cattle sale is on Thursday so I'll leave out of here tomorrow, spend tomorrow night in Elko and make the sale Thursday. Might have to hire a couple of buckaroos to help me drive whatever I buy back here." Jack was mumbling to himself while cleaning out the stalls in the barn. "I'd like to pick up at least twenty five heifers, with their calves, and two good bulls to get my herd started." He planned to hold back a few heifers each year and buy bulls as they were needed.

The ride to Elko was quick and easy through rich grazing country as spring was making itself well known along the western flank of the Ruby Mountains, and Jack Slater used the time to do more planning. He knew he would need at least two men to work the cattle and that would mean he would need a cook.

"I'll hire a cook and housekeeper in one person," he chuckled. "Maybe find a woman with a cranky attitude to keep the men in line and me out of the house," and the chuckles turned into laughter. One thing he knew, he would have to be careful who he hired to work the cattle after his altercation with Bayliss the previous week.

"I need to find out why the sheriff won't keep a deputy around Skelton, or maybe find out why the business community won't get together and hire a town marshal." He made half a dozen mental notes to follow up in Elko and an equal number to get answers to when he got back with the starters for his herd.

He left the buckskin dun at a stables and checked into the Drover's Hotel, had an early dinner after the ride into town. He noticed Ted Wilson sitting alone at one of the tables and stopped to say hello. "It's nice to see you, Jack Slater. Getting that ranch of yours put together?"

"It's a lot of work, but yes, I am. I came to town for the calf sale tomorrow, and hope I can pick up some nice heifers to get my herd started. Will you have some at the sale yard? Valley Paddock tells me you run one of the best herds in the county."

"He does, does he," Wilson smiled. "I've got some nice heifers at the sale and some young bulls, too. What are your plans for this afternoon, Jack?"

"I have to make some arrangements at the bank and then I'm free until supper."

"You be careful with that banker. He's got

the biggest mouth in Elko County, and anything you say to him will be spread around like a prairie fire. What I had in mind is a ride out to my place and maybe we could make a private deal without going through the sale yard. I've got some fine young cattle looking for a new home."

"I'd like that very much, Mr. Wilson. I'll be looking to pick up a couple of men to help me drive them back to Skelton, too."

"Are you talking permanent hands?"

"No, just for the drive south."

"I'll have Slim and a couple of the boys go with you, and Slim can give you all the background on how we do our breeding."

"That would be wonderful. I better get over to the bank and make sure everything is set up so I can pay you for all that," he laughed, shook Wilson's hand, and walked out onto Elko's main street. *This is certainly turning out to be a good day. I have to remember to ask Wilson about the sheriff. There's something wrong there.*

"Well, Mr. Slater, it's good to see you," Mr. Feemster said, stepping out of his office and ushering Jack in. "We just sent the Hamilton Mine payroll off this morning, so those businesses in Skelton will get some action in the next couple of days. What can I do for you?"

"I'm picking up the starters for my herd and need some blank checks in order to pay for the little darlings," Jack smiled. "Can you make those available, please?"

Feemster reached into the top right drawer of his large desk and produced a package of blank checks. "More than one seller?"

"I'll probably need two, sir," he said watching the banker separate two from the bundle and hand them over. "Thank you," he said, shaking Feemster's hand and walked toward the door. Feemster came around from behind the desk to walk him out.

"Oh, Virginia," Feemster said, seeing a young lady coming into the building. "So nice to see you. Jack, I'd like you to meet Virginia Bradley, daughter of our late governor. Virginia, meet Jack Slater, just arrived from Wyoming and settling in Skelton, your old neighborhood."

Virginia Bradley was a handsome and charming woman, and her companion was equally lovely. "Hello, Mr. Slater," she said with a smile. "Please say hello to my friend, Melissa Thompson."

Jack said hello to both women and asked if she was familiar with Skelton. "Yes," she said. "Papa and I had a nice ranch in The

Meadows, but when he died, I sold it and moved here. Which place did you buy?"

"I'm sorry for your loss, Ma'am. I bought the Fairly place. Needs lots of work, but it's got some fine grazing land."

"It does indeed," she said. "Mr. Fairly wasn't the smartest or most honest man, and his wife and family suffered for it. There's lots of potential with that property. Melissa is looking at some property there, now."

She turned to Feemster, saying, "We need to discuss some problems Melissa is having with the sale of that property in The Meadows.

"Mr. Slater, it's a pleasure meeting you, and I hope we see more of you around here." The smile was enchanting and Jack shook hands with the two ladies and headed out to find Wilson and buy some cattle.

I just met the governor's daughter. I wonder what kind of trouble her friend is having with buying her ranch? There are some strange things that seem to happen in Skelton, I'm thinking. As much as I like Valley Paddock, I also am starting to believe he is a fine salesman, and he walked off, snickering about that thought. *Just how many pieces of property in The Meadows have been sold because of that gentleman?*

28

Jack and Wilson agreed on a cattle deal and two days later, Jack Slater, Slim Hendricks, and two buckaroos from the Wilson ranch were driving twenty-five cows with their fresh calves and two bulls south to Skelton. "There's plenty of water, the terrain is easy, and with the calves, we'll take all the time we need to get there," Jack said and Slim agreed.

"Those calves are pretty young and they'll tire easy, besides," Slim laughed, "we ain't in no hurry, are we? Our ranch is north of Elko, where three creeks come together, and the grass is really good. I've been in The Meadows, but don't know your ranch."

"Rolling hills dropping from the shear cliffs of the Rubies," Jack said. "Lots of good water and the grass is good. People that owned my place didn't take very good care of it, though. These calves'll fatten up nice out there."

The first day was actually the hardest, getting the cattle organized into a herd, and once the cattle understood the concept, the travel was relatively easy and slow. It was on the third day, just hours from Jack's ranch, when they saw a rider coming toward them at a fast gallop. He pulled up when Jack and Slim waved at him. "What's the big hurry, Deputy?" Slim Hendricks asked when Elko Deputy Sheriff Lonnie Swickart slid his horse to a stop.

"Four men robbed the Hamilton Mine payroll yesterday, killed the men taking the payroll to the mine."

"If it happened yesterday, why are you in such a hurry today?" Jack asked.

"I gotta get the word to the sheriff right away," Swickart said.

"Have you got a posse up? Do you know who the killers are?" Jack was confused by the deputy's actions, as the man seemed to be doing the opposite of what should be done. *This deputy should be leading an organized posse and somebody from Skelton could have gotten word to the sheriff.* "Who's looking for the killers?"

"The sheriff will do all that, that's why I gotta get word to him right away," and Swickart lit out, as fast as his horse would go.

"That just doesn't seem right to me," Hendricks said, nudging his pony and getting Jack's herd of cows and calves moving again.

"There's something very wrong with how the sheriff conducts business around Skelton. There's an outlaw influence in that little town that gets away with just about anything they want, and the sheriff doesn't have a regular deputy assigned to the area," Jack said. "Now this, murder and a mine's payroll robbed, and the deputy feels it's more important to inform the sheriff than it is to catch the thieves.

"I wonder why?" Jack mused, remembering the short fight he had with Clint Bayliss, and how the saloonkeeper had said Bayliss was supposed to be baddest of the bad men in Skelton. Jack looked at Hendricks and asked, "Have you heard of problems in Skelton, as far as the sheriff goes?"

"Old Cyrus Simpson has his fingers in everything in Elko County, Jack. He treats most of the county like it's his own, and offers grief to those that oppose him, like Virginia Bradley's friend, Melissa Thompson, for instance."

"Governor Bradley's daughter?" Jack sat back a bit in the saddle wondering if that was the problem she wanted to talk to the banker about. "Tell me more, Slim. I met Miss Bradley and her friend, Miss Thompson when I was leaving the bank. Something about a problem Miss Thompson was having buying some property."

"Before he died, Lew Bradley, besides being a fine governor, ran a good cattle operation in The Meadows, as it was known then, and his strong influence kept old Simpson in check, but since his early death, Simpson has been trying to squeeze property owners and get as much ranchland as possible at a cut-rate.

"He's scared off half a dozen potential buyers and has been putting some pressure on Miss Thompson."

Jack had it in his mind that Simpson just might be behind the outlaw influence in Skelton to make people afraid to live there and sell out cheap. *I need to have a long talk with Valley Paddock, Melissa Thompson, and maybe Ted Wilson. I wonder if Sheriff Simpson is behind the payroll robbery? Maybe Skelton is more like Deadwood than I wanted to believe.* The thought also entered his mind that maybe he was just conjuring instead of seriously thinking.

Jack and Slim Hendricks got the herd moved onto some fine grass, and Hendricks left one of his buckaroos to work for Jack until such a time that Slater could get his own man hired. "You'll like working with Jack, Jack," Slim snickered, riding off toward Elko.

"Welcome to my place," Jack said, as they unsaddled at the barn. "I heard Slim call you Cactus Jack, what's your whole name?"

Laughing as he said it, "I'm 'bliged to be here, Mr. Slater. I'm Cactus Jack Farraday, out of east Texas, right along the Arkansas border." Cactus Jack Farraday was about five eight at the most, maybe a hundred and twenty pounds, and as strong as the finest piece of steel in Nevada. He always had a plug of tobacco working in his cheek, his hat was usually hanging down his back on the hurricane strings, and, as Jack remembered him saying it, "I've got two shirts and one pair of boots to my name."

"I'm glad you're with me, Jack. Let's get these animals taken care of and we'll get you set up. That building right over there is the bunkhouse but nobody's lived there for some time. It might need some fixing up."

"I'll take care of that, Mr. Slater," Cactus Jack said. "If it's got a bunk and a stove, I don't need much else. You might find me sleeping in the barn if the hay's more comfortable," he laughed, getting some chuckles from Jack as well.

"Call me Jack, Cactus, we don't need the mister stuff. Plan on eating your meals with me in the main house. We want to make sure those calves are settled in with their mamas, and that the bulls won't be wandering off."

"As long as those mamas are around, the bulls will be too," Cactus Jack chuckled, leading his horse and Jack's into the corral. They put their tack away and walked to the bunkhouse. "That was quite a shock hearing about that payroll robbery," Cactus Jack said, plopping his bedroll on one of the cots in the dusty room.

"I think that might be the opening shot of a war, Cactus. I just hope my little ranch doesn't become one of the battlefields. I guess the sheriff wants to have a lot of say in how we live here in Skelton."

"Wants to have a lot to say about how everyone lives in all of Elko County, is the way I've heard it," Cactus Jack Farraday said. "I'll get this bunkhouse shined up all purdy, and check on the kids. You'll ring the bell for supper?"

"You bet I will," Jack said. He had a big smile on his face walking back to the ranch house, actually humming a little song he remembered hearing Henry Rupert humming from time to time. *I wonder if there's a chance I might keep Mr. Farraday on my payroll. I might make Mr. Wilson beg to get him back.*

"I'll be back late this afternoon, Cactus, but I do have to go to Skelton. Check on that one calf that seems a little weak, and let's plan on branding and doctoring during these next few days. I hope to bring one or two men back with me, if I can find good hands."

They waved and Jack rode the dun toward Skelton, Cactus Jack rode his chestnut gelding out toward the west, where the grass was deep enough to hide the smaller calves. "I hope he can't find good hands," Cactus Jack mused riding at a comfortable walk, the sun shining down on his back. "Wilson's a good cattleman and Slim isn't hard to work with, but I like this Jack Slater. I'd sure hate to get in a fight with that big man, but after just these last few days, I'd sure fight with him."

He spent the rest of the day doctoring a few of the calves, moving the herd closer in to the main ranch, thinking it would be easier to separate them for branding and cutting, and enjoying the magnificent scenery in The Meadows.

Jack's five mile ride into Skelton was interrupted at about mile two by two riders waving him down. He reined up and turned to meet them. "Miss Thompson, what a pleasant surprise. Out to see your property?"

"Mr. Slater, this is a pleasure," she smiled, pulling her horse up. "This is Clarence Holloway, the man I'm buying property from. Clarence, meet Jack Slater, just bought the Fairley place."

"Heard good things about you, Slater. Good to meet you," Holloway said, shaking hands with Jack. "Don't really want to sell my place, but my daughter lives in San Francisco and is seriously ill and I'm the only family she has."

"Sorry to hear that, sir." Jack turned to Melissa Thompson. "Did the banker get your problem straightened out?"

"I hope so. It seems that someone was spreading a rumor that my line of credit was inadequate. My father is superintendent of two major mines in Virginia City, we have property in that new town called Reno, and a large investment in railroads in Nevada. Whoever started that rumor may find themselves in court when I'm through with them."

"I know you don't believe me, Melissa," Holloway said, "but I'm still sure that Sheriff Simpson is behind all this. We better keep moving. We'll be in Elko in time to file the deeds in your name and celebrate with some fine wine at supper. Goodbye, Mr. Slater."

"Keep me informed on how things go in Elko," Jack said to Thompson. "Mr. Holloway may just be right about the sheriff." They rode together the last half mile or so into Skelton, Jack saying goodbye when then reached Valley Paddock's store. "Have a safe trip," Jack said.

"I saw that nice herd you brought through, Jack. Very nice," Paddock said when Jack walked in. "I guess you heard about the mine payroll robbery and killing. Those boys at the Hamilton are still waiting for that fool sheriff to show up. This is bad business, Jack. Four men stopped the wagon, killed the driver and two guards, took the payroll and disappeared, and nobody's seen the sheriff within ten miles of the scene."

"That's one of the reasons I came to town, Valley," Jack said. "When you opened the post office and gave the town the name, did you make this a real town, or is it just a village in the county?

"The reason I'm asking is this. There needs to be some kind of organization to keep the peace, to make the rules the town would live by, and to bring some pride to the community. Is there such a group?"

"No, there isn't, and you're right, there should be. Skelton is not organized as a town, so most of our laws and rules come from the County Commission and the State of Nevada. We are authorized to form a town council and work through the county commission, but we haven't done so. The commission would authorize a budget for the council.

"Law enforcement is supposed to be provided by the county sheriff, but as you've seen, it isn't being done. We are authorized to hire a town marshal, and that would be part of the town council budget. We haven't done that either." Paddock was not a happy man, standing behind his counter, his face drawn, and his normally laughing eyes weren't dancing.

"I would suggest, sir, that you call a town meeting, including us outlying ranchers, and create this Skelton Town Board, and discuss a town marshal position. For a man like Clint Bayliss to pull a knife on a man and not get challenged by an officer of the law, is wrong, and you've told me that there is an outlaw presence in Skelton."

Paddock motioned to one of his boys to watch the store, and said that it might be time for a cold beer at Jose Torre's little saloon. "I knew I was right in bringing you here, Jack," he said, walking out onto the main street. "A town board, a town marshal, and a little pride in our community," he murmured, "and maybe an end to some of this lawlessness. Good thinking, Jack."

By the time Jack headed back to his ranch, Paddock was busy going door to door in Skelton, getting the word out that there would be a town meeting at the blacksmith shop two days from now. He even hand printed some flyers and had his boys post them around the little village. Later that night, Joe Temple was seen riding out of town after ripping one of the posters from a fence post.

29

Jack and Cactus Jack rode into Skelton several hours before the big town meeting was scheduled, paid a visit to the blacksmith shop, to say hello to Jesse Winthrop, then over to Paddock's store, and finally had a cold beer with Jose before settling in at a table at the Skelton Inn, a tiny restaurant/ hotel run by a large, effervescent woman named Irene. The lady stood as tall as Jack's six four, weighed more than Jack's two twenty five, and had a contagious laugh that could be heard in Eureka on a good day.

"You boys need some good solid food in you before this meeting tonight," she said, getting them settled with coffee and menus. "Sandra killed a wonderful kid goat this morning and it's turning on the spit now, and with my Mexican beans, you'll be ready for whatever happens later."

"You're going to be there, Irene?" Jack asked nodding yes to roasted leg of goat for supper. "This meeting affects everyone in the valley."

"Nobody wants to hear what I have to say," she said, heading into the kitchen. "You just keep pushing, Jack. Those bums, Lefty Roberts and Sonny Primm need to be run out of town, and Bayliss needs to be hung."

Slater and his hand, Cactus Jack ate quickly, and as they were getting ready to head over to the blacksmith's large barn for the meeting, Irene said, "That Clint Bayliss has been spending a lot of money the last few days. For a man that can't hold a job, he seems to have quite a stash of gold coins. Isn't that interesting, Jack?" she said, that long sly grin spreading across her broad face. She gave him a wink as he headed out the door.

"Most interesting," Jack said, tucking the information into his brain. Jack was putting a lot of things together, and they added up to trouble. The banker, Feemster, and his big mouth told Jack about the mine payroll, even when it was leaving Elko. "If he told me," Jack said to Cactus, "how many other people did he tell?" The Elko County Sheriff, Cyrus Simpson, wanted to own lots of property in The Meadows but doesn't assign a deputy to the area. "Is that why

Melissa Thompson was having difficulty with her property sale? What is the sheriff's game?"

Jack's mind continued rambling at a high lope. Irene told him about Clint Bayliss spending lots of money even though the fool couldn't keep a job. "If you robbed a payroll, would you start spending that money wildly?" he asked Cactus Jack.

"I don't know yet how I'm going to prove it, but I'd be willing to bet that Bayliss was behind that mine payroll robbery. This meeting might get very interesting, Cactus Jack, my friend," he said as they walked into a packed barn. "Looks like at least fifty people," he said, wending his way toward where Paddock was seated, near the front.

Chairs and benches were set up in a semicircle, almost in a horseshoe pattern, and just about every space was filled when Valley Paddock rose and turned to the audience. "For most of us," he began, "this is the first time that we have all been together, and I'm certainly glad that so many of us have turned out for this important gathering. Our little community, the town with so many names," and there was genuine laughter at that, "has many problems and those that want to run Elko County don't give a hoot about us."

That generated a lot of talk, some of it angry, and Paddock continued. "We have an ugly element living in Skelton, and the sheriff doesn't care. We have what seems to be fraud in some land transactions and the county attorney doesn't care. Well, I for one, care," Paddock thundered, and there was howling approval from the men in attendance. It took considerable time for order to be restored, and Paddock continued.

"Most of you have had a chance to meet one of our newest citizens, Jack Slater, and young as this man is, he is about the smartest man I've ever met. Jack, stand up and say hello."

Jack had never been introduced to any gathering anywhere, ever, and he felt the heat rise, knew his face was as red as a stormy sunrise. He slowly got to his feet, looked around the room at smiling and interested faces, waved gently, and sat back down, scowling some at a smiling Valley Paddock. "Slater is one of the reasons we're here tonight," Paddock said.

"We need to be organized as a community, he said to me one day recently. Slater said, we need to take our problems into our own hands, create a real town of Skelton, elect a town board, create a budget, hire a town marshal, and clean up our own front yard." Again, there was boisterous agreement among the men, and Paddock continued. "I have here, a list of men that own property in the area and that either have businesses or live inside our community.

"I want you to make sure your name is on this list, and if not, I'll add it. This will be the Skelton voting register, and tonight, I think we need to nominate people to run for what will be a five-seat town board, and we'll have a general election in two weeks. I want to be the first to nominate," he said, and then with a sly smile, "I want to nominate Jack Slater to the board."

Jack sat bolt upright when Paddock said that, started to argue, but heard the approval from the crowd and quietly nodded his okay to Valley. *That was a dirty trick, Valley Paddock,* he thought, but at the same time had to admit to himself that he did want to be on that town board. *This is my home and I need to help make it the kind of home I will be proud to call home.*

Within half an hour Paddock had nine men nominated to run for the five seats. "In two weeks, we'll have the election, and the five top vote getters will be the first Skelton Town Board."

A man way in the back of the barn stood

up, waving his hand. "How much of this is actually legal, Paddock? Is it like our community? It's been called The Meadows, Dry Creek, Mound Valley, even Cottonwood, now, you're the postmaster and you named it Skelton. Will the Elko County Board of Commissioners just chuckle some and ignore us, or is what we just did real?"

"It's very real, Mr. Jefferson," Paddock said. "Nevada state law calls for each county to be able to establish communities. Skelton won't be a city, yet," he snickered along with some friendly jeers, "but we can be organized as a community and the county commission can accept us and give us a limited budget. After all, most of us do pay our taxes," and there were guffaws a plenty at that.

"With that budget we can clean up our streets, and most importantly, hire a town marshal. The recent robbery of the mine payroll and murder of the wagon driver and the two guards should be evidence of our need."

The meeting broke up and Slater, Farraday, and Paddock found themselves at Jose's little saloon, along with several of the town's businessmen. "That went far better than I thought it might," the blacksmith said, settling into a chair at one of the tables. "I would have guessed that Bayliss or one of his outlaw friends would have been there to break up the meeting."

As if he worked off a script, Clint Bayliss and Lefty Roberts walked into Jose's saloon, stopping cold when they saw the group that was there. "Look at this, Lefty, it's the do-gooders society, gonna make Skelton a fine family town," Bayliss sneered.

"Don't start trouble in my saloon, again, Bayliss," Jose snarled, making sure his ten guage shotgun was under the bar.

"I'll do anything I want, Mex. Ain't nobody here tell me what to do or when to do it. That goes for you, Slater. Your days are numbered in this town, and your little meeting ain't gonna change anything I do."

Jack was sitting at one of the tables, a schooner of cold beer in front of him, wondering how he was going to prove that Bayliss was part of the payroll robbery. He contemplated just issuing a challenge, and then he remembered Irene's comments of how much money Bayliss was spending.

"Understand you been flashing some of that payroll gold, Bayliss. Sheriff Simpson isn't gonna protect you from an open murder charge. There," Jack mumbled to Cactus Jack, "it's out in the open now, for everyone to talk about; Bayliss and the rob-

343

bery, Simpson and his plans in Skelton and the valley." Slater racked back in the old cane chair, glowering at Bayliss, challenging him, threatening him.

"I think you're out of line, cowboy," Lefty Roberts said. "Mr. Bayliss is an upstanding citizen of Elko County and you just showed the man no respect."

"Yup," Slater said, still lounging back in his cane chair, but his eyes were needle points, burning holes in both men. "I got no respect for criminals, Lefty, whether they pull knives on a man, rob the mine's payroll, or kill other men."

Jack Slater had never had a chew in his mouth, only smoked one cigar, and that was years ago, but he took this opportunity to give the impression he needed to spit some chew, and aimed a perfect gob on what looked like brand new boots worn by Bayliss. "There's your respect, Bayliss," he said with a cranky smile spread across his broad face.

Bayliss jumped back, bumping the bar hard, spilling a couple of drinks. "You just bought me a fresh beer, Bayliss," Jesse Winthrop said. He had moved to the bar when Roberts and Bayliss came in. "Don't much care for people spilling my beer," the stocky man said with a sneer. "Set me up, Jose, and charge that fool there."

Bayliss's anger boiled over and he took a big step toward the blacksmith and took a fist to the middle of the forehead from an arm and shoulder that spends hours every day pounding steel with four-pound hammers. The force of the straight from the shoulder punch flung the outlaw right out the open door and into the dirt of the main street. There was no attempt to get up.

"Better go pick up your stupid friend, Lefty," Slater said. "He's gonna need help getting back to whatever sewer you boys live in." Jack's mind went into high gear when he said that. *I'll bet they haven't even thought about hiding that money. I wonder if I can get Lefty to mouth off about where it might be.* A smile slowly crept across Jack Slater's broad face.

"You filthy scum do share a cabin, don't you? Where's your third man, Sonny Primm? He in the cabin counting gold coins?" Slater could see the anger building in Robert's face, and just sneered at the man.

Lefty Roberts reached inside his jacket and came out with a little gambler's single shot pistol and started to aim it at Jack, but before he could get it cocked and leveled, Jack lunged forward and with his body,

345

drove the outlaw into the bar, knocking all the drinks over. He wrenched the little gun from Lefty's hand and slammed it across the man's face, ripping flesh away as he did so.

"You cowardly fool," Jack said, softly. He tossed the derringer to Cactus Jack, and drove his massive right fist, then his left fist, over and over into the man's head. Cactus Jack Farraday leaped to his feet and pulled Slater off Roberts, backed him up, calmed him down.

"Easy boss, don't want to kill the man." Jack was standing, every inch of his six-four shaking with anger, picked the little gambler's pistol off the table and handed the weapon to Jose. "Add this to your collection, amigo," he said, forcing a smile.

Paddock and Winthrop had Roberts up off the floor and slumped in a chair, trying to stop the bleeding from serious face wounds. "Not nice to pull a gun on an unarmed man, Lefty," Paddock said. "Where's the payroll money from the mine? We know it was you and Bayliss did the robbing and murdering. Where you got the money, that is, whatever is left from Bayliss spending so much?"

"Cabin," is all he said, and Paddock nodded to Jack.

Slater, Cactus Jack, and Jesse Winthrop walked out into the street, hustled Bayliss to his feet, groggy still from Wintrhop's punch, and marched to Bayliss's cabin, that was shared by Roberts, Bayliss, and Sonny Primm when he was in town. Winthrop kicked the door in and flung Bayliss inside. In less than ten minutes, most of the gold coin from the payroll robbery was sitting on the bar at Jose's saloon, being counted by Valley Paddock.

Winthrop got one of the young men who had been at the meeting to ride like the wind to the mine and alert them that their money was safe. He found another man and sent him to Elko. "It's important that Sheriff Simpson get the word that we have the money and the killers, but it's even more important that the folks in Elko know that we caught them, not the sheriff. You spread the word as soon as you get there."

"Tell the banker," Slater chuckled. "That way the whole county will know.

30

Representatives from the Hamilton Mine were in Skelton the next day to lay claim to the payroll money, and it wasn't until two days later that Elko County Sheriff Cyrus Simpson rode into town, supported by two deputies. There were harsh words spoken by Simpson and equally strong words spit right back at the arrogant sheriff during his short visit.

Simpson was a barrel of a man, with a bull's neck, large, deep chest that narrowed down to thick hips and legs that were short and equally thick. Slater's first thought was something about not wanting to get physical with the man. The top of his head was flat as a table and his chin and jaw were perfectly square, and the sheriff looked at the world through squinty little pig eyes buried under fly away brows.

Simpson didn't wear facial hair, wore his hair long in an ill-kept manner. *It's as if he wants to appear as ugly and mean as possible,* Jack thought, watching him approach the barn. *This man believes in intimidation and threats, and is willing to carry out the threats at a moment's notice.* Slater was quick to tell himself to be ready for anything that might happen from flashing fists to flying bullets.

The day following the meeting in town, Slater sent Cactus Jack back to the ranch, telling him, "I don't want to miss this opportunity to go face to face with this Simpson, I'll be home quick as I can." The fact that the sheriff didn't bother to hightail it to Skelton as soon as the bandits were captured, bothered, confused, and worried him. *What kind of a sheriff isn't interested in bringing captured outlaws to jail? On the other hand, why are these outlaws not particularly surprised that the sheriff wasn't right here to grab them the next morning?*

When Simpson and his deputies rode into town, Paddock, Slater, and Jefferson were in the blacksmith shop talking with Jesse Winthrop. "Welcome to Skelton, Sheriff," Paddock said, almost mocking the man. "Here to pick up your prisoners?"

"You beat a confession out of an innocent man, Paddock. I ought to arrest you," Sheriff Simpson said.

"Yup," Jack Slater said, "and after we whupped on those poor innocent little boys we went out and manufactured several thousand dollars of gold coins and hid them in their pristine little cabin. Those of us responsible for solving the crime, that is, Valley Paddock, Jesse Winthrop, and I, Jack Slater, have written reports on our efforts and they are in the hands of the district attorney, along with copies to the newspaper and to each member of the county commission.

"Just in case, you understand, that there might be some shenanigans planned for the outlaws. Here in Skelton, we like to do things right."

Paddock was standing off to the side just a bit and was positive that Sheriff Simpson was going to pull his weapon and shoot Slater on the spot. Everyone in the barn could see the anger and frustration build in the sheriff and wondered how many would die in the next couple of minutes. Many empty hands quietly moved toward weapons, but very slowly.

Simpson took a full minute to look each man in the eye, one at a time, wondering just how far they would go, how far he could go, and finally just nodded, and walked back to his horse. "Have those men at the courthouse tomorrow morning, Paddock. Alive," he said, spurring his horse, not even looking back, his deputies running for their horses.

"Man won't even take his own prisoners to jail," Winthrop laughed, watching the dust fly. "I'll have a wagon and team hitched at sunrise, Valley, and we will need an armed escort to get these men to town. Who wants to ride with me?"

"Jack, I'm not sure you should be part of the escort. You just embarrassed the sheriff something fierce and he will try to return the favor, probably by way of a Winchester." That brought a couple of chuckles, but everyone agreed with what Paddock said, and it was determined that Paddock and Jefferson would ride escort and Winthrop would drive the wagon.

"As much as I want to go with you, I agree that it wouldn't be wise," Jack said. "I'm sure I'm needed at the ranch, so I'll leave everything to your capable hands. Don't hurt the little darlings," he snickered, walking out of the barn to find his horse.

On the ride back to the ranch, Slater once again ran into Clarence Holloway. "Nice to see you again," Holloway said as they pulled their horses up. "Looks like I made my deal with Miss Thompson. I just left your place and Mr. Farraday said you were still in town. I wanted to tell you there was another piece of property for sale, right along your western line. This one is a full section."

"That's interesting," Jack said. "Who has it, I might just be interested."

"His name is James Whitcomb, and he owns a hotel in that railroad town near the California border. Reno is its name, and it's growing fast because of the Comstock mines and the capitol, Carson City. Both are accessible from the railroad, and a line south on a line called the Virginia and Truckee Railroad.

"Whitcomb wanted to run cattle on the property here, but came a cropper with the sheriff, and built in Reno. He can't sell the land because the sheriff denies anyone that tries to buy it any kind of line of credit."

"That sheriff thinks he owns this county," Jack spat out. "I don't need a line of credit, Mr. Holloway, and I would like to have my hands on that land. Do you have the particulars on how to reach Whitcomb?"

"Indeed I do, Mr. Slater," Holloway said, and the two rode back to Slater's ranch. Cactus Jack helped them get their horses settled, gave Jack a quick summary of the last couple of days, and the three went into the ranch house.

"I was expecting you yesterday, Jack," Farraday said, "so I've had the fires going good. Spring is just a bit late this year. You gents get comfortable and I'll get a pot of coffee boiling right up."

"Now that I have my papers in order, I'm going into Elko tomorrow," Holloway said. "I need to move quite a bit of stuff off the place, as you can imagine."

"I wasn't going to Elko," Jack said, "but I think I'll ride in with you. The sooner this Whitcomb feller knows I want his land, the better. Do me a favor, Mr. Holloway, please don't tell anyone about this. That sheriff has ears in every corner of this county."

"You better put some slack in that quirt you're cracking, Cyrus," Joseph P. Rogers said as Sheriff Simpson bolted into the district attorney's office in the Elko County Courthouse. "People in the county are starting to get upset with your bluster and swagger. You're mighty close to breaking the law yourself, and this last bit of stupidity with known outlaws might get you thrown right out of office."

"Bayliss and Roberts are in jail, the money has been returned, and you'll get your guilty verdict, Joe, but I'll tell you right now, those upstarts in Skelton will learn respect, and that young Mr. Slater will learn how to show respect to this lawman."

"That's exactly what I'm talking about, Cyrus. It's Bayliss and Roberts that broke the law, not Paddock and Slater. People don't bow to the Sheriff of Elko as they did to the Sheriff of Nottingham," the district attorney said, laughing as he said it, watching Simpson's face turn ugly and mean.

"Don't you get smart with me, too," Simpson said, slamming the large, heavy door as he stomped out of the office. He could hear Rogers' laughter all the way to the front steps of the stone courthouse. He stormed down the street to the Elko Bank and demanded to see Aaron Feemster immediately.

Feemster stepped out of his office, and with a smile, ushered Simpson inside. "What can I do for you, today, Sheriff?" he said, offering a chair and stepping behind his large desk. Sheriff Simpson terrified the banker, intimidated the meek man as often as he could, and Feemster knew today would be another in a long line of bad days. "Are you angry at me, sir? You certainly look angry."

"I don't want another piece of property in The Meadows or anywhere within twenty miles of Skelton sold, do you understand that? There is to be no lines of credit offered for a single piece of property."

"It's very unusual, Sheriff, and I don't believe it's legal for me to withhold lines of credit from those who qualify. You're asking me to break the law."

"No, Feemster, I'm demanding you withhold all property sales in Skelton and The Meadows, and don't forget the little problems you've had with some of our younger ladies in town. It wouldn't be right for those in the county to know some of those indiscretions, now, would it?"

Simpson swaggered out of the bank, a satisfied smile spread across that block of skin and bone he calls a head. Feemster was still sitting behind his desk, shaking as if he were suffering a massive fever, tears running down his face, fearful for his life. There was a gentle knock on the manager's door, and the chief clerk stepped into the office.

"I have a message from Mr. Vierra, sir. The bank's board of directors has called for a meeting this evening in the hotel and requests your presence. They wish to meet at eight o'clock, sir."

Feemster didn't look up, didn't want anyone to see his tear-stained face, see his red eyes, or see the fear deep in them. "I'll be there," is all he said, and waved the clerk off. *Maybe the sheriff already told them,* he whimpered, reaching to open the drawer, lowest to the right. He had his fingers wrapped around the polished handle of a Colt Army revolver, letting his fingers feel the warmth of the fine grained wood, feeling the heft of the fully loaded weapon, and slowly drew it from the drawer, letting it lie across the equally fine wood grain of his desk.

It was seven thirty that evening when patrons of the Drovers' Hotel heard a muffled shot, seemingly to come from the closed and darkened Elko Bank. Ted Wilson had just entered the hotel saloon, heard the shot and quickly walked down the main street to the bank. Several people were already there, speaking in hushed voices as Wilson arrived.

"Somebody get a deputy," Wilson said. He tried the front doors and found them locked solid when Bill Vierra sprinted onto the board walkway.

"What happened?" Vierra asked, almost out of breath.

"Sounded like a shot, inside," Wilson said. "As president of the board, do you have keys to the bank? These doors are locked solid."

Vierra produced a ring of keys, found the

one he needed, and opened the front doors to the bank just as Sheriff Cyrus Simpson rode up on his horse. "What's going on here?" he demanded. "What do you think you're doing, Vierra. Get away from that door," and he pushed the man aside.

"Hold on, Simpson," Wilson snarled, stepping in front of the burly sheriff. "Mr. Vierra is chairman of the board of this bank, I'm a member of the board, and we believe there has been a gunshot inside the bank. Don't be pushing people around, Sheriff, when you don't know what's going on." Wilson's anger was up, and he was not intimidated by Simpson, nor was he afraid of the man.

Bill Vierra stepped around Wilson and took a step inside the darkened and ornate lobby. "Looks like Feemster's office door is opened, Ted," he whispered. Looking at Simpson, he said, "We were to meet with Mr. Feemster in just a few minutes. Maybe you should go in first."

It was Wilson who stepped into the lobby and strode to the bank manager's office, not waiting for the sheriff. He found Feemster on the floor, half his head blown off and the Colt on the floor near his body. He also found a letter addressed to the board of directors, sealed in a large envelope. *Probably his letter of resignation,* Wilson thought, handing the envelope to Vierra.

It was a deputy's arrival that finally got things in order. "Let's clear the area," he said. "Sheriff, let's get some lamps lit, get those doors closed. Everyone out, please, and let us do our work." Even the sheriff walked out on the street, closing the big doors. Vierra and Wilson walked to the hotel for the meeting with the other three board members.

"This won't be pleasant," Vierra said.

"Wasn't going to be, anyway," Wilson said.

31

"That's an amazing story, Mr. Wilson," Jack Slater said. "You and the board planned to ask for Feemster's resignation, but it was because of some black mail threats from the sheriff that caused the man to kill himself. That's an amazing thing, and I hope it causes the sheriff to quit his job."

"Don't know about that, Jack. We made a copy of Feemster's letter to us and gave it to Joe Rogers. The sheriff is an elected office, so he can't actually be fired. He can resign, yes, but it would take a recall election to remove him." Wilson sat back, almost a satisfied smile playing on his face. "Of course, if the DA were to file criminal charges, that would force him out of office if he were to be found guilty."

"Any indication of that? Simpson threatened Paddock, Winthrop, and me with arrest when he came for the prisoners. He was so angry he rode off without the prisoners."

Wilson guffawed, almost spilling his coffee. "I heard rumors to that effect, but I really didn't believe them," he laughed. "Right now is a dangerous time, I'm afraid, for many of us who have opposed that fool. What brought you to town?"

"Two things, Mr. Wilson."

"Call me Ted, Jack. Makes me feel old with all that mister stuff. I'm sorry, go on."

Jack had a wry, slight smile when he asked, "What will I have to do to keep Cactus Jack Farraday on my payroll instead of yours? And, I got a handle on a section of land adjacent to mine that's available. A man in Reno owns it and has had considerable trouble selling because of interference from Simpson."

"So, I loan you one of my best buckaroos and now you turn on me, eh?" Wilson laughed, taking a friendly poke at Slater. "Gonna make that man ranch manager?"

"Yup, giving that some heavy thought."

"Just keep it in mind what I'm doing should I come to you with a problem some time or another, Jack. He's one of the best with cattle, water, and maintaining good grass. You'd have a hard time doing better." Jack's smile spread across his face as he nodded in full agreement with Wilson.

"If I were you, I wouldn't tell anyone

about that land until it's a done deal. You know Simpson will be on the warpath like a Sioux after Custer. How you gonna go about making the deal?"

"I sent the man an offer by wire and had plans to make the money transfer with Feemster. Looks like I'll have to make some other plan."

"No, you'll be fine with that plan. Bill Vierra is going to take over the manager's position until we can hire someone, and he won't take any nonsense from Simpson. I'm wondering if a quick trip to Reno might be a better way to go. Have Bill transfer funds to a Reno bank in the other man's name.

"You could come back with a signed bill of sale and have the deed transferred by the county recorder. Sheriff would never know."

"I'll give that some thought," Jack said. The two large men left the café, walking into some bright late spring sunshine and warmth. *This will make the grass grow,* Jack thought, and headed to the bank to have a talk with Bill Vierra.

Jack Slater was thinking of all the places he's been and all the people he's met. It seemed that everywhere he's been, from the day he was orphaned, there was trouble of some kind. He remembered the terrible days and nights, alone on the streets on

New York, until that copper grabbed him and turned him over to the Children's Aid Society. *Those were some incredibly nice people. I should write to Maybelle and let her know how things are, here in Nevada.*

His thoughts drifted to Fargo and the time spent on Jablonski's farm, what a miserable man he was, but how delightful Mims was, and that brought memories of the long train ride half way across this vast country, and his friendship with Ephraim Clairidge. *What a wonderful day it would be to sit across a table with that old man and talk about life, people we've known, and places we've been.* He remembered that the letter Ephraim wrote to him was still in his desk at the ranch.

Memories of Seth Bullock and Hiram Biggins in Deadwood, and Henry Rupert at the Wyoming ranch were set aside as thoughts of Oak Blossom, Evangelina, Evie flooded his mind, and as he neared the bank, he found he was almost crying. *Besides my parents,* he thought, *losing Evie was the biggest loss of my life.*

He walked into the Bank of Elko feeling sad on the one hand, and almost fulfilled with how his life was, flowing through his mind. He was greeted immediately by the chief clerk. "Mr. Vierra was hoping you would stop in. He's in his office," the clerk said, walking Jack to the door.

"Thank you," Jack said, and walked into Vierra's office.

"I'm glad you're here, Jack, there are a couple of things we need to talk about. I believe Mr. Feemster's mouth may have led the sheriff to take a look through your files here. I want you to look at what's in them and make sure there haven't been any changes made by that fool.

"And, Joe Rogers was in and said that if you should happen by, that he would like to have a talk with you. You've become quite a topic of conversation around Elko, my boy," Vierra said with a broad smile. "That report that you and Paddock sent to Rogers, the county commission, and the newspaper have stirred things up nicely."

"I wouldn't walk down the street with me, if I were you," Jack smiled. "Simpson might not hit me with his first shot. I haven't been in the county long enough to fully understand how he became so powerful, but I would guess through things like the black mail situation with Feemster. That man didn't have to die, Mr. Vierra. Lose his job, yes, but die, no."

Jack took just a short look at the file that Feemster had on his resources, and told Vierra that everything seemed to be in order. "I wonder how much of this information will be used in some way to hamper my ranching operations. As far as I can tell, nothing has been changed, altered, or deleted.

"I'm glad of that, too," he said. "I've found a piece of land adjacent to my place in The Meadows and have made an offer on it. If it is accepted, would you be able to transfer money from my account to one in Reno?"

"Absolutely, Jack. Because of the current situation with the sheriff, I assume you would want this to be held close to the chest." Both men had slight grins on their faces after that comment, remembering Feemster's big mouth. Jack thanked the banker and planned to find the district attorney right after a hearty meal at The Drover's Hotel.

"So, I finally get to meet the man called Jack Slater," Joe Rogers said, ushering Jack into his rather grand office in the county courthouse. "That was quite a report you and Valley Paddock sent. Sit down and tell me all about what went on in Skelton."

Jack was surprised by the warm, friendly reception, turned down an offer of a cigar, took a seat in a large leather chair. Rogers' office was a bit Spartan, consisting of a large desk, simple in design, two leather chairs, and some mundane bookshelves. *I'm not sure what I was anticipating, but this isin't it.*

Rogers was a slim man, well dressed with what Jack thought having a chiseled look to his face. His dark eyes were set deep in his face and his thin nose protruded just a bit. Rogers wore his hair combed straight back, and it showed a few strands of gray at the temples.

Jack spent the next fifteen minutes outlining what the situation was in Skelton when he arrived, his skirmish with Bayliss, and the call for a town meeting. "What's in the report is what happened after the town meeting. Bayliss and Lefty Roberts are very dangerous men, and both of them have pulled weapons on me, and others in our little community.

"It has bothered me since I bought my place and moved into that area that with a known outlaw presence, the sheriff never appointed a deputy for the district, and he completely ignored the payroll robbery and the murders of three men. It was all of that that led to our deciding to create a town board and hire a town marshal."

"I think it's the best thing you people

down there could have done. Of course, Sheriff Simpson will be completely against the idea and will do everything he can to keep the county commission from okaying the plan.

"I notice you're carrying a weapon, Mr. Slater. That's a good idea, considering the current atmosphere."

"Paddock and everyone in Skelton are now carrying, all the time. Is there anything else we need to do to make our plans for the community as legal as possible?"

"No, I don't think so." He sat back, gazing first at Jack, then the ceiling. "Maybe hire an attorney to draw up that town board plan to be offered to the commission. As district attorney, I would be able to assist in that, and that might add a little legal weight to the process. Other than that, all I would suggest is that you, Jack Slater, be ready to protect yourself at every moment of the day."

Jack left the office feeling much better than when he rode into town, and headed back to the hotel to write some letters, then check to see if there had been any response to his wire about the new property. *Another six hundred and forty acres added to my place and I will be able to grow winter forage and build a fine herd. I will need to visit Diamond*

Valley and buy some heifers from those fine ranches.

"You, Slater," a gruff voice said from behind as Jack walked along Commercial Street. "I been lookin' for you."

Jack turned to face a tall, thin man sporting a thin moustache and wearing a brown three-piece suit, string tie, and a derby type hat covering long stringy hair. Jack's first thought was, the man was a gambler, but didn't know why a gambler would be looking for him.

"Something I can do for you?" Jack said, remembering the district attorney's words. Jack's legs were set slightly apart, his arms hung loose and at the ready, and he wasn't wearing a smile.

"You busted up Clint Bayliss, a good friend of mine," the gambling man said, "and I don't take kindly to boys whuppin' on my friends." Aggressive in his stance and angry in his voice, he emphasized the word 'boys' with a sneer.

"Bayliss pulled a knife on me," Jack said. "You gonna be stupid, too? I don't much care for stupid people pullin' weapons on me. What's your name so I can make sure the authorities know it when they find your bloody body."

"My name's Joe Temple and you're a dead man," the gambler snarled, pulling what looked like the same type of derringer that Lefty Roberts had. Jack took a long step forward and kicked Temple's gun hand so hard, the little weapon bounced off the overhand of the store they were standing in front of. Temple's mouth opened in surprise and was filled with a massive fist that sent him flying into the street's dust.

Slater stepped into the street, picked the skinny gambler up, and drove another fist into his stomach, and followed that with an uppercut that sent him sprawling in the dirt, face first. "You ever pull a gun on me again and you'll be wearing lead with those fancy duds, Temple." Jack walked up on the porch and through a small crowd that had stopped to watch the action. One of the men handed Jack the little weapon and Jack noticed that it wasn't even cocked. He tucked it into his jacket pocket, smiling a thank you at the man.

"That fool's been lookin' for a beatin' like that for some time," the man said. "Shame you didn't finish him off."

"Don't like to shoot fools," Jack said with a smile, nodded, and walked on toward the hotel and a cold beer. "Well, that's the four of them," he muttered. "We put Bayliss,

Roberts, and Primm in jail, and now along comes Temple. Simpson's four horsemen don't make the grade," he chuckled at his own little joke, wending his way to the bar.

32

On his way to the telegraph office the next morning, Jack found Jeremy Hazelton sweeping the boardwalk in front of his hardware store. "Good morning, Jack," he said, "Did all your merchandise arrive at your ranch in good order?"

"It did, indeed, sir," Jack said, tipping his hat. "I will probably be ordering a few more things soon. It's a pleasure doing business with you." He actually sauntered down the long street toward the rail yards and the telegraph office, enjoying the bright early morning sunshine, and contemplating the expansion of his ranch.

The wire was short and to the point. "Offer accepted. Arrive Elko Saturday train. Regards. Whitcomb." That meant that Whitcomb was already on the eastbound train, since the wire was sent last night, and he would arrive in Elko tomorrow morning. "Splendid," Jack said, walking back toward the hotel. *I think I'm going to want Ted Wilson and Bill Vierra present when we sign the deed papers. Simpson is sure to try something to keep me from the purchase.*

The ride out to Wilson's ranch was pleasant, in the late spring warmth. Jack rode through rolling hills covered in grass and brush, and interspersed with flowing creeks meandering their way to the Humboldt River, filled with spring runoff. He met Slim Hendricks and a couple of Wilson's buckaroos on the trail.

"You lookin' to steal some more of our hands?" Hendricks joked. "Jackson, here," and he nodded to one of the riders, "rode into town in time to see you knock the stuffing out of some gambler yesterday. Was he part of the problem you people were facing in Skelton?"

"Sure was," Jack smiled. "Not looking for more hands, at least not yet," Jack joked back at Slim, "but I do need to talk with Ted. He at the home ranch?"

"Sure is. We'll ride in with you. That was kind of sad, about Mr. Feemster. That sheriff needs to go, Jack. We need an honest man to be sheriff."

"They seem to be few and far between around here, Slim." They rode in silence the last few miles to the home ranch. Ted

Wilson was in the kitchen with a cup of hot coffee when they walked in.

"Good to see you, Jack. So, now they tell me, you're a street fighter," he chuckled, pouring coffee for the both of them. "Was that set up by Simpson?"

"Primm was part of the little outlaw group there in Skelton, so it is possible. Bayliss and his buddies seem to be sheltered somewhat by the sheriff, and when I explained what I thought I was seeing to Joe Rogers, he didn't seem surprised."

Jack went on to tell Wilson about the return wire from Whitcomb and said he would very much like Wilson and Vierra to be witnesses when the deed was signed and the money transferred.

"Splendid idea, Jack. I know Bill will be in favor, too. The morning eastbound should be in Elko by nine or so. Let's meet at the bank at ten. While we're on the subject, have you even seen Simpson in the last two days?"

"Near as I can tell, no one has," Jack said. "Both Bill Vierra and Joe Rogers have told me to be prepared for anything, you did, too," he quipped, "and the most I've seen is a stupid gambler who pulled a gun and didn't even cock the hammer. Simpson isn't the kind of man who is going to run away from his problems. He's surely planning to attack me or the men in Skelton. It's just a matter of when and how."

Jack fought it briefly when Wilson demanded that Slim Hendricks ride back to town with Jack, and then arriving there, Hendricks took a room at the Drover's. "You need the company, Jack," is all Slim said as the two settled into chairs at a table in the saloon for cold beer. Slim and Jack spent the rest of the day rambling around town, looking at new saddles, checking out fancy dress suits and classy hat wear, ending up at the Drover's café for supper. At no time did they notice anyone following or paying any attention to them.

Jack was sitting on the edge of his bed, ready for a good night's sleep and wondering just when the sheriff would make his move. *The man was insulted, embarrassed, and made to look like a fool and isn't the type to just shrink from the problem. So, Mr. Sheriff Simpson, when are you going to strike back?*

Jack sat bolt upright about three o'clock in the morning with just one thought screaming through his head. "The ranch." *I'm in Elko, only Cactus Jack Farraday is at the ranch, and Simpson knows that.* He slammed his fist into the mattress, knowing there wasn't one single thing he could do about it. *I have to be here to meet with Whit-comb and I can't even get a message to Cactus or to Paddock.*

Cactus Jack Farraday rode in from the western range after helping more than a dozen heifers with their first-born. "Jack bought some good stock from Wilson," he was muttering to himself, coming into the main ranch at a gentle lope. He noticed a couple of riders near the house as he crossed the little creek a few hundred yards away, and picked up the pace some.

"Help you boys with something?" he said, letting his right hand hover near his Colt's familiar handle. He didn't recognize either rider, and noticed that one of them kept glancing off toward the barn area. Farraday stayed mounted, wanted to turn and look where the one rider was looking, but didn't.

"I asked you a question," he said, slipping the revolver from its leather, and pointing it at the men. "You have business here, say it now," he snarled, and was knocked off his horse as a rifle slug tore through his arm, up high, near the shoulder. The two men rode toward the main house and that's when Cactus Jack saw that each held unlit torches.

They lit the torches as Jack crawled

through the dirt trying to reach his revolver, and saw one of the men break out a window and toss the torch inside, and other threw his flame onto the roof. Jack knew he was bleeding heavy, and his arm was useless. He was able to find the weapon, and fired one shot before he passed out.

He never saw the third man, the one who shot him, the one who tossed his torch into the stacked hay in the barn, riding out with the other two. He would have recognized Sheriff Cyrus Simpson.

It was a passing rider who spotted the smoke and rode into the ranch and found Cactus Jack, unconscious. Isaac Bradley jumped from his horse and ripped Farraday's shirt apart, using it to stem the heavy blood flow. It took several minutes, and Bradley got some water to clean the wound as much as he could. The house and barn were completely engulfed and he knew he couldn't be any help there.

It was several hours before he could nurse Farraday into Skelton, actually having to tie him to his horse. He raised Valley Paddock, and the two of them got Cactus Jack inside and on a bed. It was just a few minutes and the doctor arrived and began working on the buckaroo.

"The house and barn were burned to the

375

ground, Paddock, and this man was lying in the dirt, bleeding to death when I arrived. I looked for young Slater, but couldn't find him. I hope he wasn't in that house."

"No, he wasn't, thank God," Paddock said. "He's in Elko right now. I'll send one of my boys in to tell him the bad news. Did you see anyone at all, besides Cactus Jack when you were at the ranch?"

"There was no one there, Paddock," Bradley said. "Do you have any idea who would do something like this?"

"I'm afraid I do," Valley Paddock said, feeling the anger build, wondering how Jack Slater would respond to the attack.

The young boy from Paddock's store was banging on Slater's hotel door about seven o'clock, calling Slater's name. Jack had been up all morning after realizing what he feared Simpson would do. The boy was worn out from the hard, late night ride into Elko, and it took a couple of minutes to get him calmed down enough to be understood.

"My ranch is burned to the ground and Cactus Jack was shot?" Jack read the note from Paddock again before putting it down on a table. "Is Mr. Farraday going to make it?" he asked the boy, about twelve years old.

"The doc was working on him when I left. He was talking about men with torches, and said somebody shot him from behind."

Jack took the boy in hand and went downstairs and into the café. "After we have something to eat, I want you to get some sleep, up in my room, then I'm going to send you back to Skelton with a letter to Paddock. Are you up to that?" He couldn't help remembering what he was capable of doing just a few years ago, when he was twelve.

"Yes, sir," the boy snapped back with a wide smile. "I don't really need a nap, sir," he said.

Jack snickered over that all the way through breakfast, and was still smiling when they got back to his room and he wrote a quick note to Valley Paddock. "Get this to Paddock as quick as you can. You say you're twelve, eh?" The boy nodded.

"You know, I don't think I even know your name. Where are your parents?"

"I don't know where my father is," the boy murmured, looking down, studying the dust on his boot tops. "Mama works for Irene at the Skelton Inn. My name is Robbie, sir."

"And you work for Valley Paddock?"

"He tries to get me as much work as he

can, but it only amounts to a couple of days a week. Sometimes I get to do something for Mr. Winthrop at his stables. I'm strong and want to work, but there isn't much in Skelton."

"When I get back to town, you and me and your mama have got to have a little talk. You ever done any ranch work?"

"No, sir, but I know I could learn," he said, just the slightest grin spreading slowly across his young face. Robbie tucked the letter inside his shirt, shook hands with Jack, and was on his way to Skelton.

Kind of reminds me of another young boy I'm familiar with, Jack Slater chuckled, heading out the door. It was a short walk from the hotel to the train station and he was standing on the platform watching for the eastbound train from Reno. *Paddock said my home, barn, even the little bunkhouse, burned to the ground. It had to be the work of Cyrus Simpson, and that man now has the biggest problem of his life. I'm gonna hunt that man down and drive his face into the hard rock Nevada's known for, grind it, pulverize it,* he stormed to himself, standing on the platform, his fists knotted, his eyes blazing.

James Whitcomb looked more like an accountant than a man who owned a section of fine grazing land in Elko County, Jack mused, watching the man collect his one piece of luggage. "What you've just told me, Mr. Slater makes me wonder if you're still of a mind to buy my piece of property."

"Even more so, Mr. Whitcomb. I will not let that man dictate my life. Mr. Vierra is waiting for us at the bank, and I've asked Ted Wilson to be there as a witness to our business."

"I haven't had the pleasure of meeting Vierra, but I do know Wilson. He has fine cattle and runs a good operation. I would have wanted his stock on my ranch if I hadn't let that fool sheriff run me off," Whitcomb said. "I knew I couldn't fight him."

"I'm going to take him down and out, Whitcomb. It sounds, though that you're nicely set up in Reno."

"Hotel business is good. I'm on Commercial Row, close to the train station and a busy business district. There is a tremendous number of people traveling to Carson City and of course, to Virginia City. I'm doing well, Slater, and I'm glad you're able to take this property off my hands and put it to good use."

Vierra and Wilson were waiting as Slater and Whitcomb arrived. "Bad business, Jack. The word has spread through the valley like a summer thunderstorm," Wilson stormed after hands were shaken, pleasantries exchanged, and the men were seated. "Simpson has gone too far, this time. Rogers is livid, in a rage, and has authorized warrants for the sheriff's arrest."

"That means someone has said something, because the letter I got from Valley said that Cactus Jack didn't recognize the two men, and never saw the man who shot him. If Joe Rogers issued arrest warrants, he must know something I don't."

"Your ignorant friend, Clint Bayliss, let it out during a gab-fest in the county jail, apparently. Rogers' guess is, this was a planned attack that was supposed to have followed the payroll robbery, but you fouled it up nabbing Bayliss and friends.

"What are your plans, now?" Wilson asked.

"With you gentlemen as witnesses, I'm going to buy a very nice section of grazing land from Mr. Whitcomb, then I'm going to order the material I'll need for a new home and barn, and then I believe I'm going to help Mr. Rogers catch and destroy one Cyrus Simpson," Jack said, amid laughter and back slapping.

"As big a fool as Simpson is, it shouldn't

be too hard to catch him. I've heard that skunks come to bait."

33

"How's that shoulder today, Cactus? You were groanin' some yesterday," Slater hollered and chuckled from the roof of his new home. The second floor was framed in and the roof beams were in place. Slater was fitting the cedar shakes into place as Robbie Gomez brought them up to him. Cactus Jack Farraday spent ten hours every day splitting shakes, cussing more than a swamp rat with the gout, and wanting desperately to be back in the saddle.

"Every time my shoulder pains me, I'm adding to the tally that I plan to take out of Simpson's hide when we catch him," Farraday hollered back. "Did you have to build such a big house? Ain't that many cedar trees left in the Ruby Mountains, Jack."

"One more day on the roof, Cactus, and you can go back to babysitting those calves. You got full use of that arm?" The rifle slug did considerable damage to the upper arm and shoulder, and left Cactus Jack a little lopsided from missing meat and muscle.

"Workin' a loop the last week or so. Strength is good. I'm fine, boss," Cactus yelled, "just need to get rid of the shakes," he said, laughing at his own joke, getting a questioning look from Robbie.

Jack Slater used hard work to ease the anger, almost hatred, that built rapidly when he returned from Elko and saw the wreckage of his home place. Clearing out the burned wood, furniture, mementos, and all the equipment from the barn and outbuildings took many days, gallons of sweat, and energy that came from the anger.

He brought help with him, some from Skelton, some from Elko, and much of the anger toward Cyrus Simpson was abated by the knowledge that he now owned another six hundred forty acres of fine grazing land, and more water from existing wells, springs, and streams.

Robbie Gomez started work two days after Jack got back from Elko, and the boy took to ranch work like he was born to it. More and more, Jack saw himself in the youngster and felt good about having him on the place. Gomez's mother refused Jack's offer that she come with her boy and be camp cook, preferring to stay with Irene at the café. She was just a wisp of a woman, barely five feet tall and so thin Jack swore he couldn't see a shadow when she walked across the street.

Robbie must have taken after his father, Jack thought, since the boy was rather hefty. At twelve, Robbie stood almost five feet and eight, but weighed a solid one sixty, none of which was fat. In the two weeks since Jack's return, Robbie had learned the art of swinging a hammer, using a saw, and branding and doctoring calves.

Despite all the clean up that had to be done, all the planning and work to get ready to rebuild, the ranch work had to continue, and that meant all hands were doing double duty, keeping the ranch operating, cleaning up from the burn, and preparing to rebuild.

"That boy don't talk much, Jack, but he's quick to learn and ain't afraid of askin' 'bout things. He rides good but don't know nothin' bout ropin' or workin' cattle. That makes my job safe," Cactus Jack laughed, "cuz that means I got to teach him."

"Don't be too hard on him, Cactus. I don't think he's had the best life, so far." *Watching that boy brings so many memories back. Mostly good memories, though,* he smiled, looking around his place.

The new ranch house was a two story affair with a peaked roof to keep the snow from piling up, and a wide veranda that went around the building and provided ample shade for evening 'sittin' and jawin' sessions,' as Cactus Jack called them. Jack had three men from town building the barn and bunkhouse and helping with the main house, the bottom half of which was done and occupied. Cactus Jack had two buckaroos that Jack brought back with him from Elko.

"I didn't steal 'em off Ted Wilson, either," he joked. "I hired 'em fair and square off another ranch," and he and Cactus Jack laughed over that. "When I told them you were the ranch manager, they jumped at the chance to work here, so you got yourself a crew, now."

There was a large kitchen and dining area where Jack and the buckaroos would eat, a living room/office combination, and what Jack called his library, with wall to wall shelves, already partially filled with books he bought in Elko and had shipped in from the east and from San Francisco. The chairs were massive and comfortable, and Jack spent evenings doing what he had loved from childhood.

It was a full six months before any word

came about the missing former Elko County Sheriff Cyrus Simpson. During that time all the buildings on the ranch had been completed, crops were sewn and coming close to harvest, calves had fattened and heifers impregnated, and there were two new buckaroos working the herd.

Jack, with help from Big Irene, as she now liked to be called, had convinced Robbie's mother, Sandra, to be the ranch cook, and she was good. Sandra Gomez brought a small herd of goats and a flock of chickens when she came to the ranch, so fresh milk and cheese were on the table regularly, and eggs came at breakfast, too.

Valley Paddock rode in one day with a letter for Jack. "Looks important, Jack, so I brought it out myself. It's from Joe Rogers."

Jack read the letter, motioned for Cactus Jack to join he and Paddock, and they went into the kitchen. Sandra had coffee for them immediately after they got settled at the table. "Joe Rogers says that Simpson may have been hiding somewhere in Paradise Valley, north of Winnemucca, and may have taken the outlaw's life. He is believed to have robbed a couple of wagons bringing gold from the northern mines, may have been involved in a bank robbery, and may have plans to rob the Elko Bank.

"He doesn't say how he got his information, but I know he's been sending for information every week. He wants me to come to Elko and help him put together a group to find Simpson and bring him in.

"Don't get all nervous on me, Cactus Jack, cuz I'm tellin' you right now, you can't come with me. I need you here, and you know it." Cactus Jack had been squirming around a bit, waiting to say something, and Jack shut him off.

"I know, boss," he said in that long drawn out east Texas way of his, "but I don't want to stay. I will, cuz the ranch needs me, but you better catch that miserable fool, and hit him twice or more for me when you do."

"I plan to put the big whup on him, Cactus, and I'll add some for you," Jack laughed, taking a friendly poke at his ranch manager. "Valley, since we hired Jefferson to be the town marshal, you might want to make sure he knows that Simpson might be out and about these parts. Simpson has a great hate for Skelton, so Jefferson needs to be aware.

"I'll leave first thing in the morning and try my best to keep you all posted. That corn and wheat needs to be taken care of, Cactus, and Robbie, work with your momma to get the home ranch ready for winter. Those snows will be taking aim on us pretty soon." Jack sat back in his chair and looked around the large, warm kitchen, letting a smile slowly cross his face.

"Sandra and Cactus, make a list of things you might need over the next few weeks, and if there's things we can get from Paddock, give that list to him, and I'll have the other stuff sent to you from Elko. I'm not going to make a career out of hunting this Simpson fool, but I do want to help Joe Rogers find him. We have a fine operation here and you're a fine crew," he said, and headed upstairs to pack for his ride to Elko in the morning.

A large table had been set with pots of coffee and platters of sweet rolls for the meeting of the Elko County Commission, the District Attorney, the Acting Sheriff, Ted Wilson, Bill Vierra, and Jack Slater. Micah Erickson, called Olie by his friends, Chairman of the County Commission, called the meeting to order and asked Joe Rogers for an update on Cyrus Simpson.

"Simpson has been identified in two large robberies, one just north of the border in Idaho, and the other in Winnemucca. Two of his associates were captured in the Idaho mine robbery and have talked about Simpson's plans to make more than one raid in Elko County.

"It wasn't specifically mentioned, but we have to assume the Bank of Elko will be on his agenda, and possibly something or somewhere near Skelton. What's the situation in Skelton, Jack?"

"We have a town marshal now and the word is spread to watch for Simpson and be prepared for anything. Everyone's armed and ready, Joe," Jack said. "If he shows up at my place again, Cactus Jack will take him out, and that's for sure," he chuckled.

"Good," Rogers said. "Vierra, you've hired extra guards?" He got a nod back from the Bank Manager, "And Sam, as acting sheriff, are your people ready to take out their former boss?"

"They are," Sam Chapman answered. "The Elko County Sheriff's office has been embarrassed by Simpson's antics and we'll take him down just like any other common criminal. Most of the boys can't wait," he smiled.

Olie Erickson banged his fist on the table with a friendly smile, grabbed one more sweet roll and closed the meeting. "I think we're as prepared as we can be, and I for one will be glad when the Simpson feller is locked up tight somewhere. Good job Joe, and Sam, let's go get him."

"The way Joe Rogers and Sam Chapman have things set up, you don't need me hanging around," Jack said, sitting at the supper table with Ted Wilson and Bill Vierra. "I'm heading back to the ranch in the morning. We also have a Skelton Town Board meeting day after tomorrow, and I need to be there."

"There's something Bill and I want to discuss with you, Jack," Ted Wilson said. "Next year is a big election year and many of us in Elko County have been less than satisfied with the performance of our state assemblyman, Hannity. Many of us have also been impressed with the way you conduct yourself, your ability to manage a large ranch, and your feelings toward the county."

Bill Vierra continued Wilson's comments. "The Elko County Republican Central Committee has asked us to invite you to run for that seat next year, and I can tell you right now, the bank will support your candidacy, I'm fairly certain I can get railroad support for you, and I know most of the ranchers and businessmen in the county will back you."

390

"We're not looking for a commitment tonight, Jack," Wilson added, "but it's something that we feel strongly about. You have a destiny to follow, Jack Slater, most of us could see that the minute we met you, and I hope, after you give this some serious thought, that your answer will be yes."

"My goodness," was all Jack could say, looking at Vierra, then Wilson, then at his supper plate, then slowly closed his eyes and took in two deep breaths. "I'll have to spend some time chewing on that, gentlemen. Right now, I can't even contemplate such a thing. I'm amazed, honored, frightened," he said, choking a chuckle back, and being joined in light laughter from Vierra and Wilson. "My goodness."

"I didn't get a wink of sleep all night," Jack Slater muttered, trying to get his boots on. "Winter's coming on hard and fast, my ranch isn't ready for it, I have obligations as a member of the Skelton Town Board, we're trying to find the outlaw that burned me out, and now, they want me to run for the state assembly. I would never have imagined this in a lifetime," he whispered, and the smile lit up the Drover's Hotel room number two seventeen.

Jack walked out on the main street for a

little morning exercise before breakfast and the ride home. It was just breaking dawn and there were few people on the street as he strode down the boardwalk. Three men were riding slowly down the dirt street and one in particular caught Jack's eye.

"I know that man," he muttered, and then the realization came to him. "Simpson, that's Cyrus Simpson sure as I'm standing here." He let his arm nudge that big revolver he had tucked under his shoulder, just to make sure it was there, and watched the three riders step off their horses at a hitch rack across from the bank.

Jack noticed two other horses at a rack further down, and then saw two more at one of the cross streets. "Interesting, all these horses, saddled and bridled, hitched at racks, but no one around." He spotted a young man he recognized as Percy Hazelton from the hardware store and called him over.

"Percy, do you remember me?" The boy nodded yes, and Jack continued. "I want you to run just as fast as you can run to the sheriff's office and tell whoever's working that the bank is about to robbed. Tell them I sent you. Can you do that?"

"Yes, sir, I can," Percy said. "Is that Sheriff Simpson?"

"I think it is," Jack said. "Now hurry, because I can't stop him by myself. Bring the whole sheriff's department back with you," he chuckled, and Percy Hazelton took off at a streak, running the two blocks to the courthouse. He burst through the doors of the office, waking the duty deputy with his hollering.

"Jack Slater's at the bank and he says Sheriff Simpson is there with a gang of men and they're gonna rob the bank. He said to bring the whole department and help him get Simpson." He got all that out in one breath, and the deputy made him slow down and say it all over again.

The deputy made one phone call, grabbed a shotgun, strapped his gunbelt on, and said, "Come on, kid, let's go get that outlaw." They ran as fast as they could for the bank, finding Slater tucked behind one of the buildings facing the bank. He had himself positioned such that none of the outlaws could get near their horses without him seeing them.

"Percy, you get back behind this wall here, I sure don't want you getting shot," the deputy said, joining Jack. "How many are there?" he asked.

"I've counted what I think are seven horses on the streets here, and I think some of the men might already be in the bank. Simpson and two others tied their horses there," and he pointed them out, "and then walked around behind the bank."

"Sherriff Chapman and his boys should be here shortly. I called him before I left," the deputy said.

Just as he said that, there was a muffled explosion inside the bank building that rattled windows, but wasn't really loud. "There goes the safe," Jack said. "They'll be coming for their horses, so let's be ready."

Four horses came storming down Commercial Street, with Chapman leading the charge. Jack flagged them down and explained what was happening. Chapman sent three of his men around behind the bank, and joined Jack and the deputy at the side of the building, watching Simpson's horses.

Gunfire broke the morning silence just moments later, and Jack had his revolver in hand, the sheriff had a rifle, the deputy had his shotgun, and three men exploded from the side of the bank, carrying large canvas bags, racing for their horses. Sheriff Chapman leveled the rifle and fired once, twice, and two men fell to the dirt. Jack squeezed off a quick round, blowing the knee of the remaining outlaw into many pieces.

Two of the three were still alive, but were

quickly disarmed and put in custody. Chapman left the deputy to watch them and he and Jack ran toward the rear of the bank, where they could hear more gunfire. They found one deputy shot and dead, one outlaw on the ground, seriously wounded.

Chapman spotted Simpson just inside the bank's back door, a rifle in his hands. "Give it up, Simpson, or die," he hollered. Simpson started to raise the rifle and Chapman was faster by a couple of heartbeats. Simpson took the rifle round through the middle of his chest, spewing blood from front and back.

His two compadres inside threw out their guns screaming for mercy and the deputies took them into custody quickly. "All I wanted was a little walk around town before breakfast," Jack quipped, helping Chapman get everyone put together in the same place. His wounded deputy and three outlaws were shipped off to the hospital, the dead ones were sent to the mortuary, and Jack invited Percy Hazelton to have breakfast with him.

"Sure glad you were out and about this morning, son," Jack said as they waited for their food to come. "Couldn't have caught those men without your help, and I told the sheriff so, too. Do you work in your father's store everyday?"

"Except for going to school," Percy Hazelton said. "School's good, I guess, but I sure do like working in the store. The only thing I really like about school is reading. I have a lot of books. Do you like to read?"

"I love to read," Jack said, thinking about all his books. "Papa used to read to me when I was very young. I guess that's where I picked up the habit.

"You tell your father how you helped me today, and I have to get back to my ranch. You're a fine, boy, Percy, thanks again." Jack walked down to the stables and saddled up for the ride to Skelton. "What a couple of days this has been," he said to the liveryman, with an ironic chuckle.

The ride back to Skelton was uneventful but filled with busy thoughts about his ranch, his obligations to employees, obligations as a member of the town board, and now, what to do about this concept of being a member of the Nevada State Legislature. "All of this inside of a year," he muttered, every time another thought came to him. "Wouldn't Ephraim Clairidge get a kick out of this?"

He stopped for a short visit with Valley Paddock, told about the big fight and killing of Simpson, but didn't say a word about anything else. "I think Chapman is going to make a fine sheriff. Olie Erickson said the commission could name him interim sheriff, and then he will have to stand for election next year.

"The explosion to open the safe did some damage but nothing that can't be fixed, and not a dime was lost in the attempted robbery. That town board meeting still on for tomorrow night?"

"Sure is, Jack. I'll let Jefferson know that the Simpson threat is over. He'll be relieved about that," he chuckled. "He's not been seen for three days without that rifle cradled and ready. I think he slept with it."

Jack picked up his mail and headed for the ranch. "I've got a head full of things to keep me busy but no worries about some fool shootin' me or burnin' me out," he laughed, nudging his horse in to a gentle lope for the quick ride out. He could feel winter in the air and hoped that Robbie had brought in enough wood to keep them warm. "I'm one lucky man," he said for the hundredth time that day.

34

The winter was a hard one with storm after storm blasting its way across the vast Great Basin, dumping snow that was measured in feet and carried by winds that froze skin within minutes. Jack, Cactus Jack, and the buckaroos spent a great deal of time loading wagons fitted as sleds with feed and driving them through drifts as high as the wagon seat.

"It's a good thing you were able to get a crop of grass and grains, Jack, otherwise we would have lost a lot of cattle." Cactus Jack Farraday had ridden in from the outer range, counting the herd. "Spring will be filled with the bawling of heifers calling their young 'uns," he smiled.

"You've had something on your mind, boss," he said as he and Jack walked toward the big house. "Anything I can help with?"

Jack Slater had two issues on his mind, and only one of those could be discussed with his cow boss. The other was inside a letter he had received not too long after the Simpson affair ended. It came from Fargo and was signed, Mims, and he had carried it in his shirt pocket the entire winter, pulling it out whenever he was alone and wanted some special company. He would talk to his ranch manager about the other thing.

"I've had something on my mind all winter, Cactus, and I haven't talked to anyone about it, and maybe I should. Let's see if Sandra has a piece of that pie or two left and chat some, eh?"

They had to settle for fresh, hot bread right out of the oven and hot coffee, and settled in at the big dining table. "There's a group in Elko that have asked me to run for public office," Jack started and Cactus Jack sat bolt upright at the comment.

"Well now, ain't that something," he drawled out in his best east Texas slang. "Gonna run for guvner, are you?" he kinda snickered, slathering some of Sandra's peach jam on some hot bread.

"They have asked me to run for the state legislature, Jack," he said. "The Nevada Assembly to be specific and I've nursed the idea all winter. As intriguing as the idea is, I don't think it would be in my best interest, at least right now."

"I don't know, boss. It might be in your best interest, you know, if you could get some of these water rights questions answered, get some kind of recognition of cattleman's rights as to mining issues. Think of the railroad situation and their checkerboard land patterns and how that affects grazing." Cactus Jack had changed from the simple Texas cowboy to a buckaroo cattle boss that fast, and his joking manner was set aside.

"You just nailed the issues, Cactus, and it's because I know those issues and have some serious thoughts about them, that those fellers in Elko want me to run. But I have issues, too. I have a big ranch that's just getting started. I am on the Skelton town board, and, truthfully, I don't think I want to be a politician."

He and Cactus Jack laughed at that, and caught Sandra giggling as she stirred a pot on the big wood stove. "We're building a good herd, Cactus, we need to start a stock horse breeding program, and I want to diversify more into raising grasses and grains. I'm needed here, not off gallivanting in Carson City. With that railroad as close as it is, those stock yards sitting there waiting to be filled, I'm going to be plenty busy around here."

"Sounds like you had your mind made up before we walked in that door, Jack. I know you would be an asset in the legislature, and I know how much you're needed right here," and he chuckled a bit, "and I'm glad it's you that has to make the decision. I'll back you which ever way you decide."

"That's the best news, Cactus. I think you're right, I knew weeks ago that I was going to say no to those fellers, but I had to say it outright, spell out why, and I'm glad you were the one I spelled it out to.

"I'm going to stay right here, Cactus Jack, and raise cows and horses, and send letters to whoever it is that does run for the legislature." He sat back and another thought crossed his mind, one he had from time to time. "When I was on our own farm back in New York, my pa raised hogs, and when I worked for Jablonski in Fargo, he raised hogs.

"I know hogs and cattle, I know grains and grasses. We need to add hogs to our farm, Cactus Jack. We sent hundreds of hogs to market twice a year back in Fargo, and we have a market for them here."

"I've never worked with hogs," Cactus Jack said, almost a sour look on his face. "Not sure I'd want to."

"No, Cactus, you're my cow boss all the way. I'm going to spend the winter putting this together, finding the right people, and building pens and corrals for them. No, I need you to bring us the best steers in Nevada." More hot bread was sliced, more jam was slathered on, and more genuine laughter filled the warm kitchen as the morning wore on.

It was the other issue that had Jack walking back and forth in his library, his head bent down toward his broad chest and his hands clasped behind his back. He finally sat down in a large red-leather chair, put his feet up on an ottoman, and pulled the letter from his pocket to read again.

"My dearest Jack," it began, in a beautiful hand that brought memories of Jack teaching Mims to read and write, and how he insisted that her penmanship be very good. "I've received so many wonderful letters from you and I feel horrid not answering a single one. Please don't hate me for that, but it has not been the good-old-Mims that read those letters of yours.

"Reverend Thomas died the year after you left and I was forced to take a job in one of the restaurants in Fargo, and then, on top of that, two horrible men abducted me and had their way with me. They were captured and killed by the sheriff, but I was ostracized by the community, as if it were my fault. A beautiful little girl was the final outcome of the ordeal.

"I have skimped and saved, and Maybelle is now two years old, can walk some, talks gibberish and English, and looks like I used to look. You said I was like a little pixie looking to get in trouble, and that's my Maybelle.

"Remember always, Jack Slater, that I love you, as I told you so many times when we had our suppers in that old barn. Keep writing, please, and don't hate me." She signed it Mims Jablonski as the Thomas family never did change the adoption from old Pete.

Jack cried himself to sleep the night he got that letter and didn't answer it until Christmas, when he sent a long letter and a bank draft to be cashed at the Fargo Bank. He got up from that leather chair and went into the office, sat down at his desk and pulled paper and pen.

That afternoon, Jack Slater rode into Skelton with a large envelope addressed to one Mims Jablonski, Fargo. "How is it you know this lady in Fargo, Jack?" Valley Paddock asked. "Isn't that where you grew up?"

"Sure is," Jack smiled. "We were raised as orphans on the same farm, Valley, and she never left Fargo." He had a devil's grin on his face as he walked out of Paddock's store/post office, and headed for the blacksmith's shop. *She just might leave Fargo when she gets that letter. That would put the capper on one fine year,* he muttered through his snickers, waving hello to Jesse Winthrop.

"Looks like I got about forty or more heifers gonna be kind to me come spring, Jesse. I need a box of your finest ear tags, since you're the state ag boss here. I hope I keep you just as busy as possible."

"You're full of good humor this morning, Jack," the barrel of a man said. "That thaw that started a couple of days ago keeps going, we'll be up to our butts in mud before long."

"Yup," Jack said, "and the grasses will grow and the cows will come," he smiled. "There's something about spring that makes me want to sing and jump around some. If somebody had a fiddle right now, I think I could dance some."

It was early May when Jack received a letter from Mims and after reading it, he estimated, thirty times or more, he called a little meeting with Cactus Jack and Sandra in his

404

office. He settled into his old leather rocker near the fireplace and they settled onto a couch and chair.

"Sounded important, boss," Cactus said, sitting deep into the leather couch, "what's up?"

"I'm going to be making a few changes around here," Jack said, not cracking a smile, and actually hearing Cactus and Sandra take in their breath. He couldn't hold it, though and let a big smile cross his face.

"You've all heard my story, about being orphaned and my time on the Jablonski farm in Dakota Territory, but you haven't heard all of it. There was a beautiful little girl, we were the same age, named Mims, and we were very close. I left and two years later ended up here, and now, three years later, Mims and her daughter Maybelle will be joining us here."

Cactus Jack and Sandra both tried to ask questions at the same time, and Jack shushed them. "You'll get the whole story if you just settle down," he said, giving that Jack Slater smile to them. "Mims has had a hard time, but that's over, and I've asked her to come to Skelton and be my wife. According to a letter I got yesterday, Mims will be in Elko in two weeks.

"Cactus Jack, I'd like you to be my best man, and Sandra, I'd like you to stand with Mims. Okay? And I want the whole town of Skelton to be invited, which means we'll have to put a side of beef on the roaster, and start making pies," and the laughter rang through the big ranch house.

Jack drove the team and Cactus Jack, Valley Paddock, and Jesse Winthrop rode shotgun on the trip from Skelton to Elko to meet the train and bring Mims and Maybelle home. It was a gorgeous spring day, warm, white puffy clouds dotted a deep blue sky, and the springtime mud Winthrop had foretold wasn't quite that deep.

Jack's mind wouldn't slow down, hadn't slowed since he got Mims' letter, and the ride to Elko just added kindling to the fire. Why are riding so slow? What will she look like? Will I recognize her? She named her baby after Maybelle at the Society, and that's wonderful. It was one single thought that dominated his conversation with himself.

I'm not going to be alone. Even after building the ranch, having Cactus Jack and Sandra around everyday, I've still been alone. I've been alone since that terrible accident that took my parents, but when Mims and I are married, I won't be alone. He pulled the wagon into Elko wearing a smile that lit the sky, border to border, jumped down and tied off the team near the train station, and walked with his ranch family onto the platform to await the west bound, the same one he arrived on slightly more than one year ago.

"What if she doesn't like me, Cactus?" he said, pacing up and down the long wooden walkway. "I know I've changed in these last three, almost four years, and surely she's changed." His fists clenched and un-clenched, his eyes searched the empty track demanding the train arrive, and none of the party could get him calmed down.

"The wedding is Saturday, the calf has been slaughtered and is hanging in the barn, the whole town has been invited, Valley. What if she changed her mind and isn't even on the train?"

Jesse Winthrop finally calmed the huge man down by suggesting they walk across the tracks to a little saloon and have a cold beer. "We'll hear the train in plenty of time to get back. What you need is a double shot of Kentucky, but that won't happen."

Winthrop and Paddock talked about town happenings, Cactus talked about cows and calves, and Jack listened for a train's plaintive wail. "Oh, my," is all he could say when the whistle was finally heard, and he said it several more times getting back to the station, well before the train was stopped. A whirling Dervish in the form of one Mims Jablonski was flying off her feet and into his arms as soon as the railcar doors were opened.

A tiny little girl, the spitting image of Mims, was handed down to Cactus Jack by the car porter, followed by a considerable amount of luggage. It was a scene of chaos for several minutes, and Valley Paddock finally seemed to take control and got things half-way organized. Jesse and Cactus moved the luggage to the wagon, Valley took control of Maybelle, and Jack and Mims continued to stand on the platform, holding onto each other as if separation would end all existence.

"All right, Jack, catch some air and introduce us to this lovely creature who is making a drastic mistake thinking you are such a fine catch," Valley Paddock said, giving Maybelle a gentle swing. Jack's eyes were filled with tears, as were Mims', and he wiped them on a sleeve, introducing his bride-to-be to the group.

Jack got Mims and Maybelle settled on the wagon seat while Paddock, Cactus Jack, and Jesse Winthrop mounted their horses, and they were off. "We brought a little basket of food and there's a nice spot along a creek just a few miles from here where we can stop and have a bite," Jack said. "We should be home before dark."

Home. It's really and truly my home, and this beautiful woman sitting next to me is soon to be my wife. My God, he thought, and then snickered just a little bit. "Tell me about your trip, Mims."

Mims only had three days to get settled before the big wedding, had to get un-packed, worked hours with Sandra creating her wedding dress, and spending hours with Jack, talking about their old times, her not very good times, and their future times. The first morning, Jack took her by the hands and led her to the barn where he had spread some hay, laid out a blanket, and had biscuits and jam waiting.

It was as if nothing had changed, they were fourteen, fifteen years old, sneaking some food in the barn so mean old Pete Jablonski wouldn't know. They laughed and wrestled around, laughed some more, and settled finally for some good hugs and kisses. "I've missed you, Jack Slater. Don't ever leave me again."

He rose up on an elbow and looked down into bright eyes brimming with love, and saw Mims almost as she was so many years ago. Her eyes danced and her freckles almost glowed, her hair was a tangled mess as always, and a little dab of jam was stuck on her chin. He kissed her gently and rolled onto his back, letting his hands rub up and down her back.

There were more than fifty people at the wedding and the dancing and music went on into the early morning hours. Valley Paddock officiated, and Sandra had put together an entire platoon of women who worked for days on the food. The beef was tender, the pies sweet, and it was Cactus Jack who asked after the first dance had ended, "Where's Jack and Mims?" The laughter could be heard in Skelton.

"What have we done, Jack Slater?" she asked, snuggled under a warm wool blanket, feeling her husband's great strength holding her.

"What we've done, Mrs. Slater, is make ourselves one, and we will never be alone, ever, ever, again."

ABOUT THE AUTHOR

Reno, Nevada novelist, **Johnny Gunn,** is retired from a long career in journalism. He has worked in print, broadcast, and Internet, including a stint as publisher and editor of the Virginia City Legend. These days, Gunn spends most of his time writing novel length fiction, concentrating on the western genre. Or, you can find him down by the Truckee River with a fly rod in hand.

Gunn and his wife, Patty, live on a small hobby farm about twenty miles north of Reno, sharing space with a couple of horses, some meat rabbits, a flock of chickens, and one crazy goat.

The employees of Thorndike Press hope you have enjoyed this Large Print book. All our Thorndike Large Print titles are designed for easy reading, and all our books are made to last. Other Thorndike Press Large Print books are available at your library, through selected bookstores, or directly from us.

For information about titles, please call:
(800) 223-1244

or visit our website at:
gale.com/thorndike

Printed in the USA
CPSIA information can be obtained
at www.ICGtesting.com
JSHW021026030924
69072JS00004B/4

9 781420 517231